TARTABULL'S THROW

TARTABULL'S THROW

BY HENRY GARFIELD

A RICHARD JACKSON BOOK
ATHENEUM BOOKS FOR YOUNG READERS

NEW YORK   LONDON   TORONTO   SYDNEY   SINGAPORE

Atheneum Books for Young Readers
An imprint of Simon & Schuster Children's Publishing Division
1230 Avenue of the Americas
New York, New York 10020

Book design by Jennifer Browne and Abelardo Martínez
The text of this book is set in Berling Roman and Copperplate.
Printed in the United States of America

2 4 6 8 10 9 7 5 3 1

Library of Congress Cataloging-in-Publication Data
Garfield, Henry.
Tartabull's throw : a novel / by Henry Garfield.
p.   cm.
"A Richard Jackson book."
Summary: In 1967 an encounter with a mysterious young woman from Maine involves a
nineteen-year-old baseball player in an investigation of a vicious, murderous werewolf.
ISBN 0-689-83840-9
[1. Werewolves—Fiction. 2. Baseball—Fiction. 3. Maine—Fiction.] I. Title.
PZ7.G17939 Tar 2001
[Fic]—dc21   00-027125

To Tom Gardner
and the rest of the Cove kids

ACKNOWLEDGMENTS

Tartabull's Throw, though a work of fiction, was conceived and constructed around several real events, including baseball games from the 1967 season. I owe thanks to all those who graciously shared their time and memories with me during the writing of this book.

For the chronology and factual underpinnings of that tumultuos pennant race, I referred often to *The Impossible Dream Remembered* (Stephen Greene Press), by Ken Coleman and Dan Valenti.

San Diego sportswriter and fellow Red Sox fan Barry Lorge, who was there, provided details for the chapter on Tony Conigliaro's beaning.

Former Red Sox pitcher Bill Rohr, who obviously was also there, shared recollections of his near ho-hitter in Yankee Stadium. Another former Red Sox left-hander, John Curtis, assisted with the depictions of minor-league life.

Thanks to everyone who read or heard early drafts of this book or portions thereof and offered constructive criticism, especially Mike, Ed, Susan, Jerry, Judy and all my writing buddies in Tierrasanta and Asilomar. I am fortunate to know you all.

Thanks to my editor, Richard Jackson, whose wisdom and support and keen insights helped shape this book.

Thanks to my fabulous agent, Barbara Markowitz, who never stopped believing in this project and provided advice and friendship throughout, and to Harvey Markowitz, whose judgment (aside from rooting for the Yankees) was always sound.

Finally, special thanks to my daughter and son, Polaris Garfield and Rigel Garfield, for sharing the uncertainty and insanity of living with an author and Red Sox fan in several houses on both coasts. A novel demands a lot from the author's family, and you were there from opening sentence to final draft. I wouldn't have wanted to do it without you.

CONTENTS

PART ONE

AUGUST

1.

OUT LIKE TED WILLIAMS

It's a terrible thing, Cyrus Nygerski thought as he crouched in the on-deck circle, to be washed up before the age of twenty.

But he was, he was. He contemplated his lofty batting statistics—a .175 average with two home runs and a couple dozen RBI—and the last egregious error that had prompted his manager to yank him out of the infield a week ago in the middle of an inning, embarrassing him in front of several hundred beer-sodden hometown fans. "You take that behind-the-back throw of yours," Cliff Gillespie had said with controlled fury (spitting a stream of tobacco juice at Nygerski's feet and making him dance out of the way), "and you shove it up your ass." Three runs had scored as Nygerski's errant toss on what should have been an inning-ending double play rolled lazily along the empty right-field bleachers toward Illinois.

Though all nine fielders stood in Wisconsin, the state line lay just steps beyond the decaying, open-ended ballpark. A strong left-handed pull hitter could sometimes hit a ball from one state into the other, but Nygerski wasn't thinking about that as he stood in. He just wanted the game, and the season, to be over, so that he could get the hell out of here.

He sniffed the air. There was a faint smoky smell, the accustomed background pollution, but nothing more. It was a calm evening, the twilight gathering, the worst time of day to see the ball. Sometimes, when the wind blew from the north, the smell of stale cheese would waft over the field and the town from the nearby Frito-Lay factory. Beloit was a butt-ugly factory town where blue-collar workers liked nothing better than to put away a few beers and then head out to the ballpark for a night of heckling.

It had been almost a week since Nygerski had been pulled from the lineup, and he suspected he was only being sent up now to pinch-hit because Gillespie wanted to protect his new regular second baseman from the maniac on the mound, a kid named Pinkham who threw about a zillion miles an hour with little or no sense of direction. In two innings of relief, the kid had struck out six, walked four, broken their best hitter's left wrist, and sent the batboy and the peanut salesman scurrying for cover. Although the Turtles had scored a run off the kid on a wild pitch, no one had thus far managed to hit a ball in fair territory.

The score was 8–3 in favor of the other team, though at this point in the season nobody really gave a damn who won. It was, after all, August 26, and the Turtles stood seventh in an eight-team league. Nor were any players from this low level likely to be called up to the White Sox when major-league rosters expanded on the first of September. Then again, in the surreal world of the low minors, anything could happen.

It was the bottom of the eighth, which meant that unless the kid got *really* wild or the blurs that he was throwing up to home plate suddenly became hittable, Nygerski would get just one chance at him. He watched the batter wave at a fastball (did this kid throw anything else?), and awaited his turn as the next human sacrifice.

His gaze wandered out into left field, toward the short section of stands that jutted out into fair territory near the foul line. Fallon Field had been built before World War II for the Beloit College football team, and its seating layout only grudgingly accommodated baseball. The result was the most lopsided outfield Nygerski had ever seen. The stands ended abruptly a few steps into left field, creating a dangerous obstacle for an unwary outfielder and a tempting target for a right-handed hitter who could pull the ball down the line. Beyond them, a decrepit fence snaked its way out toward a series of billboards, most of them advertising the products of small, nearby breweries. Right field, where as a lefty Nygerski would naturally hit the ball, ended over the horizon at an auto graveyard in Illinois. If the ball rolled into the weeds surrounding the rusting junkers without an outfielder touching it, the batter was awarded a home run.

The seats in left were usually unoccupied, for insults and objects had a better chance of reaching their intended targets from closer to the action. The lighting out there was poor. Sometimes couples retreated there to make out during games, and sometimes small groups from the nearby college showed up and made those stands their home. Though they were better behaved than the regular drunks who attended every game, the team's management didn't like them because they smuggled in their own cheap beer instead of buying it for an inflated price at the concession stand, and some of them smoked pot. The smell was a good deal more pleasant than the more frequent odor of processed cheese, but the security guards hired by the team took a dim view of such flagrant lawbreaking.

Tonight the left-field stands stood empty. The stadium, in fact, was nearly deserted. Beloit had fallen four runs behind in the very first inning; the verbal abuse had started early and lost most of its momentum by the third. Malcolm Wood, whose wrist at that very moment was being immobilized by a cast, had hit two homers to make the score respectable, but each time the Turtles lost no time in giving the runs back. Not a very good show for the hometown fans. Jackie Gleason was on TV at eight, and most of the crowd had left before dark, missing the kid with the great fastball and the rising of the full Moon, which Nygerski now enjoyed from his spot in the on-deck circle.

It looks just like a hanging curveball, he thought. The way pitches used to look when he had starred on his high school team in Boston, barely a year ago. Of course, the league in which he had played did not boast pitchers with ninety-five-mile-an-hour heaters or curves that fell off the table just as you started to swing. Nygerski knew he was over-matched, and by this point in the season he had the feeling that every-one in the White Sox organization knew it as well.

The batter swung wildly at a pitch up around his chin, then shrugged his shoulders and walked past Nygerski back to the dugout. In his face Nygerski read relief. Survival was more important than a point or two in the batting average. Not exactly the most confident thought to take to the plate, but there it was. Show no fear, Nygerski told himself as he stood in and affixed the pitcher with his most menacing glare. Nygerski may not have been able to hit or field, but he could glare with anyone.

The pitcher went into his windup. Nygerski heard a hissing sound and the *thwack!* of ball against leather behind him. "Stee-RIKE one!" boomed the umpire as the catcher threw the ball, now once again vis-ible, back to the kid, who was grinning.

Holy shit, is this kid fast! Nygerski thought. If he throws it at my head, I'm dead. Better just swing at the next two pitches and sit down.

And swing he did, although the next pitch sailed off to the third-base side and all the way to the backstop, where it disrupted a group of pigeons checking out some spilled popcorn. "You stink, Nygerski!" someone yelled from the seats behind him. "Helen Keller could hit better'n you!"

Nygerski chuckled to himself. That was only a half-truth, he mused. He at least could *hear* the pitches as they zipped by.

On the next pitch he closed his eyes and swung. To his amazement, he felt the ball hit his bat. He opened his eyes. He had swung late, of course, and managed to hit what looked like a routine pop fly down the left-field line. The ball arced lazily toward the rising Moon as the left fielder glided over toward the abutment of seats. Nygerski dropped the bat and watched.

"Run, you idiot!" Cliff Gillespie screamed from the dugout. Nygerski ignored him. The outfielder backed up against the stands now, right on the foul line. He patted his glove as the ball descended toward him. Nygerski didn't move. He watched the ball fall across the face of the Moon, and he saw the fielder lean into the stands, reaching his glove as far back as he could. The ball landed inches beyond it in the second row of seats, just barely in fair territory.

A stunned silence fell over the ballpark, punctuated a moment later by scattered, surprised applause. Then Nygerski felt something jab him in the back. He turned around. "What're you waitin' for, asshole?" the catcher snarled behind his mask. "Get movin'."

Slowly, savoring the moment, Nygerski circled the bases in the nearly silent ballpark. A plastic cup filled with beer narrowly missed him as he rounded third. He looked up into the stands in time to duck another cup. Several rows up, well back from the rowdies and drunks, a red-haired woman stood on her seat and clapped wildly. Nygerski lifted his arm momentarily in acknowledgment.

"Way to go, Cy," said Eddie Baker, the new regular second baseman, when he reached the dugout. Most of his teammates were laughing. "Shortest goddamn home run I ever saw," said Bull Seivers, the first baseman, who had hit twenty of them, some of them monumental shots impressive enough to keep the big club interested despite a .225 average. Cliff Gillespie, at the opposite end of the dugout, spat tobacco juice on the ground and didn't say a word.

Nygerski's home run changed only the score. Pinkham walked a couple more batters and struck out the side in the ninth, and the Turtles lost again, 8-4. After he had showered and half-dressed, Nygerski was startled to hear the manager's door slam open and Gillespie bellow his name.

"Just got a phone call from Chicago," Gillespie said, inside the tiny office that Nygerski suspected had once been a janitor's closet. The manager twirled an unlit cigar stub in his fingers. "They said you don't have to go to Peoria with the team. You're through."

"Through?" Nygerski asked.

"I believe the official term is 'unconditionally released,'" Gillespie said. "You'll be paid through the end of next week. But you can clean out your stuff tonight."

The office was so small, there wasn't even a chair for Nygerski to collapse into, or throw in frustration, or crash across Gillespie's crewcut-topped skull. Not that he was surprised. People had come and gone all season—it was the nature of minor-league baseball. Now it was his turn. Gillespie had been trying to get rid of him for months. But he had to say *something*. You don't get fired from a job—in this case, a whole career—and just walk away.

"Did you tell them," he asked, "about the home run I hit off that kid? No one else could touch him."

Gillespie's face softened slightly, from granite to a lighter grade of shale. "Only in Beloit," the manager said, "does that little can-of-corn fly ball go out. Besides, that kid's got something you ain't."

"What's that?" Nygerski said.

"A future," Gillespie replied. "You can teach control. Natural ability—well, you either got it or you don't. The big club wants to check out some other prospects. I'm sorry, Cy, but the White Sox got no use for a left-handed second baseman who leads the league in errors and can't hit his weight."

At this statement Nygerski's back stiffened. "I'll have you know that my average is now up to .179," he said. (He had done the math in his head during his home run trot.) "And I only weigh 165. Release me if you want, but get your facts straight."

Gillespie stuck the unlit cigar into the side of his mouth and opened the top drawer of the small metal desk. "Look, I know it ain't much fun, gettin' your walking papers. It's the toughest part of my job, lettin' young players go. Baseball's a demanding game. You ain't the first kid who couldn't cut the mustard. And you won't be the last."

Nygerski wondered how many times Gillespie had given *that* little speech. He sounded about as sincere as President Johnson did about ending the war in Vietnam. And that thought reminded Nygerski that he ought to get in touch with Professor Ed Fishman over at the college about his lapsed enrollment application, lest the draft board get in touch with him first.

Then again, the bus from Chicago to Winnipeg stopped in Beloit at midnight, and the weather in Canada would be nice for a few more months. . . .

Gillespie pulled something small and flat from the desk drawer. "Tell you what," he said, bringing Nygerski back to the present. "The big club's got a doubleheader tomorrow, down at Comiskey. I guess you probably know your precious Red Sox are in town. Anyway, they sent us up some tickets, and seeing as how you're free . . ." Awkwardly, Gillespie turned the tickets over in his hands. "It'll do you good to get out of this shithole," he mumbled. "God knows I've been trying for years." With a scowl that almost turned into a smile, he handed Nygerski two tickets across the desk.

"Thanks, boss," Nygerski said, in genuine surprise.

"I ain't your boss anymore," Gillespie growled at him. "And the Red Sox are gonna fold. You watch. They got no pitching beyond Lonborg. Who else they got? Buncha kids and has-beens. That don't cut it in a pennant race."

"It's the first time in my life they've been in one," Nygerski said.

"They been lucky so far." Gillespie leaned back in his chair and shifted the cigar stub from one side of his mouth to the other. "That Yastrzemski's havin' a good year. But losing Conigliaro's gotta kill 'em. Man for man, they're the weakest team in a four-way race. White Sox'll sweep 'em tomorrow."

"We'll see," Nygerski said quietly, clutching the tickets. He moved toward the door, already weary of Gillespie and his bullshit. "Thanks for these."

"Good luck, Cyrus." Gillespie did not rise or offer his hand, and Nygerski exited the tiny office.

In the clubhouse, Malcolm Wood sat with his wrist in a cast as several players crowded around him. Wood's season had been the opposite of Nygerski's. One errant fastball had ended it, but he was acting like he knew there would be other campaigns.

"Hey, Nygerski," he shouted cheerfully. "Heard about your tremendous blast. They're comparing you to Mickey Mantle." This brought a round of general laughter, and made Nygerski feel a little better as he ambled over to grab his few possessions.

"Last homer I'll ever hit in this dump," he muttered as he began jamming stuff into a large, pale green duffel bag.

"How come?" Eddie Baker needled him. "You goin' to the Show?"

There was another round of laughter.

Nygerski fixed the small, dark infielder with one of his glares. "Yeah, Eddie. I'm goin' to the show. *The Ed Sullivan Show.* Tomorrow night you can watch me juggle while riding a unicycle."

This brought more laughter and a sprinkling of derisive comments. Nygerski turned his back and fumbled with the buttons on his shirt. Most of his teammates thought him strange. He didn't care anymore.

He finished putting on his shirt and stuffing the bag. "Hey, Nygerski," Wood called over to him. "What happened, really?"

Nygerski stood up. Wood had been one of his few friends on the team, in the transitory nature of baseball friendships. "You'll never make it with a name like Malcolm," he said. "A star like you should have a nickname, you know that." Nygerski looked around the muggy, decrepit dressing room. "Baseball seasons come and go," he said, "but life goes on." And he hefted his bag and walked out the door without looking back.

At the far end of the dirt parking lot, Sammy Mavrogenes waited for him by an old Volkswagen bus stuffed with musical gear. Sammy worked with the groundskeeping crew at the ballpark to make the rent on the small upstairs apartment he shared with his girlfriend. He also played and sang in a three-piece rock and roll band, and had begun teaching Nygerski some riffs on his left-handed guitar. Sammy had provided a friendship beyond the insular, competitive world of baseball. "What took you so long?" Sammy said, throwing his cigarette on the ground and stepping on it. "I got a gig at ten."

Nygerski set down his duffel bag and opened the sliding door. "Sorry," he said, pushing aside an amp and shoving the bag in. "Had to have a talk with the boss."

Mavrogenes brushed his long curly hair out of his face and gave his friend a puzzled look. Nygerski kept his hair short for baseball. Now he could grow it down to his butt if he wanted to.

"What's with the bag?" Mavrogenes asked him as he slid the door shut.

Nygerski looked up at the full Moon, and then back at his friend. "They let me go," he said. "Guess I'll have to start looking for a new career."

"Shit. I'm sorry."

Nygerski got into the passenger seat; Mavrogenes slid behind the wheel. "You wanna beer?" Mavrogenes asked him.

"Yeah."

Mavrogenes reached behind his seat, opened the cooler there, and produced two cans of Leinenkugel. They drank silently in the moonlight as other players, coaches, and a few straggling fans came out into the darkness, got into their cars, and left. The parking lot was nearly empty when Nygerski again spoke. "Well, I can say one thing, at least," he declared, staring straight ahead.

"What's that?" Mavrogenes asked.

"I went out like Ted Williams."

"Huh?" was his companion's only comment.

"Homered in my last at bat," Nygerski said, draining his beer. "Didn't tip my cap, either. Come on, let's go."

2.

RHONDA

Rhonda Whittingham wasn't home when the cops called about her husband. She wasn't home because she was at the ballpark, watching what turned out to be her young man's last game for the Turtles. She was, in fact, the red-headed woman Nygerski waved to as he rounded third.

His nonchalant acknowledgment of her tugged at her heart, for she knew the kid didn't love her anymore, if indeed he ever had. And how could she have expected anything different? At thirty-three, she was already putting on weight in that inexorable Midwestern way, filling her mornings with a futureless job at a convenience store, her afternoons with extramarital sex, and her evenings with minor-league baseball or television. It hardly mattered—her husband, Ed, barely touched her anymore. He preferred the company of his buddies, at the factory and the bar afterward. *His* weight wasn't anything to crow about, either.

And she was still fetching enough to catch the attention of a certain nineteen-year-old second baseman, though lately his attention had been wandering. He had only been over a couple of times since the end of the last road trip, and then only because she had called him and made mewling noises over the phone. Still, she thrilled to the sight and touch of his young athletic body. She loved it when he fondled her breasts, which were the size of ripe cantaloupes. Rhonda had nicer knockers than most twenty-year-olds, and that, she knew, was because she had never let them flop around without a brassiere in the brazen way the young girls did today. But it was only natural that Cyrus looked at them. He was a ballplayer, and ballplayers, like musicians, had plenty of opportunity.

He was just a kid, for Christ's sake, with a kid's impatience and a kid's future. She had known that he would eventually grow tired of her. She should be grateful for the summer, and let it go at that.

But it still hurt. She had gotten married at eighteen, and knew somewhere in her mind even then that Ed would turn to drinking and neglect, but losing him had seemed worse. The affairs since had all been, to her, affairs of the heart. She had suffered emotionally at the end of every one. Old limp Ed, who worked at his dependable factory job and drank his beer and stoked the fire once or twice a month, had always been there, would always be there, too indifferent to suspect a thing.

And so tonight Rhonda drove straight home from the ballpark, not wishing to hang around to congratulate Nygerski on his homer and suffer his inattention, too. Ed would be home soon, anyway, because it was Saturday, and he and his cronies started drinking at noon instead of shift's end at three-thirty. And he would want her to fix him something to eat, and then more likely than not he would fall asleep in front of the television. I can look forward to another forty years of this, she thought as she aimed the big Dodge away from the full Moon toward the rolling land west of town called New Beloit. Ten years ago it had been cornfield. Now it sprouted houses, block after block of anonymous bedrooms.

Ed's Buick wasn't in the driveway. But a police car was. Rhonda felt her stomach gurgle with momentary anxiety. The police had never come to her house before. As she pulled in, two uniformed officers—

one black, the other white, symbolic of the forced integration that had come to Beloit with the proliferation of factories—emerged from the green-and-white city vehicle.

"Rhonda Whittingham?" the white officer asked.

Had Ed been arrested for something? She closed the car door behind her and looked from one stony face to the other. "Ye-es?"

"I'm afraid we have some bad news, Mrs. Whittingham," said the same officer. His partner stood a short distance away from him, his six-foot-plus frame strategically positioned between Rhonda and her front door. The white officer was shorter, with close-cropped black hair graying at the temples, and a slight paunch that strained the buttons of his starched blue shirt.

Rhonda straightened her back and looked directly into his soft, light brown eyes. "What sort of bad news?" she said.

"Would you like to go inside and sit down?" the policeman offered.

"I want you to tell me what's going on," Rhonda replied.

"We have a homicide victim we believe is your husband," the black cop said emotionlessly.

Rhonda turned her head. "We'd like you to come down and make a positive ID on the body," the white cop said. "I'm sorry, Mrs. Whittingham."

A wave of dizziness washed over her. "Homicide? You mean my husband is . . . dead?"

"We're sorry to have to tell you like this, ma'am," said the black officer.

"If, in fact, it is your husband," the white cop added quickly. "We believe it is. But we'd like you to identify him, to be sure. Would you like to . . . sit down for a minute?"

Rhonda's head felt like a Ping-Pong ball being volleyed between the two cops. Ed . . . homicide? Who would murder poor, simple Ed? Had there been a fight in the bar that had turned ugly? Had there been a robbery? Or was it—please, God—a case of mistaken identity?

"How . . . do you know it's Ed?" she asked the night, looking at neither officer.

The white cop cleared his throat. "We found his wallet," he said softly. "In the same area where we found his . . . the body. Mrs. Whittingham, I know this is hard for you. But we really need you to come with us."

Numbly, Rhonda nodded. She looked at the front of the simple suburban house, its white facade bathed in moonlight. It had been paid for by Ed's regular hours at the factory, hours whose regularity had made it oh so easy and convenient for her to cheat on him—not that he hadn't deserved it. What was she feeling? Remorse? Regret? Sorrow, not so much for Ed as for the end of the life to which she had grown accustomed? Or fear of change? It was strange—all her emotions seemed muted, distant, not hers really, not something felt so much as observed. Rhonda felt as though she were standing outside herself, watching another woman react, waiting to see what she would do. "All right," she heard herself say, her voice remarkably calm. "You'll bring me back here after?"

"Yes, ma'am," the black cop promised as the white cop opened the back door of the police car for her.

But when she saw the body, Rhonda could no longer remain calm.

"I must warn you," the small bald man with the mustache and white lab coat said, seconds before drawing back the sheet, "it isn't pretty."

And it wasn't. For Ed had not just been killed—he had been slaughtered. This wasn't murder, it was overkill. Until now, Rhonda's only experience with dead bodies had been at open-casket funerals of relatives, where the deceased's face had been professionally smoothed into serenity for the peaceful journey into the next world. But Ed's face had not yet been visited by the after-death makeup artists. One eye was gone, and deep red gashes ran diagonally across his face. Rhonda gasped. Before the coroner could stop her, she yanked the sheet out of his hands and threw it back, revealing Ed's entire body.

His throat and a chunk of his ample belly had been ripped from him, and his blood-caked face still bore its final expression of terror. Ed had gone out of this life screaming.

And looking at his brutalized body in the harsh white light of the morgue, with the little man holding the sheet and the two cops like statues a few steps back from the table, Rhonda could only communicate with her dead, disfigured husband by screaming back at him.

Her hands at her face, she backed away from the table and into the black cop, who awkwardly handed her off to his partner. She gasped for air, started to scream again, stopped herself, and buried her head into the policeman's shoulder instead. Silently, the little coroner covered Ed's mutilated face. Rhonda shook uncontrollably as the cop draped a wooden arm around her and said nothing.

"It's him, then, I take it," the black officer said after several seconds of strained silence.

Rhonda raised her head. "It's him," she whispered, drawing away from the white cop, to his evident relief. "But . . . *why?* Who did this to him?"

"We don't know, ma'am," the black cop said, looking at the spotless linoleum floor.

"You . . . don't *know?*" Rhonda croaked in astonishment. Neither policeman would meet her eyes. The coroner stood on the opposite side of the table, a short distance from Ed's draped body, and blinked at the three of them, obviously waiting for them to leave his sanctuary. Rhonda shuddered. Alone with the dead. Who would want a job like that?

The white cop cleared his throat. "We, ah, don't have a suspect at this point," he said. "The place your husband was last seen was at a bar on Riverside Drive. . . ."

"Al's Tap," Rhonda said. "He goes there all the time."

"Right," the officer continued. "We spoke with several of his friends, who were there with him, watching the White Sox game. They said—

and I'm sorry to have to tell you this, ma'am— they said he left the bar in the company of a young woman."

"*What?*" Rhonda was dumbfounded. In all her years of cheating she had never once suspected that *Ed* could be fooling around. She had met him unannounced at Al's Tap countless times; he had always been with his cronies from the job, talking sports or shooting pool. She had never smelled another woman on him, or found lipstick on his clothes, or caught him in a serious lie, and she had put down his lack of interest in her to low sex drive brought on by an accumulation of alcohol. But maybe she had been naive. "Who was she?" Rhonda asked the policeman.

"We don't know," he replied. "We thought maybe you could help us out with that. From the descriptions we got, she's in her early twenties, with long dark hair, blue eyes, ah, nice figure—"

"Doesn't sound like anyone who'd be hanging around with Ed," Rhonda snapped. Involuntarily, she looked over at the sheet. The man in the lab coat jerked his eyes away.

"Come on," the black officer said, pushing open the door. "I think our business here is done."

In the hall, mercifully away from Ed's mutilated body and the expressionless coroner, Rhonda continued the disturbing conversation. "You haven't found the girl?" she asked the two cops. Three sets of rapid footsteps echoed in the corridor as Rhonda hustled to keep pace with the much taller officers. Apparently they didn't like being inside this building any more than she did.

"No, ma'am," the black cop said. "But we're looking."

"One thing we do know," his partner added, "none of your husband's friends could recall ever having seen her before. She was a stranger. So chances are she was a stranger to your husband, too."

Thanks, Rhonda thought. If you're trying to spare my feelings, I'll give you points for that. But that doesn't change the fact that Ed's dead. It doesn't take away what was done to him. Is it retribution for my sins?

"And they said she was acting strangely," the black cop said.

"Strangely? How?"

The officers looked at one another. They were in the lobby now, where a plain, fortyish, blond receptionist sat behind a desk. "Good night now," she said automatically as they pushed open the door and stepped out into the humid, moonlit night.

"The bartender said she was talking weird, claiming to be a witch, stuff like that," the white cop said. "She was saying strange things, making predictions. Apparently she predicted the White Sox would lose. When they *did* lose, a couple of your husband's friends took exception, and the bartender asked her to leave. He said your husband followed her out the door and didn't come back."

"You think Ed was killed by this woman?" Rhonda asked them both.

"We honestly don't know," said the black officer. "Kind of rough stuff for a young lady, though. We may be looking at a jealous husband or boyfriend, or it may have been a random thing, a robbery maybe, where your husband tried to fight back. We just don't know. Right now we don't even have a murder weapon."

"Anyone have a grudge against your husband?" the white officer asked as they approached the parked police car. "For any reason? He owe anybody money, or did anybody owe him?"

Rhonda shook her head. "I can't think of any reason *anyone* would do this to him," she murmured, belated tears trickling from the outer corners of her eyes, not in sorrow for Ed or herself but for the senselessness of it all. She wiped at her face with the back of her hand. Wordlessly, the black officer handed her a handkerchief, which she accepted with mumbled thanks.

"Where . . . was he . . . when you found him?" she asked.

"In the park, by the river," the white cop said. "A couple of college kids stumbled across the body. There wasn't anyone else around."

"No one goes in that park after dark," Rhonda said. "Except for drunks and dope addicts."

"And kids who don't know any better," the black cop added.

Rhonda shook her head. She felt the tears again, and blinked them back. "It doesn't make any sense," she said.

"Mrs. Whittingham, is there someplace we can take you?" the white officer asked her. "Your parents' house, friends, relatives? You name it, we'll take you there."

Rhonda dabbed at her face with the handkerchief and shook her head. "Just take me home," she said.

"You sure? It might not be a good time to be alone."

"Just take me home," she repeated. "I've got a car. I'm a grown woman."

"All right," the officer said, opening the car door for her. "You need anything, you just give us a call."

She didn't say another word as the officers drove her home. At the deserted house she assured them several times that she would be all right. They did not leave until she had unlocked her front door and let herself in, and they made her promise to call them if she thought of anything, no matter how seemingly insignificant, that could lead them to her husband's killer.

Rhonda did not immediately call her parents, or any of her friends. Dazed, she wandered aimlessly around the house, looking at all the things that belonged to Ed—his clothes in their closet, his sports magazines in the living room, his tools in the garage, the half-empty six-pack of beer he had left in the refrigerator. Everything was in its place, except her husband. The reclining chair she had bought him three Christmases ago stood empty in front of the TV. It would never feel his weight again.

In the side pocket of her purse her fingers unzipped an inner lining and extracted a folded piece of paper, on which some weeks ago young Cyrus Nygerski had scrawled the number of the phone in his apartment. Two thin streams of tears ran down her face as she dialed the number.

The phone rang and rang and rang.

3.

CASSANDRA

In the pinkish-gray light of predawn, a solitary figure shouldered a duffel bag as he made his way along the deserted streets. Raised near the ocean, Cyrus Nygerski had never gotten used to the arbitrary way the days began and ended in the continental heartland. The Moon had already descended behind the rolling suburbs; in thirty minutes or so, the Sun would pop a limb above the freeway beyond the cornfields. Sunrise in the Midwest was like a bus schedule, he thought as he headed for the bus station. East and west, he pictured other towns in other cornfields, waiting their turn on the turning Earth. There was little sense of the drama, so subtle and yet so evident, of sunrise in an Atlantic port, when the fish and the birds and the very molecules of the air and water seemed to come alive. The landmass all around him swallowed edges, mocked boundaries, resisted definition.

He walked south, down a street laid out along Earth's axis, perpendicular to the east-west avenues that likewise had no natural obstacles around which to bend. Beloit, except for the Rock River, which meandered through its concrete heart, was a grid. The bus station, as most bus stations in midsize cities seem to be, was in the worst part of town, which in Beloit happened to be one block north of the state line on the east bank of the Rock River. There were no cars on the streets. It was 6 A.M. on a Sunday, and the blue-collar town was sleeping.

He would be gone, long gone, when it awoke. His baseball career was over. His reason for living here was over. Rhonda would miss him, he thought, and he supposed that he would miss her, too—his affair with her had been a valuable part of his education. But he had made no effort to contact her to say good-bye. She was a married woman, and many years too old for him, and what he felt as he walked toward the bus station was not regret but relief.

He'd sat in the bar and watched his friend's band, and had offered Mavrogenes the other ticket to the doubleheader in exchange for a ride to Chicago. Mavrogenes had declined, citing his job with the Turtles. Nygerski had tried to hit on a pretty, frizzy-haired college girl, been rebuffed, and crawled out to the parking lot to sleep in his friend's van. He had woken at first light and slunk away, without saying good-bye to Mavrogenes, either. Cyrus Nygerski hated good-byes. He thought of them as preludes to death.

Two pigeons, the first life-forms he had seen since setting out, scuttered out of his way as he approached the tiny bus station. He kicked an empty Pabst Blue Ribbon can off the sidewalk into the street and opened the door.

"Can I help you?" said a small man of about sixty at the counter in front of a wall full of baggage tags. He had white hair and wire-rimmed glasses, which perched halfway down his thin nose. A narrow gray-and-blue-striped tie with a Greyhound tie clip constrained a prominent Adam's apple that bobbed up and down when he talked, making the whole tie move.

"Um . . . Chicago, one way," Nygerski said. "Leaves at six-fifteen, right?"

"That's correct," the man said. He shook back a sleeve and looked at his wristwatch. "It's running a few minutes late this morning, but it should be here within the half hour. Any baggage?"

Nygerski tried not to be mesmerized by the tie. "Just this, and I'll keep it with me," he said, hefting the duffel bag.

The man began preparing the ticket as Nygerski took in the small station: back-to-back plastic seats, three pay phones along one wall, a stack of metal lockers with keys, and vending machines offering newspapers, candy bars, cigarettes, and coffee that looked and tasted like used motor oil. He bought a *Chicago Tribune* and sat down to read the sports section.

The Red Sox had beaten the White Sox while the Twins had lost to Cleveland. Detroit had won also, and on this last Sunday of August the American League standings looked like this:

	W	L	Pct	GB
Boston	72	56	.563	—
Minnesota	71	56	.559	¹/₂
Chicago	70	56	.553	1
Detroit	·71	57	.555	1

"The Red Sox have not been in first place this late in the season since October 1, 1949," the newspaper said. Nygerski had been a baby then; the Red Sox had lost the pennant on the final day to the dreaded Yankees, who, Nygerski noted with satisfaction, were now lounging in ninth place, fifteen games back.

Man, what I'd give for a *Boston Globe* right now, Nygerski thought as he skimmed the pro-White Sox article. He chortled when he read the comment by Eddie Stanky, the White Sox manager. "So, they're in first place for a day. Big deal. Their food will taste better. We'll take two tomorrow and be right back up there."

He turned to the box scores. As he did so, the door to the tiny station opened and a young woman entered. She glanced quickly over at Nygerski, who was not able to duck behind the newspaper in time, and their eyes met. Hers were bright blue. He forgot, momentarily, about baseball.

He watched her over the top of the paper as she stepped to the ticket counter and set down a small metal suitcase. Nygerski had the sudden feeling he had seen this woman somewhere before. Should seeing her here mean something to him? Where does such a feeling come from? he wondered. Surely the girl was a complete stranger. Nothing in his conscious memory could account for the sense of familiarity, or of fright. Her darting glance had alarmed him; his palms had begun to sweat, and he had become aware of the beating of his heart.

"Has the bus to Chicago left yet?" she asked the man behind the counter.

The clerk looked up at the clock. "Should be here within ten minutes," he said. "You need a ticket?"

"Yeah. One way, with a connection to Boston."

Nygerski's ears perked up. He scrutinized her over the top of his paper, ready to raise it in front of his face should her eyes dart his way again. But she ignored him as the old man prepared her ticket.

He had caught the trace of an accent in the few words she had spoken; her A's, like his, were flat, and out of place in the Midwest. She had long, very dark, straight hair, which had not been combed. It fell over a denim jacket with a rip halfway up one sleeve and a streak of dirt running diagonally down the back. Her blue jeans were likewise covered with dirt and grass stains, and he could see a large hole in the knee closest to him. Her back was turned at the moment, so that he could not see her face, but from his first look he guessed her to be near his age. His limited experience with women made such guesses hazardous. He had learned to keep them to himself.

He ducked behind the paper as she accepted her ticket and turned from the window, toward him. Where had he seen her before? And what was it about her that frightened him?

She walked past him to the coffee machine. He observed that she was neither tall nor short nor skinny nor overweight. Beneath the jacket she wore a loose-fitting white shirt that was as dirty as her jeans. She plunked a dime into the coffee machine and watched the cardboard cup plop into the dispenser and fill with hot liquid.

Nygerski tried to rekindle his interest in the sports section, but the presence of the girl was too powerful to ignore. She took the cup of coffee and raised it to her lips as she looked out the dirty plate-glass window. "Ugh!" she exclaimed. She turned around suddenly and looked right at him. He hoped his involuntary shudder was invisible. He swallowed, and forced a smile.

"They have the worst coffee in these places," she said directly to him. "It's practically undrinkable."

Her blue eyes would not let go of him. He noted that the whites around the irises were bloodshot, and that dark gray bags underlined each eye. In addition, one eyelid drooped lower than the other; he saw it twitch several times as she stared at him. Her face looked gaunt, haunted. Nonetheless, she was a very pretty woman. Beautiful, in fact, even if she did look like she needed a bath and a week of sleep.

"Motor oil," he managed to mutter.

"I'm sorry?"

"It tastes like motor oil," he said, embarrassed by the sudden attack of shyness. "I try to avoid it, myself."

"Oh." She laughed, and the gaunt look faded, along with some of Nygerski's fear. But he couldn't shake the sense of familiarity. She took another sip of coffee and grimaced. "It's better than nothing," she said.

Several seconds of awkward silence passed. She stood before him, her coffee in front of her face, making no move to take the seat next to Nygerski. He made no move to get up.

"Going to Chicago?" she asked him.

"Yeah," he said, folding the paper. "You?"

"I'm going to Chicago, too," she said, nodding. "It's on the way home."

"Where's home?" he asked.

"Maine."

"No shit! I'm from Boston."

She laughed again, displaying an array of crooked yet somehow lovely teeth. He admired her small, pointed chin, her long neck, the patch of skin around her collarbone where he could see a small scratch. She's exquisite, he thought, even though she's a mess. Where had he seen her before? And how could he possibly have forgotten?

"I know," she said. "I can tell by your accent. Better get up, the bus'll be here in less than a minute."

"How do you . . ." Nygerski did not get the sentence out before a Greyhound bus pulled up in front of the big window, darkening the tiny station. Sheepishly, he stood up and hoisted the duffel bag from the chair beside him. "You got good ears," he mumbled.

"Sixth sense," she said. "My name's Cassandra."

She extended a thin hand. Nygerski noticed as he took it the amount of dirt under the fingernails, and the large purple bruise beneath the nail on the index finger. "I'm Cyrus," he told her, feeling as he did so that it was unnecessary, that she could read him at a touch. It was a ludicrous feeling, and yet there it was. "Have we . . . met before?" he asked her.

She laughed again. "Not in this life," she said. "Come on, the bus is waiting."

They found a pair of unoccupied seats two-thirds of the way to the back of the bus. Nygerski swung his big duffel bag up onto the overhead rack and held out his hand for Cassandra's case. Its modest size belied its weight. "Damn," Nygerski said as he hefted it into a spot beside his own bag. "What's in this thing?"

"My life," Cassandra said.

The bus was moving before he sat down. In two minutes they were on the interstate, the smokestacks of Beloit enveloped by the cornfields. Nygerski wondered if he would ever see this place again, and guessed he wouldn't.

Cassandra leaned back in the window seat and closed her eyes. "Did you catch that guy's tie, how he made it move up and down? Gawd, I feel dizzy."

Now it was Nygerski's turn to laugh. "You must've had as little sleep as I did last night."

"I can never sleep when the Moon is full," she said, turning to look at him. Her left eyelid twitched several times; the girl seemed unaware of it. Nygerski awaited further explanation—of why her clothes were torn and dirty, where she had picked up the scratches on her neck, how she had come to be in Beloit, Wisconsin, of all places, on a summer Sunday.

When it became clear that she was not going to elaborate, when indeed she turned her eyes away from him to look out at the monotonous vista of corn rushing past the window, he continued the conversation. "Where you from in Maine?" he asked her.

"Little place called Deer Isle, on the coast," she said. "You've probably never heard of it."

"That bridge still standing?"

Cassandra turned to him and smiled broadly. "You *have* heard of it!"

"I've sailed under that bridge," Nygerski said. "Heard a lot of rumors about it."

"Christ, everybody on Deer Isle's got bets on when that bridge is going to fall down. When were you there?"

"Summer before last. I crewed on one of those big tourist schooners out of Camden. It was a blast."

"You know where Rum Runners Cove is?"

"I must have seen it on the charts. It's an incredible area, all the coves and islands and little out-of-the-way harbors. It's another world."

"Yeah, it's pretty," Cassandra said, in a tone that sounded oddly flat. "Not much to do there, though, really. Not like Boston." She closed her eyes again and leaned her head against the window.

Nygerski watched her for a minute, thinking this a signal that she wished to sleep. When she did not open her eyes he unfolded the newspaper to the box scores. Reading in a moving vehicle usually nauseated him, but he hung in long enough to note that Earl Wilson had won his eighteenth for the Tigers, and that Don Drysdale, who was having a bad year, had pitched a strong game for the Dodgers. The Red Sox were sending Gary Bell (9–10) to the mound in the first game of today's doubleheader against Paul Klages (2–2).

He forced his eyes to the window to ward off carsickness, and was surprised to see Cassandra looking back at him. Her closed lips formed a thin smile, and again it seemed to him that he must have seen her before. Maybe in Maine, that summer? If so, why had it not remained in his memory, as this bus ride surely would? He had never seen eyes like hers. They were blue not like the sky but like an aquamarine crystal, broken into a thousand pieces.

"So you're from Boston," she said. "How 'bout them Sox?"

He tried to hide his surprise. "You like baseball?"

"I can tell that you do," she said, nodding at the paper in his lap.

"It's not just that—I've played some ball," he said, with an equal mixture of pride and sadness.

"I'm not surprised," she told him. "You move like an athlete. What position do you play?"

"Second base," he said. "I played for the local minor-league team here."

"But . . . that's all over for you now, isn't it?"

Nygerski gulped in amazement. "How do you know that?" he asked her.

"You're traveling alone, without lots of luggage, you're wearing shitty clothes, you haven't paid much attention to your hair this morning. You used the past tense. And, I don't know, you seem sort of defeated. Like you're looking back, not forward. Everything about you says leaving, not arriving."

"I got released yesterday," Nygerski mumbled.

"I'm sorry," Cassandra said.

Suddenly he had an inspiration "But they gave me two tickets to the Red Sox game," he said, reaching into his inside jacket pocket and pulling them out. "Today. In Chicago. And I've got no one to use the other one."

A cloud crossed Cassandra's features, and was gone almost before Nygerski could be puzzled by it. "Did I say something wrong?" he asked.

"No, no." She smiled at him. "A baseball game, you said. You have tickets to a baseball game."

"A doubleheader, actually. Red Sox and White Sox at Comiskey Park. Epic battle for first place in the American League. First game starts at one. You wanna go?"

She didn't answer for a moment, and Nygerski feared she would turn him down. "Sure," she said, finally. "Sounds like fun. As long as I can find some place to get cleaned up first." She reached over and touched the hand holding the tickets. There was that crooked smile again. "Thank you, Cyrus," she said. "They're gonna win, you know. The Red Sox."

"The game, you mean?"

"The pennant. They're gonna win."

He tried to sound calm. "Well, we'll see," he said. "There's three other teams."

She patted his hand and closed her eyes. "Trust me," she said. "They're gonna win."

He watched her again as she leaned back in her seat and began to doze off. What was her story? he wondered. What was she doing here, on this bus in the middle of the country? She had said she was going to Maine, going home, but where had she come from? Where had she been, and for what purpose? And why had she suddenly popped up in his life, along with a profound feeling of déjà vu? Who *was* she? "Cassandra," he said softly.

She opened her eyes sleepily and looked at him.

"About what you said . . . that I look like I'm leaving, not arriving?"

"Yeah?"

"It just occurred to me that I could say the same thing about you."

Cassandra looked down at her dirty clothes. A thin smile formed on her lips. "How observant you are, my friend," she said. "Leaving is the story of my life."

4.

TARTABULL'S THROW—I

Cassandra slept most of the way to Chicago. Her sleep was fitful—she shifted positions, smacked her lips, and muttered words and half-sentences that danced on the edge of coherence. Eventually she rested her head on Nygerski's shoulder, and that seemed to comfort her, for she settled down after that. Nygerski, who had been awake most of the night, tried to close his eyes as well, but found the physical contact arresting enough to drive away sleep.

Instead, he watched the cornfields and small towns roll by outside the window, stealing a look every thirty seconds or so at the sleeping girl beside him. Her breath, heavy and regular, felt warm against the flesh of his neck. Still, she was not totally relaxed. Every so often he would see the closed left eyelid twitch, or one of the corners of her mouth move, as if she was puzzling over something in her dreams. She's very beautiful, he thought again, resisting the urge to stroke her hair, lest he wake her. Several strands lay across her pale cheek, partially concealing a dark bruise there the size and shape of a guitar pick. What had happened to her? Asleep, her face had lost the haunted look he had noticed in the bus station. But he could see fragments of dirt and dead leaves in her hair, and she smelled like the outdoors. No—

that wasn't it exactly. She smelled like . . . like something wild and not altogether good, yet still compelling. Nygerski thought of bacon. His stomach rumbled, reminding him that he had not had breakfast.

He let her sleep through several stops as the cornfields between towns gave way to sustained suburbia. Through Elgin, Des Plains, Harwood Heights they passed, the day growing brighter and busier around them. Even on a Sunday, Chicago bustled with activity. Not until the tall buildings of downtown hove into view and the driver announced that the bus would arrive at Union Station in fifteen minutes did Nygerski nudge the sleeping woman beside him. "Cassandra, wake up. We're almost there."

She stirred slightly and smacked her lips again. Her head remained on his shoulder.

"Hey," he said, shaking her gently. "You're missing the sights."

"Safe," she mumbled in her sleep, cuddling against Nygerski's neck. There was that smell again, like spoiled meat, but too faint to repulse him. The touch of her felt awkward and wonderful. Her left eyelid twitched rapidly.

He smiled. There was something about watching another human sleep, especially a person of the opposite sex, that aroused feelings of warmth and tenderness. He decided to give her a few more minutes.

Her lips parted with a sound like a Band-Aid being removed. Her head rolled back and forth on his shoulder. "You're safe," she said, quite clearly.

The bus exited the interstate highway and slowly maneuvered its way onto surface streets. Nygerski shook her shoulder. "You're dreaming, Cassandra. Wake up. We're in Chicago."

She snuggled close to him, and Nygerski saw the corners of her mouth curl upward. Her left eyelid had stopped twitching. The bus turned a corner, and her weight pressed against him.

And then she blinked, raised her head, looked out the window and finally at him. She blinked again; the left eyelid twitched once and then was still. "We're here," she said, surprised.

"Sleep well?" he asked her.

She looked at him and laughed, then shifted away from him on the seat. "Considering where I am, yeah." She rubbed her eyes and stretched her arms upward. "On a bus, I mean."

"What were you dreaming about?"

A puzzled look crossed her face. "Dreaming? I don't think I was dreaming about anything. Why?"

"You were talking to yourself. In your sleep."

"Oh." Nygerski thought there was an edge of nervousness in her laugh. "My friends tell me I do that," she said. "So I guess I was. But I don't remember any dreams."

Ten minutes later they walked into the main lobby of Chicago's cavernous Union Station, just two more weary travelers in the nation's Midwestern hub on the last Sunday of August. It was nine in the morning. Sunlight streamed through high windows below the domed ceiling. Other travelers hurried past them without a second glance, their footsteps echoing on the stone floor. Announcements of impending departures and arrivals of buses and trains floated through the air over the PA system. Nygerski and Cassandra turned to one another with the same thought.

"What would you say to—" he began.

"I'm so hungry, I could eat a horse," Cassandra declared, riding over his unfinished invitation to breakfast. "Let's get something to eat, okay?"

He grinned, not at all disturbed that she had read his mind—or had she merely read his stomach? "My sentiments exactly," he said.

"First I gotta find a rest room," she told him. "And you look like you could stand some freshening up, too."

Nygerski ran a hand through his short, uncombed hair. "Yeah, I guess I could," he admitted.

"Meet you back here in fifteen minutes," she said. And without waiting for an answer, she was off, walking briskly down the hall in the direction they had come, carrying the silver case like it weighed nothing.

Nygerski was back in five, after combing his hair, throwing some water on his face, and taking care of other necessities. He bought an Oh Henry! bar and a street map of Chicago, and sat down on one of the wooden benches to locate Comiskey Park.

Ten minutes passed, then twenty. He had intended to save half the candy bar for Cassandra, but after twenty-five minutes his hunger got the better of him and he decided it would be all right if he just saved her a quarter of it. Five minutes later he was beginning to think he'd been ditched. He got up and wandered toward the glass doors. Pigeons and people passed by on the sidewalk. Three of the birds fought over a discarded food wrapper. Nygerski's stomach rumbled.

He returned to the bench, picked up his duffel bag, and polished off the rest of the candy bar. He folded the map and shoved it into the back pocket of his jeans. What now? The game didn't start for three hours, but the demands of his stomach were more imperative. He didn't want to believe the girl was gone. But he had known her, he reminded himself, for less than four hours, and half that time she had been sleeping. He didn't really know her at all. Yet he couldn't escape the feeling that he should have, that there was a connection between them, that she had some significance in his life. Then again, maybe it was wishful thinking.

He stood there, thinking wishfully, for five more minutes. It had now been three-quarters of an hour since she'd left him. Apparently she wasn't coming back. Okay, so he'd eat, and then head for the stadium and try to scalp the other ticket before the game started. He didn't want to think about how easily she had hurt him.

And then, just as he was steeling himself to go, he caught sight of a dark-haired woman in a bright red minidress far down the hall. Her walked was brisk but unhurried. And she was carrying a silver case. It was her!

He set down the duffel bag with a feeling of immense relief, which he tried to erase from his features as he watched her approach. The change in her was incredible. She had brushed out her hair; it fell in sleek waves over her sleeveless dress and bare shoulders. Her light makeup erased any trace of the fatigue that had surrounded her eyes back in Beloit. Now they sparkled beneath groomed eyelashes and mascara. The guitar-pick bruise was visible but faint under the blush she had applied to her cheeks. Thong sandals had replaced the old sneakers she had worn on the bus. And the dress showed off a lovely figure. Nygerski could not keep his eyes from her legs.

She flashed him her wide, crooked smile as she entered the lobby, and his irritation at her for keeping him waiting melted like ice cream on a sidewalk. "I found a great little restaurant," she said as she came up to him. "It's only a block away. First I want to put this in one of those lockers. I don't want to lug it around. You might want to get one, too. Come on, they're down here."

He hurried to follow her down another arm of the station. Heads turned as he hustled to keep up with her. He found himself suddenly wondering about the men in her life, and why she would be traveling alone. This woman was a complete mystery to him. He knew nothing about her. But she was doubly beautiful now that she had cleaned up, made up, and dressed up—and he, Cyrus Nygerski, had a date with her for this afternoon's doubleheader. Things could be worse.

Cassandra insisted on separate lockers, though her suitcase and his bag would have fit in one. He didn't argue. She took a small black purse out of the suitcase before locking it away. She led him back through the lobby and out the big double doors onto the street and into the glaring August sunshine. He felt light and almost naked without his few meager possessions, and a little giddy in the company of such a good-looking woman. But most of all he felt hungry.

The restaurant was small, boisterous, and crowded. Almost every seat had a view out the window. Nygerski ordered eggs over easy with bacon and toast, coffee, and a large glass of orange juice. Cassandra astonished him by ordering a steak, rare, with baked potato and salad, and a large mug of beer. She gulped half the beer down in the first swallow. Nygerski raised an eyebrow. "Kinda early in the day, isn't it?"

She laughed good-naturedly. "Not when you've been up all night," she said. "We women are in tune with the Moon, you know. When it's full, it tends to make us manic." Her eyes smiled mischievously at him over the rim of her glass.

When the steak came she attacked it with the same enthusiasm, and Nygerski devoted his full attention to the food in front of him. When the waitress returned to check on them several minutes later, Cassandra ordered a second beer and asked him if he wanted one.

Nygerski shook his head. "I'm not really much of a drinker," he confessed. "It slows me down."

She laughed again. "There are times," she said, "when *nothing* slows me down."

Why does that not surprise me? he thought as the waitress refilled his coffee cup. Aloud, he said, "So you're going home. To Maine."

"That's right," she said through her teeth as they worked on a large piece of steak.

"How long were you in Beloit?"

She chewed several more times before washing the meat down with a swallow of beer. "Few hours, maybe," she said. "I don't really remember. I was hitchhiking. Got a ride."

"So where've you been?"

She laughed again, but not so gently. "Fill him with food, he fills up with questions."

"I'm sorry," he said. "If it's none of my business, I'll—"

She cut him off. "San Francisco," she said. "I spent the summer in San Francisco."

"Oh."

"I had a . . . relationship . . . with a guy. It didn't work out."

Nygerski shoveled the last bite of his egg onto a piece of toast and raised the whole operation to his mouth, avoiding a reply.

"He was a Negro," she went on. "In Maine, that's still taboo. But nobody turned an eye in San Francisco. It's a whole different world out there."

"'The Summer of Love,'" Nygerski said, quoting a newspaper article he'd read about the gatherings of young people in California and their frequent run-ins with the law.

"It was incredible, Cyrus. It's just like in the song—people really do go around with flowers in their hair. And barefoot, and in costume. You'd see people with guitars and flutes on streets corners, just having fun. Every day there'd be something happening. The cops could be a drag sometimes, but there were always more of us than there were of them."

"How about drugs? I heard lots of people were getting strung out on drugs."

Cassandra shrugged. "I met a couple kids who were into heroin," she said, "and *they* were pretty strung out. And acid . . . I heard about people having bad trips, but I never had one, and neither did anyone I knew. You ever take LSD?"

Nygerski shook his head. "I'm a babe in the woods," he told her. "Marijuana and beer's about the extent of it. Dope interferes with baseball."

"But acid is different," Cassandra said. "It opens doors in your mind. You learn things that stay with you long after the drug's worn off. It makes you feel like all your abilities are enhanced. It's like . . . like you can see all the possibilities, all the interconnectedness of things. . . . I can't explain it, really. It's something that has to be experienced."

Having nothing to say to this, Nygerski took another big bite of his breakfast.

"I stayed in an old Victorian house with about sixteen other people," Cassandra continued. "It was hard to tell who lived there at any one time, people came and went so often. In the evenings we'd sit around, get high, and play music, and all the guys would try to think of out-landish ways to keep their asses out of Vietnam."

The mention of the war brought Nygerski up short. Cassandra must have seen it, for she said, "How about you? What's your story? You been drafted?"

He nodded. "I *still* hurt from that physical, and it was almost a year ago."

She laughed. "So why aren't you—"

"Over there?"

"Yeah."

"I got out of it so far on account of my mom being on her own with my sisters. My dad left when I was ten, and we've been pretty much dirt poor since. I got a contract to play baseball for money—not much, but enough to make me look like the family breadwinner. And just to be safe, I applied to college."

"How old are your sisters?"

"Fourteen and twelve."

"I have a ten-year-old brother," she said. "His name's Timmy. He's the smart one in the family. Gets all A's in school, already beats me and my dad at chess. Plus, he's become a real baseball nut. I called home last week to tell my folks I was coming, and Christ, all I heard for fifteen minutes was the Red Sox this and the Red Sox that."

Nygerski beamed. "Hey, I don't blame him. They're in first place in August. It's almost a miracle. They've stunk for as long as I can remember."

Cassandra insisted on paying for breakfast; Nygerski put up a feeble argument, just for show. He was unemployed now and would need to watch his money.

"Let's get to the ballpark," he said when they were outside. "We got two hours. You wanna walk or take a cab?"

"How far is it?"

"About four miles," he replied, pulling out the map.

"Oh, let's walk. It's a beautiful day for a walk. And I feel good."

Just then, a red and white city bus pulled up next to a bench beside them. White letters above the windshield called out its destination: COMISKEY PARK.

"On second thought, let's take a bus," she suggested. Nygerski and Cassandra looked at each other for a moment, then erupted into laughter.

Comiskey Park, home of the Chicago White Sox, was already beginning to fill by the time Nygerski and Cassandra arrived, more than an hour before the start of the game. After the tiny stadium in Beloit, Nygerski felt overwhelmed by the spaciousness of the old stone ballpark. Their seats were on the third-base side, a dozen rows behind the visitors' dugout. Players for both teams stretched, played catch in the outfield, swung bats at phantom pitches, and milled about in small groups. Several members of the grounds crew dragged a chain-link blanket around the wide dirt crescent anchored by first and third base, reminding Nygerski of packhorses. People drifted in and began to fill the seats around them.

"Pretty good seats," Nygerski commented. "It's a lot bigger park than Fenway."

"And it's gonna be full of people rooting for the Red Sox to lose," Cassandra told him.

"Not all of us," Nygerski corrected her. "Look."

He nodded, and she looked to her right, toward an old man and woman approaching them from the end of the row of seats. The woman's permed white hair, knee-length blue dress, and doughy roundness bespoke New England winters over a woodstove in the kitchen. The tall, slightly stooped man leading her sported an even more readily identifiable badge of regional affiliation: a Red Sox cap.

"I believe our seats are right next to yours," he said to Cassandra, checking the number on his ticket.

"If so, you're in the right place," Nygerski piped up. "We're Boston fans, too."

"Y'don't say?" The old man's lined face lit up. He turned to his wife. "Hear that, Martha? These folks are rootin' for the Red Sox, too. Looks like we got us a cheering section. Where you folks from?"

"I'm from Boston, and she's from Maine," Nygerski said.

The old man's lips drew back from his yellowed teeth in a grin of joy. "Converse McLean, Epsom, New Hampshire," he declared. "This here's my wife, Martha. We've been Red Sox fans since the days of Babe Ruth."

"They're going to win," Cassandra said.

"By gawd, I hope you're right, young lady," the old man rejoined, taking the seat next to her. He held out a bony, long-fingered hand; Cassandra grasped it.

"I'm Cassandra Paine," she said. "And this is Cyrus. We don't know each other's last names yet."

The two men reached across Cassandra and shook hands. Martha sat down on her husband's opposite side. "Where in Maine?" she asked Cassandra.

"The boonies. Penobscot Bay area. My little brother listens to all the Red Sox games on the radio. We get the Boston stations over the water."

"I have relatives in Ellsworth," Martha said.

"Really? That's not far from where my folks live." And with that, old home week began. Martha and Cassandra had gotten a good way through their family histories before the old man, bored, turned to Nygerski.

"You hear about Ken Harrelson?" he asked.

Nygerski nodded. He had read about the acquisition of the slugging, outspoken first baseman in the newspaper.

"Has he joined the team yet?" Nygerski asked the old man.

McLean shook his head. "Tomorrow in New York. Which is where we'll be, too."

"Yeah? You're following 'em? Cool."

"Our daughter and her family live in Joliet," Martha McLean explained to them both. "And my husband can't be persuaded to take a trip without it tying in with the Red Sox somehow. So I said we could catch a game here and in New York, and he agreed to the trip. First time we've been anywhere in years."

"First time the Sox have been worth the trouble since forty-nine," the old man said, looking at his wife. "You know Larry would've wanted us to be here. And Patrick, too, God rest his soul." He turned to Cassandra and Nygerski. "Larry was my son. Born in nineteen twenty-three, three years after the Red Sox sold Babe Ruth to the Yankees. Boy, not many people remember those days, but let me tell you, before the Black Sox scandal, before everything in baseball started bein' about money, Boston was the class of the American League. Between the turn of the century and the Great War, we won five World Series Championships. The nineteen eighteen Series was played in September, a month early, because a lot of the players were going into the service. The Babe was a pitcher then, but he batted fourth in the order. He won three games for us. Next year he played outfield and didn't pitch so much, but he hit twenty-nine home runs. More than anyone had ever hit before. And he didn't even play every day. Oh, you could tell he was going to change the game."

"But they traded him," Nygerski said.

"Sold him!" McLean cried, his indignation surprisingly immediate over a forty-seven-year-old wrong. "Harry Frazee sold him, to pay off a failed theater production. To the Yankees! The Yankees were nothing until they stole Babe Ruth from us. Nothing! And you know what? We ain't won the World Series since."

"But what does all this have to do with your son?" Cassandra asked.

A misty look came into the old man's gray-blue eyes. "My son *and* grandson," he said softly. He looked at his wife, seemingly lost for a moment.

"Tell them, Connie," she urged gently. "They're Boston fans. They'll understand."

The old man licked his lips. "Larry served under Eisenhower in Germany," he said. "It was early nineteen forty-five; the war was won. The Germans were blowing up bridges as they retreated, and the Americans would have to stop and repair them before marching on to join up with the Russians. Larry was killed helping to rebuild a bridge."

"Oh, gosh, I'm sorry," Cassandra murmured.

"Patrick was a baby. Never saw his dad. And he was too young to remember forty-six, the year after the war, when the Red Sox finally made it back to the Series."

"Which they lost," Nygerski put in.

"Which they lost," the old man echoed. "Pesky held the ball! Enos Slaughter scored from first on a double, and Pesky held the ball. If he'd made the throw, Slaughter would've been out by a mile. But they lost, and they lost the playoff in forty-eight, and they lost to the Yankees in forty-nine on the last day of the season, and nothing's gone right since."

Nygerski started to say something, but the old man cut him off. "Patrick," he said, swallowing hard, "was shot down over North Vietnam in March. Two other pilots saw his plane hit the ground and explode."

Wordlessly, Martha McLean reached over and entwined her fingers with her husband's. "So you see?" McLean concluded. "My boy and *his* boy both lived their entire lives without seeing the Red Sox win. I'm the last one left, and I'm going to be here to bear witness when the Red Sox rise again. I'm going to be here to witness it, for *them*."

Nygerski was too stunned to say anything. Cassandra found words first. "Well, I hope they win it, for your sake alone," she said, patting his upper arm. "And I have a feeling they will."

McLean returned her smile. "The optimism of youth," he said with a sigh. "I hope you're right." They were announcing the starting lineups, putting the names and numbers up on the scoreboard. The old man took out a game program, opened it up to the scorecard in the center, and began writing in the names of the Boston players.

A roving peanut vendor caught their attention. Cassandra turned to Nygerski. "I'd like some peanuts and Cracker Jack, but a beer would be nice, too. Get you one?" She stood up.

"Where are you going?" The anxiety she had caused him at Union Station was fresh in his mind.

She laughed at his worried look. "To the concession stand. Do you want a beer?"

"Oh. Sure. Yeah, a beer would be all right. Thanks."

He took note of the heads that turned to follow the short red dress across the row of seats and up the aisle. She moved quickly, gracefully, weaving her way between incoming fans like a Christmas ribbon, until she disappeared from sight underneath the second section of stands.

He didn't see her again until the national anthem had ended and José Tartabull stepped into the batter's box for the Red Sox to begin the game. Nygerski had been searching the nearby stands for her in vain; now, at the first pitch, she materialized by his side, with peanuts, two hot dogs, and two large beers.

And something else. "Here," she said when they were seated with their food and drinks. She placed a small square of paper, about the size of a postage stamp, in his hand.

He squinted at it. A white piece of paper with a purple blob on it. "What's this?"

"It's what we talked about earlier," she said quietly. "It's time you became experienced."

His eyes widened. "Is it . . . ?"

She grinned broadly and nodded. "I may have left my heart in San Francisco, but I brought some of this with me. It's good."

"So . . . what do I do?"

"Just put it in your mouth and let it dissolve," Cassandra explained. "You can wash it down with the beer, if you want."

"And then what happens?"

"Nothing—for about an hour, hour and a half. Don't worry; you'll know."

Nygerski considered the piece of paper with its purple Rorschach test.

"And you won't be traveling alone," she added, holding up a similar paper square. She winked at him with the eye that twitched, and popped it in her mouth.

Nygerski waited a moment, shrugged, and did the same. It didn't taste like anything. "Am I supposed to hear Jimi Hendrix music in my head, or something?"

She laughed. "Anything can happen with acid," she said. "I saw the real Jimi, in June, at Monterey. A bunch of us went down in this old farm truck. We all dropped. It was fantastic."

Nygerski took a swallow of beer and turned his attention to the field, where the Red Sox went out quietly in the top of the first. As Gary Bell took his warm-up tosses, Nygerski leaned over toward the old man and peered at his scorecard. "The usual lineup, it looks like," he said.

"Yeah, except they got the old man catching. Elston Howard. Can't get used to him without a Yankees uniform."

"He'll be good for us down the stretch, though," Nygerski said.

"Well, he's been around," Converse McLean grumbled. "I s'pose he's worth having in the clubhouse just because he's got pennant race experience, even though he can't get around on a fastball anymore."

"He been playing much?" Nygerski asked.

"Some. We're not strong at catcher. Team's strength is supposed to be up the middle, and look at what we've got. Mike Ryan, Andrews, and Smith. Three kids."

"They've done all right so far," Nygerski commented.

"Yeah, but they're young. And young hitters get into slumps. But, by gawd, management seems serious about winning this thing. They brought in Bell, and Howard, and now Harrelson. Be good to have some pop in the lineup behind Yastrzemski. I guess he'll play right field, in place of Tony C."

"No one can replace Tony C.," Nygerski murmured with a touch of reverence.

"I know, son, I know. But baseball is like life. You've gotta pick up and go on. It'd be more of a tragedy if they gave up, if they didn't replace him, if they played the rest of the season with José Tartabull in right. I like Tartabull, but he don't hit homers and he's got a weak throwing arm."

The home crowd stirred as the White Sox scored a run in the bottom of the first, but Boston came back with two in the third to take the lead. Nygerski kept waiting for the acid to kick in. Periodically he looked over at Cassandra; every half-inning he asked if what was supposed to happen was happening yet. But mostly he watched the ball game, and talked baseball with Converse McLean, and basked in the late August sunshine. Which seemed especially bright today, on the shimmering, emerald outfield. The stadium buzzed noisily, though Nygerski noted that it was only about two-thirds full.

In the fifth inning, Carl Yastrzemski hit a tremendous home run into the right-field bleachers to make it 3-1. Nygerski watched the arc of the ball as it soared away from him against an electric-blue sky, leaving a vapor trail in his mind. It landed among some empty seats, and a blur of human life scrambled after it.

He turned to Cassandra. He noted the curve of her breasts beneath the scarlet dress, the contours of her legs. . . . Her lips parted, and she smiled that crooked smile at him again.

"They're not hittin'," Converse McLean said beside him. "Yaz can't do it alone."

In the next two innings, Bell, the Boston pitcher, flirted with disaster constantly. The White Sox managed several hits and walks but did not score. The Red Sox hitters went meekly down, one by one, until Yastrzemski, with two out in the seventh, launched another home run into the right-field stands. This time Nygerski saw the whole flight of the ball like time-lapse photography. He saw the seat in which it would land when it was still in flight, and he saw that a little black kid would win the race for the souvenir. He saw several players emerge from the Boston dugout and clap Yastrzemski on the back as he crossed home plate. It all seemed eerily familiar to him, like he had seen it before. The home run did not surprise him at all. And he knew, somehow he just *knew*, that the Red Sox would score no more runs this day.

"They ain't had a hit since about the third inning, except for those two home runs," Converse McLean said.

Nygerski turned back to the game with an increasing feeling of dread. And in the bottom of the inning the foreboding in his mind manifested itself as the Boston defense made an error and the White Sox scored two runs to cut the lead to 4–3. Bell was obviously tiring, but Dick Williams, the Boston manager, made no move to take him out.

The stadium began to swirl around Nygerski, colors blending with noises and smells to assault his senses. The straight lines of iron railings and foul lines oscillated, the planes of grass and outfield walls seemed to breathe, in and out, up and down, like waves beneath a pier. Colors grew brighter. Words in the foam of conversation in the crowd rose up, distinct, and splashed him in the face with new meaning. The percussive sounds of bat against ball and ball against glove backed the symphony all around him.

And the sense of doom was palpable. The brilliant blue of the sky was now dotted with clouds, bright on the upper limbs but dark underneath. The Chicago crowd, silent for most of the game, now buzzed with anticipation. Nygerski knew the LSD was asserting itself in his brain, and he tried to focus on the game despite the sensory overload. Fear prickled the inside of his chest, and he tried to force it down.

The batter hit a high pop fly behind home plate, toward the stands in front of them. Nygerski got a good look at the catcher as he threw off his mask. It wasn't Elston Howard. He knew that Elston Howard was black—the first Negro, in fact, to play for the Yankees, years after Jackie Robinson broke in with the Brooklyn Dodgers. Only the Red Sox had been slower to integrate. But the man who made the catch at the railing was a little too tall and reedy for a catcher, and unquestionably white.

"Wait a minute," Nygerski said to the old man beside him. "Did they change catchers?"

"What're you talking about, boy?" said Converse McLean of Epsom, New Hampshire.

"I thought Howard was catching."

"Who?"

"Elston Howard."

"*Elston Howard?* You mean the old Yankee catcher?"

"Yeah." The stadium bent and curled; now Nygerski felt his mind bending as well. What the hell was going on here? "We talked about him, before the game. Don't you remember?"

"Christ, boy, Elston Howard retired. The Yankees benched him, and he called it quits."

Nygerski pursed his lips. "Let me see your scorecard," he said.

"Be my guest," the old man replied diffidently, and handed it over.

Nygerski scanned the lineups. The White Sox had made several substitutions, which the old man had penciled in. But the Red Sox had made none. And listed in the seventh spot in the batting order was Mike Ryan, catcher.

"I'll be goddamned," Nygerski said weakly. He looked at Cassandra, who smiled at him, her pupils dilated. Her dark hair shimmered against the red dress.

"Enjoying the game?" she asked him.

"Something's wrong," he said.

She smiled enigmatically, her crooked teeth lovely in the sunlight. "I said you'd know, didn't I?"

"This isn't right," he insisted. "Something's changed."

"You better believe it," Cassandra replied.

The White Sox got another hit in the eighth but did not score. Williams stuck with Bell. The Red Sox went out in order in the ninth, still leading, 4–3.

Nygerski squirmed in his seat. I'm a ballplayer, he thought. I'm a *good* ballplayer. What am I doing watching this game from the stands? I should be down there. He shook his head to banish the thought. He reminded himself that he had been released from the low minors. What the hell was he thinking?

"Three more outs," McLean said, in a near-whisper, as Bell came out to pitch the ninth.

But the first batter, Ken Berry, brought the crowd to its feet with a double down the left-field line. The noise washed over Nygerski like a wave. "Oh, Christ," McLean muttered, beside him. The next batter was in the batter's box; the noise had not died down. The batter bunted the first pitch toward first base. The Red Sox made the play, but Berry went to third.

He's going to score on a fly ball.

Nygerski looked quickly at Converse McLean and Cassandra, but neither had uttered the words. Yet he had heard them as clearly as if they had been spoken directly into his ear.

He's going to tag up and score, and tie the game.

Nygerski looked around at the people in the nearby seats, wondering where the voice was coming from. But no one had said a word to him.

Cassandra flashed her crooked smile again. "*Now* you're experienced," she said.

The scoreboard announced Duane Josephson as a pinch hitter for the pitcher. And Dick Williams came out of the Boston dugout, heading for the mound.

"Christ almighty, it's about time," McLean said, joining Nygerski and a few other scattered fans around the stadium in applauding Bell as he left the game. "Pitched a hell of a game, though. The boy put in a day's work."

The reliever was a young Negro named John Wyatt. As he took the first of his warm-up pitches, Cassandra touched Nygerski's arm. "I have to go," she said.

Nygerski actually *felt* his face fall. For a second or two all the muscles, including the ones for speech, simply stopped working. He managed a string of one-word sentences. "What? Now? Where?"

"Home," she said. "It's getting late. I've got to go." She stood up.

Wyatt continued his warm-up.

"Cassandra, we've got a game on the line here!"

"I can't stay, Cyrus. I have to go."

She reached into her purse and pulled out a small, silvery object on a chain. "Here," she said, grabbing his wrist with one hand and placing the object in his hand with the other. "I want you to have this."

"Cassandra, wha—"

But she was already turning to leave. He looked at the gift: a small silver star inside a circle, about the size of a silver dollar. "Cassandra, wait!" he called after her.

Cassandra began pushing her way down the row of seats. Astonished, Nygerski started to follow her. He looked back at McLean and his wife, but their attention was riveted on the field. "Cassandra, wait!" he called after her. The organist played "Charge!" and the crowd roared. The colors of the ballpark swam around him, including a streak of brilliant red making its way down the aisle toward the exit nearest the field.

Duane Josephson stepped to the plate.

"Cassandra!" Cyrus called. The red dress and naked legs seemed to dance in front of him as she freed herself from the seats and floated, tantalizingly out of reach, in front of the stands. He looked desperately back at his seat, once, and then at Cassandra, moving away from him. Then he went after her.

He was down by the dugout, pushing his way through the first row of seats, when Wyatt delivered his pitch. He heard the crack of the bat and saw the spaghetti arc of the ball. The noise of the crowd behind him rose in his ears like wind. The right fielder, José Tartabull, charged toward the ball. Nygerski saw that he would catch it before it fell in front of him, and that Berry, the runner on third, would try to score. Human bodies surged to their feet around him. Nygerski looked wildly around for Cassandra, but he could not see her through the crowd. Someone pushed him forward; he stumbled, and his knee hit the cement hard. Wincing, he struggled to his feet. In front of him, Berry took off for home plate as Tartabull uncorked his throw.

And a ribbon of red, punctuated by long dark hair and fine white legs, moved through the crowd behind home plate, into an opening there that led to darkness underneath the stands. Nygerski's vision filled with her until there was nothing in the stadium but swirling patterns of red, black, and white. Ball and runner converged on the plate, on the catcher waiting there at the crux of the impending collision.

The players in the dugout and the people in the stands pressed forward. Berry went into his slide. And Nygerski could see that Tartabull's throw was high, too high. . . . The catcher stretched to get it. He had the ball, but Nygerski was sure that his feet were out of position, he didn't have the plate blocked, and the runner would score. . . .

He saw the slide, the catch, the desperate, lunging, sweeping tag, the swirling red dress and long white legs in the dark space behind the plate. The crowd roared as ball, catcher, and runner converged in a cloud of dust. He saw the umpire throw his arms out to his sides, and he heard him bellow: "Safe!"

And then all Nygerski could see was Cassandra.

5.

ON THE STREETS OF CHICAGO

On the streets of Chicago, the beast walked.

It moved stealthily, on all fours, slinking from shadow to shadow under the watchful eye of the full Moon. It avoided the main thoroughfares, where a crowd of people might have spotted it and robbed it of its most potent weapon—surprise. Instead, it moved through alleys, past warehouses, and along deserted residential streets, heading north, paralleling the shore of the nearby lake. Its ears rose like twin daggers from its tapered skull, angled slightly forward, now and again swiveling to the sides, fine-tuning bits of incoming information that could help it pinpoint prey. Occasionally it stopped to sniff the air. Stray cats caught its scent or dusky outline and hurried away. Always it remained out of the sight of people, noting their presence, waiting in the shadows for the right opportunity. Its hunger grew.

Though feral and single-minded, the animal combined the intelligence of the human it had recently been with the cunning of the wolf it now resembled. It knew that among humans there were those who moved on the fringes of their communities—outcasts, drifters, unwanted and virtually unseen. It sensed that in this decaying urban environment, such humans would not be hard to find and kill, and it began looking for them instinctively.

The werewolf had no need and little inclination to cover its tracks, for its emotional storage bank had no niche for either guilt or a sense of right and wrong. It was driven by supernatural lust for violent death, and if it could not find a person, any large animal would do. But humans were best. The fear was most palpable in them. Anticipation drove the animal's efficient but unhurried gait as it padded softly toward that part of the city where it could isolate a man and bring him down. It was that fear, as much as the flesh and blood of its victims, that fed the beast's hunger. The terror of the final seconds of a brutally ended life was the drug on which the animal depended and toward which it directed all its keen senses. Nothing must be permitted to get in the way of that fear, of the animal drinking it in, consummating once again its coupling with the forces of evil, which are always ready to move in anywhere good leaves a vacuum.

Werewolves have been around almost as long as humans have. We have yet to learn everything there is to know about our strange Universe, even the increasingly comfortable space surrounding our home planet. There are mysteries here on Earth that still elude explanation. Why, for instance, would the one planet in our Solar System bearing life capable of contemplation have a single lifeless satellite whose apparent size in the sky is the same as its star? We get better solar eclipses than anyplace in the Cosmos. A simple physical coincidence? Or an indication of some sort of resonance between light and dark, of powerful forces shrouded by antiquity and fear? The Sun is the life-giver; the Moon is a dead rock. We fear what we cannot explain, and death is the biggest mystery of all.

Every large American city experiences several unsolved murders every year. And police will tell you that criminal activity and mayhem increase during the two-to-three-day period of the full Moon. Since the early days of hunting and gathering, the Moon has had that effect on us.

It drives the tides, and also the incompletely understood emotion cycles of the human psyche. The full Moon makes some people restless, some manic, others crazy. And in rare and extreme cases, it causes certain humans to actually alter their physical shape and give themselves over completely to the bloodlust of evil and the aphrodisiac of fear.

Near midnight the beast found what it was looking for in the parking lot of a deserted marina. There were no boats here anymore, and the dock was a twisted wreck ending just beyond the small waves that lapped at the haphazard heaps of boulders and slabs of cement. The streetlights that had once illuminated the parking lot had long ago been extinguished by well-aimed rocks; now they loomed like vultures in the moonlight, casting long, overhanging shadows onto the cracked asphalt. Near the shore, to one side of the broken-off dock, a small ground fire burned in what remained of a fifty-five-gallon drum. Two men sat beside it, sharing a bottle of wine.

The men slumped and their shoulders sagged, indicating the passage of hard years. Each wore an army jacket to keep out the chill coming off the lake. One of the men wore a baseball cap from which curly white hair protruded at right angles to his head; he had a bushy white beard to go with it, and a nose red from drink. His companion wore a dark woolen cap and a three-day growth of stubble, punctuated by a cigarette drooping from his thick lips, a long ash dangling precariously from the end. The first man passed him the bottle, knocking off the ash. A second bottle, empty, lay on the ground beside them.

The animal took all of this in at a glance. It did not need to hide as it stalked across the parking lot toward them, for the men, facing the water, were engaged in spirited reminiscing and could not have heard its padded footsteps over their own wine-lubricated voices as it moved in for the kill.

"Remember that time back in forty-five, Bill?" said the man with the white beard. "We came down here and took off with that sailboat?"

"The *Hazel O'Leary*," the other man responded. "I still remember her name." He raised the bottle toward the water. "Here's to the *Hazel O'Leary*," he said. He took a long drink, then passed the bottle to his friend.

"Betcha can't remember the names of them two girls we was with," the white-haired man said.

"Yours was Betty. Mine was . . . oh shit . . . dark-haired little thing, cuter'n hell. Christ, I can't remember her name. 'S been more'n twenty years, for Chrissake."

The white-haired man guffawed. "He can remember the name of the boat, but not his girl," he said, slapping his knee. "No wonder you ain't never been married. That, and you have wine with breakfast."

"Most days, wine *is* breakfast," Bill replied, and they both doubled over in laughter, oblivious to the beast behind them contemplating dinner.

"It was Betsy, not Betty," the man with the white beard said. "And I forgot your girl's name, too. But I sure remember that night. What a night that was. Made it all the way up to Sheboygan before they caught us. Quite an adventure. Folks who owned the boat was awful good about it."

"Those were the days," Bill replied, accepting the bottle and tipping it up. "We got back from Europe and just wanted to raise a little hell. And it was okay, back then. We didn't hurt nobody. We didn't smoke any of that marijuana and run naked in the streets. We was just happy 'bout winning the war. Weren't no harm in it. Not like today." He passed the bottle back to his buddy.

"Ain't never gonna be like it was back in forty-five," the man with the white beard lamented, taking a mournful swallow. "War over, money and jobs and women for the pickin'—"

"And the Cubbies won the pennant," Bill put in.

"And the Cubbies won the pennant," white-beard rejoined, raising the bottle. "Here's to the Cubbies."

"The Cubbies," Bill cried, accepting another drink. "May they rise again. And may we live to see it."

The beast growled, close behind them.

The white-haired man turned. "Holy shit, Bill . . . ," he whispered. Bill's attention was on the bottle of wine pressed to his lips, and the memory of the 1945 Cubs. The beast growled again, and lowered itself to spring.

"Easy there, boy," white-beard's voice quavered. "Nice doggie . . ."

With a low snarl, the black-furred shape was upon him. Bill barely had time to lower the bottle and throw it at the creature before his friend's life was terminated in a blur of teeth, tissue, and blood. He staggered to his feet, tried to run.

But the beast saw everything in its peripheral vision, and reacted with clarity and purpose. In two bounds it brought the drunken man down. He, too, died quickly, his throat ripped open before so much as a cry of panic could emerge from it.

There had been frightfully little sound. The beast had done its work with cool efficiency. For several minutes it fed quietly, gaining strength from the flesh and lifeblood of its victims. Soon it moved off, along the shore. A highway of moonlight led away from the deserted marina into the depths of Lake Michigan. The beast looked up at its source and howled softly, melodically.

The two mutilated bodies would be discovered the following morning by three teenage friends playing hooky from school to go fishing in the polluted water. The men would have no identification and no next of kin to come forward. Two bums, killed by some sicko for their wine and the change in their pockets, or simply for the thrill of it. The police didn't have enough resources to spend a lot of time on crimes like this. They happened too often, and with too little consequence to anyone who mattered. Would the world really be that much worse off without two winos? Oh yes, evidence would be gathered, photographs taken, case files opened. Perhaps one or both of their names would eventually be learned. Their bodies would be cremated if not claimed. And then they would be relegated to the slag heap of unsolved crimes, assigned lowest priority as newer and more significant carnage came in.

Every big city has similar killings every year. A few, more than the statistical average, happen on nights when the Moon is full—nights when shape-shifting beasts walk among us, watching, grinning, feeding on our fear.

6.

THE MORNING AFTER

He hadn't slept.

Slanted sunlight stabbed through the long windows into the marble lobby of the train station. It found the wooden bench on which he sat, and the newspaper in his hands. Dust danced in its beam. Down the hall a janitor pushed a dust mop. A few early risers pattered quietly over the stone, on their way, as he was, to other places in other cities. It was not yet six in the morning, and most of Chicago was still in bed.

Cyrus Nygerski folded the newspaper and spread it across his legs, where the sunlight could not bleed the words through from the other side. He reread the box scores and the story of the doubleheader. The White Sox had won the second game, 1–0. The Red Sox had been lucky to get a split, the paper said. Only a great play by Elston Howard on the throw to the plate had saved the first game. The story intimated that the umpire had blown the call. Tartabull's throw had been high, and Ken Berry had reached the plate at the same time the ball did. The ump had called him out, preserving the Red Sox victory.

What had Nygerski seen, then? A trick? A fantasy? A drug-induced hallucination? The paper said the runner had been out, but Nygerski had seen him score, amid the kaleidoscopic images that had flooded his mind in his altered state of consciousness. And Elston Howard hadn't been the catcher. Elston Howard! What would the Red Sox possibly want with Elston Howard, a washed-up, thirty-eight-year-old catcher who didn't even hit .200? He'd been hurt early in the season, and the Yankees had benched him. Nygerski remembered hearing that he had announced his retirement, earlier this month.

And yet there he was in the box score, and in the story about the game. And instead of dropping both ends of a doubleheader and falling a game behind the White Sox, the Red Sox had gained a split and were headed to New York at the top of the standings.

In spite of everything Nygerski thought he remembered.

There were other memories as well, crowding against those his objective senses told him must be real. Memories of a stellar minor-league season, and interest from the big club, and a telephone call to his manager from Chicago. And the girl, Cassandra, and another chance meeting, in another bus station. *Had* he seen her before? "Not in this life," she had told him. Yesterday the sentence had sounded like flirtatious banter. In the harsh light of morning, with the girl gone, it seemed more like a riddle.

Everything in his life had turned upside down since he had met her, barely twenty-four hours ago—the strangely familiar, uncommonly beautiful, wildly unpredictable girl who had told him the Red Sox would win the pennant and slipped him a tab of acid with his beer. "Now you're experienced," she had said to him, just before she left, just before the throw.

That LSD was strange stuff indeed. Most of its effects had worn off. But he still felt nervous, on edge, unsure of himself, and he knew it would be hours before he would be able to close his eyes. He had tried to follow her, with shapes and colors swirling all around, out through the stadium gates and into the parking lot. But he had not seen her again. And he missed the home run that won the game for Chicago. "Some kid fresh from the minors," an usher told him when he asked.

"First big-league at bat, he wins the game with a pinch-hit homer. It's our year, son. Our year."

He had combed the stadium for the girl all during the second game, no longer caring who won, but she had disappeared as completely as the Red Sox offense. She was gone, a meteor across his life, leaving only a sizzle and a blinding flash of light.

The weird doubling of images that had reached its height in the ninth inning of that first game had abruptly ceased an hour after the end of the nightcap, and he had spent the rest of the night walking the streets of Chicago under the pale glow of the full Moon, hoping to spot a dark-haired woman in a red dress. Cassandra. Her name was Cassandra. From the moment he had first seen her, almost exactly twenty-four hours ago now, he had felt that it was no mere accident that she had crossed his life. What an odd feeling to have about someone you met by chance in a bus station. And yet there it was.

But had it really been a chance meeting? Or had she sought him out, to show him something important, some lesson he was supposed to absorb and follow? Who was she? And why did he have this profound feeling of loss, now that she was gone?

And what would he do now? Yesterday it had been important for him to be in Chicago; it had been his destination, and he had had a reason to be here. Now he felt small and unimportant.

Absently, his hand reached for the silver amulet around his neck, the star inside a circle, that she had given him. He remembered that she had been to San Francisco and was on her way to Maine. He had a ticket to Boston in his pocket, on a train that left in an hour. He had no idea what he was going to do when he got there. Find a job, maybe. Or look for a college that would shield him from the draft. Or maybe take a midnight bus to Montreal, hide out in Canada, brush up on his French. Now that his baseball career was over, maybe he'd try his hand at hockey.

He laughed at himself. Lack of sleep had made him giddy, even in his thoughts. Maybe he'd be able to get some rest on the train. He needed time to think, to sort things out. His past was a collage of contradictory images. His future was a blank slate.

He fingered the train ticket in his pocket. One way, to Boston. Home. Somewhere in his duffel bag was his mother's last letter. He had read it quickly and then folded it and put it aside. It was filled with banalities and the hope that his season would improve. He had written to her only once all summer, several weeks ago, in the throes of a slump that had ended only with his benching and eventual release. She would have no idea that he had been let go, because it had never occurred to him to call her. Now, however, the familiarity of his boring family seemed like exactly the respite he needed, before he decided what to do with the rest of his life. She would be surprised to see him. But he knew she would pamper him and prepare his favorite meals, and that his younger sisters would be jealous at his reception. The special treatment of first-borns, he thought with a smile. He remembered Cassandra telling him that she had a younger brother.

He turned from the sports section and skimmed through the rest of the paper. In the back of the regional section a small item caught his eye. The story was only four paragraphs long, but it hit Nygerski like a sledgehammer.

MAN FOUND SLAIN IN RIVERSIDE PARK

BELOIT, WIS.—Police are still searching for clues in the brutal slaying of a factory worker Saturday evening in a park alongside the Rock River.

The slashed, mutilated body of Edward Whittingham, thirty-seven, an electrician at the Alden-Manchester Company, was discovered at approximately 10 P.M. by two students at nearby Beloit College.

Whittingham's throat had been cut, and he had been slashed several times across the face and upper body.

Though police have not ruled out an animal attack, the case is being treated as a homicide, according to police chief Neville Watts. "At this point we have no suspects," Watts said, "although we are pursuing some leads. We urge anyone with any information to come forward."

Whittingham, a lifelong Beloit resident, began work at the Alden-Manchester paper machinery plant in 1958. He was married and had no children. His wife, Rhonda, was in seclusion yesterday with her parents in Janesville and could not be reached for comment.

Nygerski lowered the paper and stared out the window. His first thought was a selfish one: Jesus Christ, I got out of there just in time. He had met Rhonda's husband only once, at the ballpark, and to Nygerski's knowledge Ed had had no suspicions about their affair. But he wondered if his name would come up in the murder investigation. He wondered what Rhonda would tell the cops, or her parents, or her friends. And he wondered, finally, what Rhonda felt, with her husband dead and him gone without so much as a good-bye. Would *she* think he had done it? Of course he had an alibi, and Mavrogenes would tell the truth if it came to that, but what did Rhonda think of him this morning? He didn't know.

The paper slid from his hands to the floor, catching the sun. Nygerski barely noticed it. He felt weak, alone, and confused. His ticket east protruded from his pocket. He was profoundly glad it was there. No one in Beloit, Wisconsin, knew where he was at this moment, nor which train would carry him away from the Midwest, where his baseball career, and his youth, had ended.

When he heard the boarding call for his train to Boston, he hefted his duffel bag, ignoring the newspaper splayed out on the bench and the floor beside him, and walked slowly to the platform, looking around at the other passengers as he went. There were a few young women in the crowd, but none with long dark hair and eyes like blue glass broken into a thousand pieces. Even after he stowed the bag in the overhead compartment and settled into a window seat, he kept watching for her, hoping she would come running up to the train at the last minute, her hair streaming behind her, the compact silver case in one hand. In a few minutes the train began to move.

He wanted to sleep, but could not. Staring out the window, he watched the steel mills of East Chicago and Gary, Indiana, roll by. He had never seen anything so ugly.

After a few minutes he got up and walked the length of the train, looking into the face of every passenger. She was not onboard. He returned to his seat and wished that he had kept the paper so that he could reread the sports section and lull his mind toward numbness. He leaned back in his seat and closed his eyes, listening to the rhythmic pounding of the metal wheels on the metal rail as the train rolled eastward toward New England.

He would have to find her, that was all. She had told him where she lived in Maine, and he knew he would be able to locate it. The directions were already in his mind somewhere. The girl had shown him something about his life he had needed to see. He intended to see her again, to ask her what she had been doing at that Beloit bus station that morning, and why she had disappeared in the ninth inning at the ballpark. Something had happened in that ninth inning that had jarred his sense of reality, and even under the aftereffects of LSD, Nygerski knew it was important. He would find her, and he would make her tell him what she had done to him, and why he could not escape the feeling that they had met before.

PART TWO

THE DREAM SEASON

7.

THE KID BROTHER

They *had* met before.

I know, because I was there, when my sister brought Nygerski to Maine in April 1967, the year the Red Sox almost won the pennant. And who could forget Cyrus "Moondog" Nygerski, the answer to baseball's most famous trivia question?

He wasn't called Moondog then, of course. My sister would hang that name on him, on the night before his moment of fame. He was just Cyrus, and he was quiet and thin and not that tall, not really what you'd call physically imposing. But there was a quality of self-possession about him you don't see in many nineteen-year-olds, a grace and economy of movement that served him well in athletic endeavors.

Cassandra brought Nygerski to Maine in April, before the season started. Our dreamer father was trying to make the rundown camp he'd bought with two of his law school friends into a working camp and year-round home, and our mother was contemplating leaving him. She *had* left, in fact, albeit temporarily, when Cassandra arrived, unannounced as always, with a new young man in tow. Most of the guys Cassandra brought home antagonized the shit out of our father, for he had the barely concealed opinion that the so-called baby boom children

were spoiled brats who didn't know the value of a dollar or the right-
eousness of hard work. But about Nygerski he was pretty much silent,
for there was something in the young man's dark eyes and quiet manner that commanded respect. I know I was in awe of him. He was a
lefty, like me, and during the week he spent at Rum Runners Cove, he
showed me how to hold and release a curveball, and how to look a
grounder into the glove. For he was a real, live professional baseball
player, with a real contract and orders to report to some little town in
Wisconsin in midmonth, and to me that was about the best thing in the
world a person could be.

I was ten in the summer of 1967, and my sister, Cassandra, was
twenty. The other families we knew all had five or six or eleven kids,
but we had just two, because something inside Mom didn't work right,
and Cassandra and I were the only pregnancies that took. We were
unusually close for two kids so far apart in age. For instance, I knew that
Cassandra had dropped out of her sophomore year at the University of
Maine before spring break and headed for Atlanta with a young black
man who was active in the civil rights movement. I knew because she
told me, over the phone, and I participated in her deception of our
father. He sent the five hundred dollars she asked him for to her off-
campus house in Orono, where it was dutifully picked up by a roommate and sent south. Even at ten I worried about her—a pretty white
woman on the arm of an articulate Negro in a time and place so inflamed
by violence and passion. And even at ten I had the feeling that the
man, and not my sister, was getting more than he bargained for. Had
our father known, he would have gone ballistic, but we both took
pains to keep it from him. I remember being touched that she trusted
me—not realizing then that she was simply using me for her own pur-
poses. But then, that's how women like my sister get much of what
they want in this world: through the unwitting cooperation of those
who admire them.

When she brought Nygerski to Rum Runners Cove in early April, no one was more surprised than I. But the timing could not have been better. Because our family, like the world around us, was in turmoil, and Nygerski provided welcome, if temporary, relief from our absorption with ourselves. Our mother was back in Ohio, fed up with my father's promises and April snowstorms. She wanted to miss winter's final blast this year, she said, the day before she left. My dad's partnership in the property at the cove was being torn apart by divorce and financial problems, and the sixties were exploding all around us—the war, drugs, rock and roll, racial unrest. My sister was in the middle of it, as she seemed to be in the middle of everything.

Nygerski and Cassandra arrived in the back of old Fred Doyle's pickup truck, he with an old green duffel bag and she with the silver suitcase our mother had given her when she went away to college. Fred was a carpenter and clam digger who lived a few miles away from us on the eastern shore of Deer Isle. "Found 'em hitchhikin' 'bout a mile up the Sunshine Road," he told my father over a beer. 'Tweren't for me, they'd be theyah still."

Cassandra gave me a big hug and whispered in my ear, "Just go along with whatever I say, okay? I'll fill you in later."

Cassandra and Nygerski both had beers going, too. Cassandra had arrived with the remains of a six-pack tucked under her arm in a paper bag. My father arched an eyebrow when she pulled out the cans, but what could he say? Cassandra was old enough to drink and had inherited his love of beer. Our whole extended family drinks beer, except for Aunt Polly, who hasn't touched a drop of alcohol since the day her husband died. It's mostly a social thing, but Cassandra drank at least in part to suppress demons, something that would get her in trouble in later life.

It was established quickly that Nygerski was from Boston and played baseball, and I believe my father stopped giving him the evil eye the minute he found out Nygerski really did have a contract to play minor-league ball for the Chicago White Sox. What was less clear was how he and my sister had met. I knew she'd been in the south, and that big-league teams had spring training camps in Florida, but my dad assumed they'd just hitched down from Orono, where, as far as he knew, she was still enrolled. "How're your classes?" he asked her.

"They're okay." We stood in the kitchen, where everyone always seemed to congregate in that big, drafty, two-story house at the cove. The living room was large and comfortable, the dining room boasted a huge table and a great view of the water, and there were several cabins in various states of repair scattered around the property, but when guests arrived they were always entertained in the kitchen, around the funky old wood cookstove and never far from the refrigerator.

"Passing everything?"

"Uh-huh." It was clear Cassandra didn't want to elaborate on the subject. "I'm on vacation now, though. Thought I'd come down for a few days."

"Sure. Well, lots of work to do. Painting, if it stays warm. And there are always alders." Dad looked out the window, past the coffee cup full of pencils, the notepad, nails, and other clutter, to the outdoors. The tide was halfway up the cove, coming in. "Your mom's in Columbus," he said.

"Yeah, I know. I called, remember?"

"That's right."

"Dad, maybe she just needs a break from this place," my sister offered. "It *is* awfully isolated, especially when we're the only ones here."

Amen to that, I thought. I had heard talk about Maine since I was a baby. When my folks bought into Rum Runners Cove and started going there in the summer, I thought it was great. The other families had kids my age, and the Maine coast offered unlimited activities for boys with imaginations. But my dad's decision three years later to pull up and move there permanently had deeply divided our family. Cassandra had been all for it; my mother and I had not.

"You're right—she'll be back when the weather gets warm," my father said, more to himself than to Cassandra. He looked out the window and sighed, for it was one of those days of promise Maine teases you with in early April to make you think winter is over. Most of the buttons on Fred's flannel shirt were undone, revealing red suspenders over a simple white T-shirt. I had been running around barefoot all day, and Nygerski had shed his dungaree jacket and arrived with it over his arm. And Cassandra wore nothing heavier than a red cardigan sweater, also unbuttoned. Buds were popping on the trees, the grass needed mowing, and you could almost *hear* the alders encroaching on the side of the house. Those damn trees with their spidery trunks as thick as broom handles grew faster than anything I'd ever seen. But it was the first week of April, and experience had taught us all to expect the worst. In two weeks, give or take a day or two, the emerald field outside the window would be covered in new snow.

"I thought Cyrus could stay in the Near Cabin," Cassandra said, steering the talk away from our parents' marital problems. "That little potbellied stove's still out there, isn't it?"

Our dad nodded. "You'll have to haul some wood," he said to Nygerski. "Nights're cold."

Nygerski nodded. "I don't mind," he said.

New England conversations can drive outsiders nuts. Everything is said in the spaces between the sentences. My relatives could stand around that kitchen for hours, some leaning against the countertops, others sitting crosswise or backward on straight-backed chairs, and no one uttering a sentence with more than five words in it. Outsiders mistake this quality for unfriendliness, when it is nothing more than an abhorrence of waste, whether in language, movement, or material goods. It's an admirable worldview that is rapidly disappearing under an avalanche of excess.

"Well, we'll have to call your uncle Bill and get some lobsters," my father said. At this I brightened, for in the month since Mom left we'd been getting by mostly on burgers and potatoes and soup. I always liked it when Cassandra came home, because my folks treated it like a big deal.

My father was the first person in his family to leave the Maine coast for anything other than war service or seafaring, and the rest of the family never forgave him for it. Dad went off and got himself an education and, by the time I was born, was a partner in a law practice in Columbus, Ohio, where he had met and impregnated my mom with Cassandra when Mom was only seventeen.

His brother Bill, five years younger, stayed home and became a lobsterman. By 1967 the oldest of his three sons was helping him out full-time on the boat. Uncle Bill had a piece of land out on William's Point, at the very end of the paved road, and he built a dock out near the mouth of Rum Runners Cove, on the far side where the deep water is, where he moored a series of progressively larger lobster boats. On the other side of the cove was an old camp, abandoned since World War II, with a large house and several falling-down cabins, surrounded by sixty-four acres of rocks, spruce trees, blueberries, and alders, fronting on a pebbly beach and half a cove of mudflats.

When the camp's absentee owner died, and his heirs, who had no Maine connections, decided to sell the property, Uncle Bill told my father about it. In 1962, when I was five, my father and two of his lawyer friends purchased the place, and thus began our annual treks to the coast of Maine, and our family's essential conflict.

My father dreamt of restoring the camp to its former glory, of putting up new cabins and renting them out to summer visitors, of a fleet of small sailboats in the cove and clam bakes on the beach. My uncle Bill thought the sheltered cove would make a darn good place for a commercial lobster pound.

Most of the family, of course, sided with Uncle Bill. Starting up a summer camp for the offspring of rich out-of-staters seemed a mighty highfalutin and chancy thing to do. A lobster pound made rock-solid Maine coast sense. Just about the only dissenter was Aunt Polly.

Cassandra and I called her Aunt Polly, but she was my father's aunt, actually, and next to him the least popular person in our entire extended family. Her unpopularity stemmed from the dubious circumstances surrounding her husband's death, and her ability to see things invisible to the rest of us. She knew, for example, about the fire that burned down the grocery store and two other buildings in the heart of Deer Isle village, as it was happening, six miles away. We all saw the hazy orange glow in the sky and wondered, but Aunt Polly said with complete certainty, "It's Pinkerton's. There'll be nothing left in the morning." And she could clean us out at the poker games we played for fun with pennies. Cassandra said it was because she could read our minds. I put it down to a combination of experience and luck. But Cassandra—who always was Aunt Polly's favorite—became a pretty fair poker player herself, good enough to get through college without having to take a part-time campus job.

Aunt Polly said my father was right—tourism, not lobstering, was the future. "Chrissake, Bill," she had said at one of the few family gatherings to which she was invited, "them lobsters can't breed half as fast as you and your friends pull 'em up. Folks from away, they breed, too, but there ain't no one trapping *them*. Twenty years from now, you'll be lucky to haul enough to feed the guests at Clayton's camp." Uncle Bill had scoffed, and his sons had rolled their eyes, for it was plain that their eccentric old aunt did not know what she was talking about. Hell, there were *plenty* of lobsters.

But it was my dad, Clayton Paine, who bought the place, along with Bob Woolf and Fred Granger, two Yale Law School classmates. They worked feverishly to fix it up. For the first few years we went to Maine for four weeks in the summer, and the Woolf and Granger kids became our companions in clamming and blueberry-picking expeditions, rowboat races in the cove, and hikes around the point while the grown-ups cut alders. My dad was always pining about Maine when we lived in Ohio, and driving us all nuts with his talk of nor'easters and lighthouses.

As if he could've become a lawyer and made all that money by staying on Deer Isle and hauling lobsters.

When he announced that he wanted to quit his firm and open up his own law office on Deer Isle, and take us there to live year-round, my mother was wary, but eventually she went along with him. I give her credit for sticking it out through two full winters and most of a third.

I was eager to get Cassandra away from my dad so that we could talk. After Fred left I helped Nygerski carry his stuff to the Near Cabin as Cassandra showed him the way. Late afternoon clouds had moved in to block the Sun. There was some wood in there, and I ran back to the house to get some newspaper, making sure it didn't have today's date on it, because it always drove Dad nuts when someone burned the paper before its day was over. We started a fire and hauled more wood from the shed. "The Woolfs are coming," I informed my sister as the three of us pulled up wooden chairs to the stove. We could see sparks and flames through the gaps in the cast iron as the wood crackled furiously. The little cabin was already warmer than the house would be until July.

"Really? When?"

"Tomorrow or the next day."

"Wow. That'll be different, seeing them in April."

"Yeah. Dad called 'em, told 'em to come up."

The town plowed the road down to the house after we moved in full-time, but I still had to walk a mile to catch the school bus. On cold days my dad drove me. Cassandra came down from Orono on vacations and some weekends. My folks made a point of quartering Cassandra's male friends in the Near Cabin, a simple, one-room structure built with logs cut lengthwise and the flat sides facing in. It was still without electricity but had been newly equipped with a woodstove and strips of pink and silver insulation. Cassandra and I had rooms in the drafty house during the winter, but in summertime, when all three families were there, we kids slept in cabins, segregated by gender, of course.

The older girls, including Cassandra, adopted the Green Cabin, just back from the bank atop the beach, in which the boats were stored in winter. It had no electricity or heat, but it did have a certain funkiness, with raspberry bushes growing up through one side of the porch and alders coming up to the back windows at night, scratching and peering in. They had put up tapestries and lit the place with candles in cork floats and wine bottles. The older boys, like Roger Woolf and Sam Granger, claimed the Near Cabin, up the road from the house, while my friends and I were housed in a new, large, electrically wired structure that went up the first summer my father owned the place, steps from the house and painted red to match.

The Far Cabin, an unimproved twin to the Near Cabin, remained standing—barely—out by the bend in the road. Wendy Woolf, who painted and sometimes exhibited her work at a summer gallery, had claimed it as her art studio. It had no heat and no insulation, and you could see sunlight through gaps in the walls. There was a toolshed my father wanted to expand that spring that made a triangle with the house and the Red Cabin, where the cars parked. And there was an old outbuilding behind the house, with running water, which housed two bathrooms and a gigantic claw-footed tub—all we had for bathrooms until my father had one put in the house that first winter.

"They've been arguing about tearing down the Far Cabin and putting a bigger building there, like a guest house," I told my sister. "Wendy's wailing about it, of course. Bob wants to wait till the whole thing with the Grangers gets settled."

"Daddy ought to get one thing done at a time," my sister said, not unsympathetically. "Just now in the kitchen he was talking about expanding the shed."

"He's doing it," I told her. "He's had three guys here working the past two days."

"Well, he should get that done first. The Grangers—they're still getting divorced, right?"

"Far as I know," I reported.

"And they both want their third of the property."

"Yup."

Cassandra looked at Nygerski. "Can you imagine? Three lawyers buy a prime piece of property on the Maine coast, and all they can do is squabble over it."

I had been studying Cassandra's new friend since his arrival. He was taciturn but not nervous, and he stretched out now in the simple wooden chair, his feet under the stove, utterly at ease in his body. He didn't say much, which is considered a virtue in Maine. Now he said only, "Well, that's lawyers for you."

"So tell me what's really happening," I prodded my sister. "I thought you were in Atlanta."

"I was," Cassandra said. "And Memphis, and Washington, D.C. And New York, which is where I bumped into Cyrus."

"Literally," Nygerski said, grinning a little.

"What do you mean?" I asked.

"I mean, she crashed into me at the bus station, and here I am." He looked at the watch on his right wrist. "That was, oh, about eighteen hours ago."

"So you just met?"

Nygerski and my sister nodded in unison. "She was running full tilt through that crowded bus station and blindsided me," he said. "When I came to, I was on a bus to Maine." He looked at Cassandra, and his grin widened.

"That's not true . . . ," Cassandra said.

"You still haven't told me what you were running from," he retorted.

"You wouldn't believe me."

Silence engulfed us for several seconds as my sister and Cyrus Nygerski stared pointedly at one another.

"Where were you going?" I asked him.

"Home. My mom's house, in Boston. Cassandra talked me into coming up here instead."

"Just like that?"

"Just like that," he said. "I've been to Maine before. Crewed on one of those tourist boats a couple years ago, out of Camden. And I've got a week."

"When does your season start?"

"I have to report on the sixteenth."

"A man," Cassandra said to the stove.

"What?" Nygerski and I said together.

"A man," my sister said. "I was running from a man. A very smart and good man, when he *is* a man. When he's not . . ." Cassandra's eyes pointed at the stove but focused somewhere far away. We waited for her to continue.

"I'm not following you," Nygerski ventured finally.

Cassandra shook her head. "No, it's too scary. Too much unfinished business."

"What are you talking about?" he said.

"I don't want to think about it yet," she averred, snapping her head back and looking around the small cabin. "I don't want to think about *him*."

"The man who was chasing you?"

My sister nodded. "He has no idea about this place. He knows I went to the university, and he knows where my friends up there live, but here, I'm safe from him."

"Why are you afraid of him?"

Cassandra looked directly into Nygerski's dark eyes. "Because I think he's a killer," she said.

8.

AUNT POLLY

We couldn't get her to say anything more. Cassandra wanted to show Nygerski the cove before it got dark, and she made a point of insisting that I come along. She seemed reluctant to be alone with him.

We peeked into the Green Cabin, where the boats were stored during the winter, and then continued down to the shore. All the while Cassandra took pains to include me in the conversation, steering it to subjects within the boundaries of geography or family. Nygerski listened but didn't say much.

The next morning at breakfast Cassandra asked my dad if she and Cyrus could borrow the car to go see Aunt Polly. Again, she invited me along.

Aunt Polly lived by herself in a small house overlooking the harbor in Stonington, the larger of the two towns on the island, at the very southern tip. Her house lay along the third street up from the docks, one block east of the big green opera house (on which the words OPERA HOUSE were painted in bold white letters that a sailor with binoculars could read at a considerable distance). Her front yard was a slab of granite a foot or so higher than the street. A few tufts of grass and some flowers grew in the fissures in the rock; she had a birdhouse on a metal pole, and a birdbath made of cobblestones and cement. That birdbath had been there from time immemorial; I never knew and never asked if it had been made by Aunt Polly, her late husband, or somebody else.

Aunt Polly never had a driver's license or a car. She was married, long before I was born, to a drunken lobsterman who fell overboard in the fog and drowned. The townspeople had only Aunt Polly's word on that, though, for Polly was his crew for the few turbulent years they were together. According to most people who knew them, Polly could handle that lobster boat better than her husband could. She could sure as hell steer by compass course in the fog and get back into port without hitting any of the underwater ledges that the glaciers left as mines for the first European explorers. Those ledges still wreck boats today, but the locals know them and can feel their way through, and Aunt Polly could do it as well as any of them.

One day in the early fifties Aunt Polly emerged from the dense fog at the docks of the Stonington Lobster Company without her husband. All the lobstermen knew about Albert's drinking, and that he occasionally beat his wife to keep her in line. Hell, Polly's husband had boasted about it to his friends. But wife-beating has a long, if not honored, tradition in rural Maine, and back then it was considered almost acceptable. People looked the other way and didn't say anything. Those lobstermen must have suspected that Aunt Polly had seized an opportunity for revenge, but she never wavered from her story, and the body was never found. But her husband's mysterious and untimely death made her something of an outcast in the community, and her other eccentricities only increased her isolation. By the time I was old enough to know her, she had sold the boat and saw few people outside the family.

We have a big family, though, and Aunt Polly enjoyed her own company, so she didn't suffer from loneliness. Uncle Bill and my father went to see her from time to time, as did their sisters and their kids. And she was especially close to Cassandra. When we still lived in Ohio and only came to Deer Isle in the summer, Cassandra visited Aunt Polly whenever she could, often several times a week. What a teenage girl and an ostracized old woman had in common I couldn't imagine, at least not before the summer of 1967.

Aunt Polly's living room was furnished simply with sturdy New England furniture like tourists pay a lot of money for on their way back home along southbound Route 1. It was all made on the island—the couch, the straight-backed chairs, the no-nonsense coffee table with thick, stubby legs and a fist-size knot missing near one end. Aunt Polly herself sat in a rocking chair made from the ribs of an old rowboat. There was a radio in the room but no TV. The main window, opposite the rocker, provided an ongoing view of the comings and goings in the harbor and beyond, and Aunt Polly said that was all the TV she needed.

In her kitchen Aunt Polly kept a huge collection of herbs and spices, some in jars, others hanging from the ceiling beams, the shelves, and the corners of the cupboard. Inside the cupboards, along with the plates, bowls, bean pots, and casserole dishes, were perhaps two dozen glass figurines, many in the shape of wild animals, and glass balls of varying colors and sizes. Hanging here and there on fishing wire were collections of shells from Maine and other places. None of these things cluttered the house in any way, however. The view to the outside remained predominant.

We talked. Mostly I listened, because I was a kid and along for the ride. If I hadn't come, I'm sure my dad would have put me to work, trailing after the carpenters or cutting grass or hauling off alders or painting something. Nygerski didn't say much, either. Aunt Polly asked Cassandra about college, and my sister told her frankly that she had dropped out and accompanied a young black man to a series of civil rights rallies in cities up and down the east coast. This would have been shocking news to my father, but Aunt Polly just nodded and rocked. She always had an air about her that made it seem as though she knew everything already. It was impossible to be anything less than completely truthful around her.

"And where did you meet this nice young man?" Aunt Polly asked, nodding ever so slightly at Nygerski.

"In New York. I bumped into him at the bus station, the day I decided to leave James. It was like he was put there, in my path. And I had the strangest feeling that we should know each other."

"Perhaps you do," Aunt Polly said. She swiveled her neck and faced Nygerski, who had taken a chair while Cassandra and I sat on the couch. Her face was deeply lined but did not seem old—there was a quality in her pale green eyes that defied age, that would look the same at seventy as it had at twenty. "Memory is a tricky thing. *Time* is a tricky thing. We think we are its masters, with our clocks and schedules, but all of that is an elaborate illusion. Perhaps you've already met—in the future."

"Come on, Aunt Polly, talk sense," I said. I loved my Aunt Polly and worshiped my sister, but even at ten I had little patience with their mystical bullshit.

Aunt Polly's youthful eyes flashed at me. "It happens frequently," she said. "For example, love at first sight. What is that, if not recognition? Or any of the so-called psychic phenomena—"

"None of which have been conclusively proven," Nygerski said. I liked him already. A fellow skeptic.

But Aunt Polly just smiled, and rocked slowly back and forth. She had been looking at Nygerski strangely since the moment we had arrived, as though trying to place him in context. Aunt Polly usually ignored strangers, but she conversed with Cyrus like he was an old friend she hadn't seen in a while. She liked that he argued with her. I guess Aunt Polly didn't get much chance to debate the nature of reality.

"It's a human conceit, time," she said, looking at each of us in turn. "It's something we made up, to give the illusion of order to things. And sometimes our efforts have only made matters more confusing. It's only been in the last couple hundred years that there's been one calendar. Before that, men used to fight over the date. The Spanish had their

Catholic calendar, which was ten days ahead of the Protestant calendar the English used. And the international date line is only a hundred years old. Before that, it was impossible to tell one day from the next."

"You're talking about ways of measuring time," Nygerski said. "Not time itself. Even if Monday is really Sunday, you're still a day older the next time the Sun rises."

Aunt Polly leaned back and favored him with a knowing smile. "The Sun, the Earth, the Moon. Have you noticed that everything used to measure time moves in a circle? Yet we cling to the notion of time as linear, and insist on living our one-way lives, never glimpsing the possibilities."

"But we still are born, grow up, grow old, and die," Nygerski insisted. "In that order."

"Yes, and we create the concept of time in our own image," Aunt Polly replied. "But I remember the day we heard the news that the great ship *Titanic* had gone down off Newfoundland. One of my daddy's friends had gone to Boston for the opening of the new baseball park, and another was off the Grand Banks, fishing. The fisherman came home, icebergs and all. The man who went to Boston got into a bar fight down there and was stabbed to death. He was in the wrong place at the wrong time, as they say. Like the *Titanic*."

"All of that proves nothing," Nygerski mumbled, but without much conviction.

Aunt Polly turned in her chair. "Cassandra, I've told you about the Hole, haven't I?"

My sister shifted uncomfortably. "It was a long time ago," she said.

"What's the Hole?" Nygerski asked.

"A dangerous place," Aunt Polly said. "A place best stayed away from."

"A kid drowned a couple years ago, swimming near there," I put in.

"He wasn't the first," Aunt Polly said seriously. "Fool summer kids got the idea that because the water comes in over the mudflats, it'd be warmer than out by the bay. And maybe it is, though this water was meant for fishin', not swimming. It's calm in there, and sheltered. Those kids didn't think a thing could go wrong, not on a beautiful summer day. They didn't know about the Hole."

"What *is* the Hole?" Nygerski asked again.

"Howley's Deep Hole," Cassandra said. She rose from the couch and walked to the far wall, where a nautical chart hung in a glass frame. Deer Isle dominated the chart's center; at the top was a chunk of the mainland and the legend; at the bottom was Isle Au Haut and the open sea. All the landmasses, including the hundreds of small islands, were yellow. The deep water was white. Gradations between the two colors—browns and blues—indicated land exposed at low tide and shoal areas.

"Here's Rum Runners Cove," she said, pointing. Then she pointed to a much larger finger of water just to the south of it. "And this is Dyer's Inlet." She traced the finger into the main body of the island. "And these," she said, indicating a narrow spot between two points of land, dotted with asterisks representing rocks, "are the Narrows. It's hard to get a canoe through here, much less a real boat. But look." Beyond the Narrows the water bellied out again, into an almost completely enclosed tidal lagoon. Nygerski got up and went over to inspect the chart more closely. I got up also, though we had the same chart on the wall at home and I had seen it a million times. But Nygerski was fascinated. "See how shallow the water is," my sister said. "Two, three feet at low tide. A lot of it's mud—you always see people out there clamming. There's no place more than ten feet deep. Except right here."

The numbers on the chart, indicating depth at mean low tide, were single digits throughout the lagoon and out into the inlet beyond the narrows. But the spot to which Cassandra pointed was clear white. Two tight concentric circles surrounded an impossible number: 200.

"Wow," Nygerski commented.

"Two hundred feet of water at low tide," Cassandra averred. "How-ley's Deep Hole. Now, think about this. Glaciers are big. They distribute their weight fairly evenly. That's why the hills around here are low and rolling, and that's why there are a lot of shoals and islands before you get to open ocean. They pressed down the whole coast. But the Hole is like someone thrust a knitting needle into the Earth. So, the question is, how did it get there?"

"Maybe a meteorite," I said. It was my favorite theory.

"It's never been accurately measured," Aunt Polly said. She rocked gently, her gaze fixed on the sea beyond the town. "No one really knows how deep it is. Or if it has a bottom at all."

"It says two hundred on the chart," Nygerski said, tapping the glass.

"Old Saul Howley only had two hundred feet of lead line," Aunt Polly replied, continuing to rock slowly back and forth, her eyes on the ocean. "He never expected to find such deep water in there. And he took his soundings more than a hundred years ago."

"And no one's measured it since?" Nygerski was incredulous.

"A few people have drowned trying," Aunt Polly said, with no change in inflection.

"Drowned? How?"

"Currents," Cassandra answered. "Tides. That basin has only one way to fill and empty with each tide." She pointed at the narrow band of water between the two points of land. "The volume of water that has to come through here is incredible. It creates a reversing rapids—when the tide's coming in, you can't get out, and when the tide's going out, you can't get in. The only time you can get a boat through there is right at high tide. At low tide it's calm, too, but it's too shallow. And the Hole itself . . ."

"Yes, what happens there?"

"Whirlpool. Like the water's being sucked into the Earth. I've seen it."

Cassandra's statement brought Aunt Polly back into the room. "You stay away from that Hole," she warned, her eyes fixed on my sister. "Them who go too close to that Hole . . . they don't come back."

"How many people have drowned there?" Nygerski asked.

"Maybe half a dozen," Aunt Polly told him. "Maybe more. The Hole doesn't like to give up its victims. Only two of the bodies were ever found."

"What happened to the others?"

No one answered for a long moment. Then Cassandra said, "They're still down there, I guess."

"Or," Aunt Polly said deliberately, "they went somewhere else."

"You mean, like Jake Weed?" Cassandra murmured.

Aunt Polly nodded. "Yes. Like Jake Weed."

Nygerski looked back and forth between the two women. Despite the difference in their ages, anyone could have seen the family resemblance in this moment. Then he looked at me. I shrugged. "Who," he asked the room at large, "is Jake Weed?"

Aunt Polly stopped rocking and rose deliberately from her chair. "If you've got time for a story and another pot of coffee," she said, "I'll tell you."

9.

JAKE WEED'S STORY

Europeans settled the Maine coast from the islands in. They arrived on boats, and boats remained the primary link with England and France for hundreds of years. The islands offered trees for shipbuilding, deepwater anchorages, and freedom from the accursed blackflies that swarmed on the mainland. And the ocean around them teemed with food. In the 1800s there were more than three hundred island communities along the coast. Only a handful, on the big islands like Vinalhaven and Isle Au Haut, remain today.

Jake Weed was born on Isle Au Haut in 1871. As a boy, he crewed on sailing vessels to Boston, Newfoundland, the West Indies. When he was home, he fished and lobstered, and he came to know most of the favored spots around Isle Au Haut and Deer Isle. By the time he was twenty, he was much sought after as a mate and helmsman, for he knew every inch of these waters and could find his way to port between the ledges even in the thickest fog and the worst storms.

Like most Maine fishermen, Jake Weed could not swim. The water's so cold, most of 'em figure they'd rather get the suffering done with quickly if they go overboard. In due time he married a girl from Deer Isle, and built a house down there on Dyer's Inlet, not far from your

Daddy's place. There were only two or three houses down there then, but now there's a cluster of 'em, and since most of the people down there are related in some way to old Burt Dyer, they called it Dyerville. Jake gave up his travels and gave himself to lobstering and making a home for Annabelle and their baby girl.

Jake hadn't been to sea for several years when lumber baron Thomas Shess offered him the job of navigator on the *Eleanor Rose*, a handsome seventy-five-foot schooner setting off for Jamaica with a load of lumber. She would return with rum, already outlawed in Maine but too lucrative for a man like Shess to ignore. Jake wavered at first, but there was good money in the job, Annabelle was pregnant again, and the ocean was his life. No local man was more capable. The *Eleanor Rose* sailed from Stonington in May of 1897, on a Friday—thumbing its nose at superstition—and arrived in Jamaica without incident.

The return voyage was not so fortunate. Thirty miles off Matinicus Rock, in a sea made choppy by a wet easterly wind and a falling tide, the fog closed in around the *Eleanor Rose* like a vise. Night fell, and Jake summoned up all his navigational skill to try to feel his way up into Penobscot Bay. He knew the tide would set them to the west of their compass course, and he tried to gauge the current's strength from the action of the waves and the feel of the boat.

Captain Sewall Chason was an impatient and stubborn man who had been in Shess's employ for twenty years. He was an excellent seaman. But he was from Boston, and did not know the local waters. Of the twelve-man crew, only Jake and two other men, Bobby Soule and Raymond Eaton, were from Deer Isle. The rest were a ragtag assortment of sailors and adventurers from various ports along the Atlantic seaboard. There was even a black man from Jamaica. According to Jake, he was treated the same as everybody else onboard.

They all had one thing in common, though. Not one of them could swim.

Captain Chason was eager to get ashore and unload the illicit cargo, for he had another job waiting, this one a shorter but equally profitable run to Saint Pierre and Miquelon for French brandy.

They were headed for Burnt Cove, on the western flank of Deer Isle. The tide was strong, for it was new Moon, and Jake warned the captain not to turn north into the bay until they could be sure they were past the islands and ledges off the southern tip of Vinalhaven. The captain, noting the boat's speed through the water, overestimated her speed over the bottom, and feared that Jake was taking the *Eleanor Rose* too far east, into the treacherous waters off Isle Au Haut. Jake argued back that the tide was stronger than it seemed. They had been hard on the wind for hours—unusual for a return voyage to Maine—making tortuous progress. Captain Chason listened to his vanity and impatience instead of his navigator. He ordered the helmsman to turn north too soon. The *Eleanor Rose,* chugging northward with sheets eased, struck a submerged portion of Halibut Ledge, ripped a hole in her hull, and went swiftly down. Eleven of the twelve men and almost all of the rum was lost, but Jake managed to grab a wooden hatch cover and, clinging to it, he floated for most of a freezing night. His feet finally struck bottom, and he stumbled up a beach of pebbly sand to the high-tide mark, where he passed out.

When he awoke and the fog lifted, he recognized where he was—Skunk Island, off the eastern shore of Vinalhaven. He could see Deer Isle in the distance, but no trace of his crewmates or the wreck of the *Eleanor Rose.* Well, almost no trace. Scouring the intertidal zone, he came across a bottle of Jamaican rum, wedged between two rocks and miraculously unbroken. He was good and drunk by the time a lobsterman out of Stonington spotted him waving and jumping up and down on the shore and rescued him.

Only three bodies were ever found. Matt Soule was one of them, and all Deer Isle turned out for his burial and the memorial service for the two dead local men and their shipmates. The island mourned for a time and then went about its business. The quarries got busy, and men were coming to Stonington from all over New England for jobs. The wreck passed from daily conversation. Jake returned to Annabelle and to lobstering.

But the brush with death changed Jake's mind about one thing. Without anyone's knowledge, except maybe Annabelle's, he hired a summer woman named Sally Elliott to teach him how to swim. They met once a week at a spot up on Eggemoggin Reach, where there weren't any houses and the water's not too cold. Someone might have seen them occasionally, but you know what it's like here: People mind their own business. His fellow lobstermen would have ridiculed him had they known, but by the end of the summer he was confident that he could rescue himself should the need ever arise again.

Lobsters weren't scarce in those days, and a man could make a pretty good living. There weren't no reason to be secretive about the best spots. But Jake got to thinking about Howley's Hole and the basin around it. Lobsters could get in there, all right. If they were close to the Narrows on an incoming tide, they'd get swept right in as they crawled along the bottom. And then, Jake figured, they'd have no reason to leave. All that deep water to themselves, and no one setting traps for 'em, because it was so much trouble getting a boat in and out of there. Of course, the lobsters didn't figure this out for themselves, because, as everybody knows, lobsters are one of the stupidest creatures the Almighty ever put on this Earth. If they weren't such good eating, they'd be absolutely useless.

Anyway, Jake lived out near the Hole and could get there overland. He decided to leave an old dinghy on the shore there, which is mostly grass and weeds, and he set three or four traps in the water around the Hole, though not too close to the Hole itself. And he tended 'em once or twice a week after his regular day was through. Well, I'll tell you, Jake started hauling some impressive lobsters out of there. Everyone would ask him, "Jake where are you gettin' them huge lobsters?" And he'd smile and say he got 'em by the Brandies, to the south of Isle Au

Haut, or off'n Rich's Point, because sometimes other lobstermen pulled up big ones there. But he didn't tell anyone about his secret spot.

One day in the fall of that same year, Jake got to his traps out by Howley's Hole later than usual. There had been some rough weather out to sea, and the wind was still blowing, but it stays pretty calm in by the Hole, surrounded as it is on all sides by the land. About the only effects of storms in there are higher and stronger tides. Jake hadn't checked those traps for going on a week, and despite the wind and the mare's-tail clouds he figured he'd better go have a look. He launched the dinghy on a falling tide in midafternoon. It was well into October, and the days were growing short, but Jake didn't plan to be out more than an hour. Everything would've been fine, too, if the line on the first trap hadn't snapped just as he got the damn thing halfway into the boat. It teetered on the gunwale and then slipped overboard. Jake lunged for the trap and nearly fell overboard himself, but he managed to grab a corner of the trap and keep it from going to the bottom forever. And a good thing that was, for there were four lobsters in it, one of 'em a three-pounder.

Jake took out the lobsters and pegged them, and then spent several minutes splicing a new line onto his trap while the boat drifted. I suppose he must have thought about taking the trap in and repairing it onshore, but Jake liked to make a buck like anyone else, and that trap had just yielded four lobsters. He wanted it back in the water right away. So he spliced on the line, and by the time he was done the Sun was ducking behind the trees. He set the trap and went to check his others. All had lobsters. By the time he got to the last trap, the Sun had set, and the full Moon rose over the trees by the Narrows. Jake realized that the Moon was a mixed blessing. It would help him see to get back to shore, but also meant that the tides were bigger than usual. And the tide had been falling the whole time Jake had been out. He would have to haul the dinghy, lobsters and all, over an expanse of mud.

He had that last trap almost into the boat, when something big underneath the water tugged back hard on the line. By this time Jake had drifted perilously close to the Hole, where the bottom falls away. He was standing upright in the little dinghy, feet planted far apart, bringing in the line hand over hand. The sharp tug pulled him off balance. If he cried out, no one heard him. He tried to grab the boat as he went pinwheeling over the side and into the cold water. He still had the line in his hand. Somehow that line got wrapped around the upper part of his leg, and the weight of the trap made it tight and dragged him beneath the surface.

Down, down, down he went, into the swirling darkness. He struggled against the line, but only managed to wrap it more tightly around his leg. His lungs screamed for air as the water sucked him down. He must have thought how ridiculous it was, to survive a shipwreck at sea only to drown in his own backyard. He kicked off his boots and let them sink to the bottom. He thought of Annabelle and their two children, one born, the other still in the oven. He thought of all the good people of Deer Isle who would turn out for his funeral. And then, just as it seemed his lungs would burst, he remembered the pocketknife in his jeans. With the last of his strength, he pulled the knife free and opened it, and began sawing frantically at the line that anchored him to the trap, invisible in the depths below. The rope bit deeply into his leg, doubled over on itself so tightly that he could not get his knife between the strands. Knowing he had only seconds, he cut the line below him. Suddenly buoyant, he surged toward the surface. He thought he would black out before he made it, for he estimated later that he had been dragged down at least ten fathoms. He gasped for air as he broke the surface, and again tried to pry loose the rope from his leg. It wouldn't budge. Jake saw the dinghy, bobbing gently a short distance away in the moonlight. He had no feeling in the leg below where the line wrapped around it, but he was too weak to care. He managed the few strokes he needed to reach the boat, hauled himself aboard, and collapsed.

Had he not been near death, he might have wondered where his lobsters had gone. He might also have noticed that the Moon was in a different part of the sky and that the tide had come in—both of which were impossible, since a man can survive but a few minutes under water. After he recovered, the memory of his near-drowning at the Hole would become more and more vague, like memories of a dream, until Jake could not be sure what he remembered and what his oxygen-starved brain had conjured up.

In the morning two fishermen found him drifting in the dinghy out by Guardian Rocks, two miles from the Hole. He'd drifted through the Narrows and all the way out of Dyer's Inlet into the main body of the bay. He was still unconscious, the rope still cinched around his leg. The leg was black and waxy and, it turned out, useless—he'd lost circulation in it for some twelve hours. Jake ended up being hospitalized in Portland for several weeks. Medicine in those days weren't what it is today. They amputated the leg. It was the only thing they could do.

When Jake recovered from the operation he was in for another shock. Annabelle came to visit him in the hospital. When he had last seen her she had been swollen with impending childbirth, but now she was barely showing. The trees outside his hospital window sported young buds instead of the brilliant colors of autumn. Confused, he asked for a newspaper. It was April, several months *before* the wreck of the *Eleanor Rose*. Jake didn't have a clue as to how it happened and, as you can imagine, he began to wonder if he hadn't suffered some sort of brain damage while he was underwater, and hallucinated those months that hadn't happened yet, including the shipwreck. Everyone else seemed to think everything was normal, but Jake had, in fact, traveled back in time. He had enough common sense not to shoot his mouth off about it, but after a few days he convinced himself he wasn't going mad. It had really happened.

Jake was fitted with a wooden leg. And he returned to Deer Isle, and to lobstering. Annabelle told him to take it easy, but he had a growing family to feed and, leg or no leg, Jake never was a man of leisure. He learned to walk, though with a limp he'd keep till the day he died, and he rigged the equipment on his boat so he could get to it more easily. The sea has a long history of peg-leg sailors. He amused his buddies by jabbing his knife into his artificial limb in front of people who didn't know about it, and one time he got angry at another lobsterman and brandished the leg like a club. When he went down to Howley's Hole he discovered that he did not have any traps there, and he did not set any.

And then the memories of the time he'd lost, the time he'd traveled back over, began to fade, and he wondered anew if he had dreamt those months or actually experienced them. But sometimes he would experience odd bits of foreshadowing, as though remembering things that had not yet happened. Occasionally he would know what someone would say before the words were said; at other times he would have premonitions, feelings he couldn't place but that stirred him to action. He told no one about them. The strongest of his premonitions involved the *Eleanor Rose*, which was then fitting out for her voyage to Jamaica.

He approached Thomas Shess and offered his services as navigator. Shess said he would have loved to have him, for Jake was, as I've said, the most knowledgeable sailor in the area. But the financier was reluctant to take on a man who had so recently lost his leg. Captain Chason said Jake would be in the way. But Jake was adamant. He *had* to be on that ship! Finally, owner and captain relented, and when the *Eleanor Rose* set sail in the new time line, Jake was once again aboard her.

Well, you can guess the rest. The *Eleanor Rose* completed her journey to Jamaica, and just as before, an east wind came up and the fog surrounded her as she approached Penobscot Bay on her way home. But this time Jake would not be swayed by the impatient captain. Chason called Jake every epithet in the book, and some that weren't in there yet. He pulled rank and ordered the helmsman to change course. "Do that and we'll all die," Jake said. But the helmsman obeyed his captain.

Jake had to do something. Waiting until the captain's back was turned, he swung his wooden leg in a well-aimed arc and coldcocked Chason on the side of the head. The captain crumpled to the deck unconscious. "Hard about!" Jake cried, just as the crew heard the unmistakable sound of breakers against exposed rock. The *Eleanor Rose* swung wide of Halibut Ledge and sailed to safety.

Jake was hailed as a hero. When the hapless Captain Chason came around, with the ship safely in port, he couldn't discipline Jake, for every member of the crew knew that Jake had saved their lives. And from that time on, Jake held a special place in the hearts of his fellow islanders. People who had barely spoken to him before now brought him gifts every holiday. He became a beloved figure around the docks, limping around on a series of wooden legs local carpenters fashioned for him for free. He kept lobstering, and on those occasions when one of the men got lost or into trouble with a bit of weather, Jake was always first to volunteer for the rescue party. He and Annabelle went on to have six more children, and today his descendants can be found all over Deer Isle, Isle Au Haut, Swans Island, and a half dozen towns on the mainland. Jake's son Tom worked on the crew that built the Deer Isle bridge. The *Eleanor Rose* sailed these waters for many more years, until some Californian bought her and took her through the Panama Canal to the Pacific. She was finally scrapped in San Diego, so I hear. But it was Jake, not that boat, who people around here remembered and cared about. When he died, people came from all over the coast to pay their respects. He'd kept mum about his trip through the Hole. In fact, he'd almost forgotten about it. But his friends and relatives never forgot him, and what he had done.

As Aunt Polly finished her story, she leaned back in her rocker and looked at each of us in turn. Nygerski frowned. I didn't know what to think. But Cassandra's lips were pursed; she seemed to be in deep thought. "A real hero," she murmured. "And all it cost him was his leg."

"There are always costs, my dear," Aunt Polly said. "Nothing of value is ever achieved without a price. I think Jake would have said it was worth it."

"How could he swim to the dinghy," Nygerski asked, "if he had traveled back in time to before he had learned to swim?"

Aunt Polly smiled thinly. "You don't believe me, do you?"

"It's a lot to swallow," Nygerski admitted.

Aunt Polly nodded. "It is. You travel back in time, you can change anything. You could even go back, if you could go back far enough, and kill your parents before you were born. And then how would you have been able to go back and kill them, if you had never been born? It's a famous paradox, and no one's come up with an answer for it. But Jake only went back a few months. And he was underwater for just as long as his lungs could hold out. A few more seconds and he would have died. So maybe it's only possible to take short trips back in time—a few months, a year at the most. I don't know."

"Could one of *us* travel back in time?" I asked her.

"Don't you go near that Hole, Timmy!" Aunt Polly's expression changed. She stopped rocking and glared at me. "I told you, most people who've fallen in the water there have drowned. Jake's the only one I know who lived to tell about it. It's a dangerous, dangerous place. A place best avoided, if you want to grow old, like me."

But Cassandra's manner disturbed me. She stared out at the islands as though deep in thought. As though looking for a ghost ship, lost in time.

Nygerski was still skeptical. "So you're saying it's possible to go back and change things?"

Aunt Polly laughed pleasantly. "Young man, we are changing things every day. Every minute of every day. Every action you take has an outcome; every word you say has consequences. And everything you do or don't do constitutes a choice, with repercussions no one can predict. There are millions of ways for things to happen."

"But only one way they actually do," Nygerski insisted. "The rest is 'what if?' You can't be dead and not dead at the same time."

Aunt Polly looked at him hard before answering. When he didn't show the slightest sign of being unnerved, she smiled slowly and said, "I wouldn't be so sure. You see, there's more to the story. Cassandra, what was mother's maiden name?"

Cassandra came back from someplace out among the islands and turned to face Aunt Polly. "Grammy Bea?" she said. "It's Soule."

Aunt Polly nodded. "My mother—your father's grandmother—was the third daughter Matthew and Wilhelmina Soule had after the voyage of the *Eleanor Rose.*"

Understanding dawned on Cassandra's face, as it did on mine, for the first thing we did was look at one another. "The man who was buried . . . ," Cassandra said haltingly.

". . . after the wreck," Aunt Polly finished for her, with an emphatic nod. "Were it not for Jake Weed, none of us would be here." Her eyes returned to Nygerski. "Except you, of course."

Nygerski stood up and walked to the window, to a spot behind Cassandra where she could not see his face. "Let me get this straight," he said, taking two steps and swiveling on the balls of both feet, then repeating the maneuver in the other direction. "You're all supposed to be dead. No, worse. Nonexistent. You were never supposed to have been born."

"There's no 'supposed to' about it, young man," Aunt Polly said. "Things aren't 'supposed to' happen any way at all. The reality in which the *Eleanor Rose* sank off Vinalhaven is just as real as the reality we're sitting in now."

"Right. Only in that other reality, none of you are here. You're Fig Newtons of my imagination."

I laughed, but Cassandra turned around and scowled at him. "Don't make fun of things you don't understand," she said.

"Oh, come on," Nygerski scoffed. "You don't really expect me to believe this, do you? Everyone knows time travel is impossible. Time only goes one way. Past, present, future. You can't go back, except in movies."

His outright disbelief emboldened me to ask the question that had been on my mind ever since Aunt Polly had finished her story. "If Jake forgot he'd actually gone back in time and changed history," I said, "then how do *you* know about it?"

"He confided in Matt, who told Mother, who told me." Aunt Polly looked up at Nygerski. "It's a family legend, lad, and we hold it close. You should consider yourself privileged to have heard it. Not many outside the family have."

"I want to see this place," Nygerski said. "This Howler's Hole, or whatever."

"It's not hard to get to from the cove," Cassandra told him. "You just take the canoe across to the other side, walk across the blueberry field and the dirt road, and you're at Dyer's Inlet. If it's high tide, you can go through the Narrows. Tim and I have done it a bunch of times."

"You be careful around that Hole!" Aunt Polly warned. "It's claimed the lives of better swimmers than you."

"Aunt Polly, we always wear our life jackets. But most of the time it's nothing more than a spot of really deep water. No whirlpools or anything. Nothing like the current coming in and out of the Narrows."

"On the dead low tide, when the full Moon occults Jupiter, that's when it's most dangerous," Aunt Polly said. "According to the legend."

"Mom and Dad would never let us go at night," I put in.

But Aunt Polly was looking only at Cassandra. "I know what it is, child, to see things," she said, slowly and seriously. "You have a gift. Use it well, but use it sparingly. Respect its power. Don't try to control things you can't. And stay away from the Hole. You understand me?"

For the moment, for the two of them, Nygerski and I were no longer in the room. Slowly, Cassandra nodded. "Yes, Aunt Polly," she said. "I understand."

10.

THE HOLE

Of course Nygerski had to see the Hole. Jake Weed's story had affected him like a sign on wet paint—he had to touch it himself to test its veracity. "There's not much to see from the shore," Cassandra told him. "It's just a deep spot in the water. You'll be disappointed."

But Nygerski would not be dissuaded. So Cassandra took a right about a mile before the dirt road to the Cove, down another dirt road in even worse condition. A lot of people know about Maine now, but in 1967, it was pretty much a backwater, outside of tourist towns like Boothbay and Bar Harbor. There wasn't anything quaint or touristy about Dyerville. The settlement (for it was far too small to call a town, lacking a post office, school, or store) consisted of perhaps a dozen houses and trailers, a tiny Baptist church, and a dock. A few old American cars with fins on the back and the creeping cancer of rust beneath the doors and around the rear wheels, and several snowmobiles covered with tarps for the upcoming summer, stood in makeshift driveways. Beside some of the homes, small plots of earth had been turned for vegetable gardens. Two lobster boats were moored out in the inlet, and half a dozen skiffs lay atop the grassy bank onshore, next to several piles of brightly painted buoys and a wall of wooden lobster traps.

"Not a lot of money here," Nygerski observed as they drove through. An old man waved at them laconically from his front porch.

"No," Cassandra said. "But wouldn't you rather be poor here than in the bad parts of Boston, or New York? At least you can go clamming, or feed your family by jacking deer. Rural poverty has a lot more dignity."

"What's jacking deer?" Nygerski asked.

"You shine a flashlight into a deer's eyes at night," I explained. "The deer's blinded, so it freezes. Then, blammo!"

"Like shooting polar bears from a helicopter," Nygerski commented.

"It's totally illegal, but people do it," Cassandra said. "Beats starving."

The dirt road snaked past the settlement along the waterfront and then turned back into the trees and thinned further, into dual tire tracks with a grass median. "The Narrows is over there," Cassandra said, pointing into the trees on her left as she drove. "Jake Weed's old house is right up here." And as she spoke, the car rounded a curve in the road and came out into a large field, which sloped gently downward toward calm, mud-green water. At the far edge of the field stood a gabled two-story house. The windows were boarded up, and the porch had fallen away, leaving a doorway to nowhere three feet above broken, rotting boards. A small outbuilding had collapsed entirely, and the alders had gathered around its corpse like a pack of hyenas.

"No one's lived here for as long as I can remember," Cassandra said. "Jake had heirs, but I guess they all moved to Stonington. Left this place to the Dyers. It's a shame nobody's wanted to fix this old house up. Some of the locals think it's haunted."

"By whom?" Nygerski asked.

"Dunno. Some fisherman who drowned, probably."

The road curved again, past a small wooden shack even more dilapidated than the houses in Dyerville proper, and as it reached the water it did not so much end as peter out, into a wide peninsula of flattened grass surrounded by tidal shallows and delineated by several silvery trunks of driftwood that someone had dragged from somewhere. We parked next to an old red and white Plymouth station wagon that listed to one side. The tide was out, and the flats lay exposed. I could see several clammers out there, their backs bent as they turned and poked through the mud near the receding water.

We got out of the car and walked through the scrub grass and onto the granular mixture of rocks, shells, and bits of dried seaweed that lined the shore. The rim and fingers of this placid little lagoon formed a vast mudscape, littered with small smooth mounds where clam forks had overturned the exposed bottom on other low tides. But at the center was open water, a stone's throw across and darker green than at the edges. From this pool of water flowed a stream that ran between the mudflats on the two shores around a bend toward the Narrows. You could tell whether the tide was coming in or out just by watching that current at the spot where the two shores came together. But out in the middle the water looked calm and harmless.

"So where is it?" Nygerski asked my sister.

"You're looking at it," Cassandra said.

"You're kidding! That water right there is two hundred feet deep?"

"That's just what it says on the chart," Cassandra reminded him. "It could be a lot deeper."

The three of us stood there in silence for several minutes, each lost in our own thoughts. My friend Elroy Woolf and I, both drawn to scientific things, had spent hours in the Red Cabin at night debating the origin of the Hole. I clung to my meteorite theory, while Elroy maintained that it was probably a sinkhole—an underground air pocket that collapsed when the glacier pressed down on it.

Squishy footsteps scrunched down the dirt road toward us, and we turned to see old Clem Dyer, all seventy-odd grizzled years of him, ambling in hip boots down to the clam flats with hod and fork. He saw Cassandra's long hair and stopped. A smile made wider by the absence of his four top front teeth spread beneath his red wool cap and white whiskers. "Well, I'll be!" he exclaimed, approaching us. "If it ain't Cassandra!" His gray eyes flicked to me long enough for him to say, "Hullo, Timmy." Then his attention returned to Cassandra. "When'd you get back?"

This reception was typical in two ways. People on the island paid a great deal of attention to my sister, and any time she turned up on Deer Isle, they assumed she was "back," rather than visiting. The attention was understandable; she was twenty and even I had to admit she was pretty. But it still ticked me off when people ignored me or paid me only cursory attention in her presence. And I thought men like Clem were pathetic, the way they fawned all over her with their tongues practically hanging out.

But Cassandra got through a lot of her life on charm alone, which accounts for why I have none—she got my share as well as her own. She could talk to anyone, from the president of the United States on down to a feebleminded old coot like Clem. She returned his feral smile, dominated by long canine teeth that framed the gap in the middle, with a smile of her own. "Just got back yesterday, Clem," she said. "This is my friend Cyrus, from Boston."

The old man squinted at Nygerski. "Boston, eh? I stay away from them big cities. Ain't even been to Portland since fifty-nine."

"No reason to go," Cassandra said.

"Ayuh," he replied.

"Cyrus here is a ballplayer," Cassandra said.

"A what?" The old man smiled vacantly at Cassandra and nodded his head.

"A ballplayer," Cassandra said, louder, for Clem's hearing wasn't what it used to be. "A baseball player. He plays baseball."

"Oh." Reluctantly, Clem shifted his attention from my sister to Nygerski. "What team yuh play for?"

"The Beloit Turtles," Nygerski said.

"The what?"

"The Turtles. The Beloit Turtles. They're a minor-league affiliate of the Chicago White Sox."

"Oh, the White Sox. You play for the White Sox?" Clem's eyes widened; many little red blood vessels were visible in the whites.

Nygerski laughed and looked at Cassandra. "Well, not yet," he said, and laughed again. The old man laughed, too, but it didn't seem like he knew why.

"How's the clamming been, Clem?" Cassandra asked him.

"Oh, 'bout the same," he drawled happily. "Gettin' a late staaht." He nodded toward the other figures out on the mudflats. "Guess I better get out thayah." And he tromped off, scrunching and squeaking in his high rubber boots.

"Friend of the family?" Nygerski asked Cassandra, when Clem was out of earshot.

My sister and I laughed. "Everybody knows old Clem," she said. "Drunk as a skunk most of the time, but he don't mean nothin' by it." My sister was a lot better than I was at slipping into the local vernacular.

"He lives in that last house we passed," I offered. "Sometimes he shows up at the drugstore in town. Buys ice cream for kids. Adults avoid him."

We watched him wade out onto the mudflats, select a spot, and start digging. Farther up toward the narrows, two men loaded two buckets of clams into their dinghy and began dragging it over the mud toward the water. "They're done early," Nygerski observed.

"It's almost dead low tide," I said. "They came by boat, so they gotta get back out through the Narrows before the current reverses. Those other guys'll leave pretty soon, too. Clem and whoever came in this car can take their time."

"So where is your house from here?"

Cassandra pointed toward the trees lining the water where it narrowed and began funneling out of the basin. "Over there. Out through the Narrows and across two blueberry fields and a dirt road. It's less than a mile as the crow flies, but it's a six-mile drive."

"And people come down here to swim? Why?"

"Water's warm," my sister told him. "At least, a lot warmer than most water around here. The Sun bakes the mudflats, and then the tide comes in over them. Warms up the water." She paused. "Not so many people come down here anymore, after that kid drowned a couple of summers ago."

"How'd he drown?"

Cassandra shrugged. "Swam out too far, I guess. Got caught in the current, panicked, and got tired. Had two friends with him, but neither of them saw him go down. And no one sure as hell saw him come up. They found him on the rocks by the Narrows, all bloated, two days later."

The two men nudged their dinghy afloat, and one of them started the tiny outboard engine. It sounded like a bumblebee in the distance. The little wooden boat moved slowly out into open water.

"Well, you seen enough?" Cassandra asked Nygerski. "It doesn't look like a dangerous place, but it is."

"Yeah, okay."

But as we walked back toward the car, Nygerski posed another question. "Cassandra, those people your aunt Polly mentioned, who disappeared into the Hole and were never found . . ."

"Yes?"

"Well, didn't anybody ever try to recover the bodies? I would think the families would insist on divers, at least, if not dragging the bottom. It seems weird for people to disappear, in an enclosed area like this—"

"Almost enclosed," she corrected him.

"Well, all right, almost enclosed. It's still weird that no one tried to find them."

"Oh, they tried," Cassandra said as she opened the driver's side door. "But, number one, you can't get a boat of any size in here to drag the bottom, and two, it's hard to find divers on Deer Isle to go into the Hole. Everyone's aware of its reputation as a spot where people drown. Eventually they did find two guys to go down there, together, but they didn't get close to finding the bottom of the Hole, let alone a body."

We got into the car, and Nygerski took one final look out at the deceptively placid pool of deep water, no bigger than a midsize pond. I could see on his face that he had more questions. But we drove the six miles to Rum Runners Cove in near-silence, with no more discussion about the Hole.

We returned to find the cove transformed. A red Volkswagen bus and a yellow Beetle were parked between the house and shed, and kids, dogs, and camping gear spilled out onto the grass beside them. The Woolfs had arrived from Connecticut.

11.

A DEER IN THE WOODS

There were seven Woolf kids, born like batches of pancakes at regular intervals across the arc of the baby boom. Roger, the oldest, was one year younger than Cassandra; then came Betsy, Holly, Jeff, Elroy, Martha, and Kelly, the baby. Elroy was my age; we had been friends since babyhood. Jeff was fifteen, and too cool to hang around with the two of us.

In addition to the kids, Bob and Wendy Woolf had a succession of dogs, this year two black Labradors who chased each other around the cars and baggage, barking. I was nearly knocked off my feet by one of them as I got out of the car. The Woolfs weren't good at training their dogs. Years earlier they had owned a beautiful female husky, high-strung even for that notoriously nervous breed. Three-year-old Lauriann Granger had surprised the dog in the kitchen, sneaking up from behind and throwing her arms around its neck. She had paid with five stitches across her cheekbone. Later the dog had to be put down for raiding a sheep pen near the family's winter home in Connecticut. These Labs were just as unruly if not as prone to viciousness.

Because supervising such a brood taxed the energies of two mere mortals, the Woolfs sometimes hired nannies—college girls, usually—

when they came to the cove in the summer. This occasionally created a rift in my parents' already strained relationship, for my father flirted with the baby-sitters shamelessly. He did have something of a wandering eye, my dad, and my mother knew it. I looked over at him now, on the steps talking animatedly with Bob and Wendy Woolf, and I could tell that he was both happy to have the place abuzz with activity and disappointed that the Woolfs had not brought a nanny on this trip.

They were a handsome, all-American couple, Bob a couple inches taller and thinner through the midsection than my father, with close-cropped blond hair; Wendy robust and curvy, brown curls framing a face that seemed always ready to erupt into laughter. But it was Elroy I wanted to see, for he was my best friend in the world. I never saw my old friends in Ohio anymore, and I had made no solid new ones among my schoolmates in Maine. Although Elroy and I saw each other only for a few weeks every summer, we had many of the same interests, and for those few weeks we were inseparable. It was strange and wonderful to see him in April.

"We're here for the whole week," he told me as I helped him lug his stuff to the Red Cabin. "Spring vacation."

"I got spring vacation, too," I said, dropping his backpack on the cabin's bare wood floor between two pairs of bunk beds. I'd be sleeping there, too, along with Jeff, for the room I had inhabited all winter belonged to Bob and Wendy Woolf. The older boys would join Nygerski in the Near Cabin, while the girls would sleep in the house.

"We'll have to go check on the fort."

"It's probably pretty muddy in the woods," I told him. Elroy didn't know Deer Isle at any time of year other than summer. By now I had slogged my way through a couple of Maine winters and knew it wasn't all like Winslow Homer paintings and Robert McCloskey books.

"It's pretty warm out," Elroy said, taking off his jacket and tossing it onto a bottom bunk. "I thought it'd be colder than this."

"It snowed less than two weeks ago," I replied.

Yes, and my dad kept saying winter wasn't over yet, even though flowers were blooming, buds were on the trees, and grass was poking up everywhere through the mud. That didn't mean, he said, that we wouldn't get one more big dumping of snow before spring arrived for good. The prospect of a late-season storm had scared my mom all the way back to Ohio—that and a fight she had had with my dad a couple days before she left, about lipstick on one of his shirts.

"Tim, we gotta go see the fort!" Elroy insisted. "To see if it survived the winter!"

"It was still there in December," I reassured him. "I went out there on snowshoes."

"Snowshoes?" he gasped, horrified. "That means you left tracks! Somebody could have followed them and found the fort!"

"Elroy, no one was around but me and my folks."

"You didn't tell your cousins about it, did you?"

"No." I shook my head emphatically. "Swear to God."

"I think we should go out there tomorrow morning," he said.

"We might have trouble getting across the cranberry bog," I said. "And there's still patches of snow in the woods. We'll have to wear boots."

We set out early, right after breakfast. Almost everyone was still sleeping off the big lobster dinner we'd had in honor of the new arrivals. Meals around that huge dining room table were one of the joys of life at Rum Runners Cove. The table took up most of the room, and when all three families were there, dinnertime could truly become a circus. We never, for example, *passed* the ketchup—we slid the bottle across the table's wide wooden surface at high velocity. When we had lobsters, the shells were deposited into two large bowls at the center of the table, and many of the behind-the-back throws, fadeaways, and bank shots off the milk bottle missed their mark. The house smelled of lobster for days afterward.

Uncle Bill and his family were there, and after dinner Bob Woolf pulled out a guitar and we all sat around singing folk songs by the fireplace. Elroy and I excused ourselves after a while and went out to the Red Cabin. The others were still singing and carousing as we drifted off to sleep.

To get to our fort, we first had to traverse a series of room-sized rocks, some carpeted by moss, others bare, that collectively we called simply "the Ledge." This glacial deposit extended well back into the woods from a spot on the road just out of sight from the house, beyond the Far Cabin. It's much grown-over now, but in my youth it was quite open and walkable, and from its crest you could see out over the cove, across William's Point to Dyer's Inlet, and out to the ocean and Isle Au Haut in the distance. Midway across the Ledge was a cranberry bog that in spring and early summer was full of water. Stepping-stones at challenging intervals for a ten-year-old provided a way across, but if you missed one, you got wet up to the knees. At the far end of the Ledge was a six-foot cliff that one could walk around—but why do that if you could climb it? Beyond this point the woods began in earnest.

We had been wise to wear our boots, for the forest floor was wet and squishy, with patches of dirty, granular snow lingering in the perpetual shade. The fort could not be seen from very far away, for the materials of its construction gave it natural camouflage in a world of tree limbs and fallen branches. We were almost upon it when we saw the deer.

I had seen deer before, of course, usually fleeting glimpses of them running through the woods. But this deer wasn't about to run anywhere—not with its throat ripped open and half its guts torn out. It was a young buck, with six points on each of its two antlers. Its lifeless eyes bulged, and its mouth was open, as if frozen in midscream. It had been dead for some time, for white maggots churned in the wounds, and something else had eaten away the flesh on the side of its face and along its shoulder and foreleg down to the bone. But the passage of days had not dimmed the horror of its death. Something had violently claimed this deer's life.

Stunned, Elroy and I looked at one another. "Let's get out of here," he choked.

Dumbly, I nodded, and we ran, boots squishing through the thawing forest floor, jumping over downed limbs and dodging standing trees. We ran until we reached the Ledge and scrambled down the face of the kid-sized cliff. "Tim, slow down!" Elroy called after me as I bounded across the rocks. All I wanted to do was get as far away from that deer as possible. My family had never hunted, but I had seen gutted deer carcasses in the fall strung up like drying overalls, and the fact of their deaths had never bothered me. This was different.

"Hey! What the heck's gotten into you guys?"

We stopped. Cassandra's friend Cyrus Nygerski stood looking at us from the other side of the cranberry bog. It was, as usual, impossible to read the expression on his face. I wondered briefly if my sister had played poker with him yet. He would have given her a challenge.

"What are you running from in such a hurry?" he asked as we caught our breath. "You look like you've just seen Bigfoot."

Elroy and I were still too stunned to make a coherent reply. My friend bent over, his hands on his knees, panting, and for a moment I thought he was going to puke. But he was just out of breath. I guess I was in better physical shape, for I was first to recover. "Wh-what are you doing here?" I stammered.

"Just out for a walk," he said, nodding at the bog. "How'd you get across there?"

"Used those rocks," I said. "Step carefully." I needn't have admonished him. Nygerski, the athlete, was nothing if not nimble, and he joined us on the other side of the bog without getting so much as a toe wet.

"Where's Cassandra?" I asked him.

"She took off, with Betsy, in your dad's car. Said she wanted to go see some silversmith somewhere. Made it sound like it was important."

"Silversmith? You mean Charles Hayes?"

"That's it," he said. "Must be the place we passed on the way in, up by the bridge. The Hayes Gallery."

"Yup," I said. "My mother worked for him the first year we lived here.

Until he fired her and hired his twenty-one-year-old girlfriend to take her place." Charles Hayes was not held in high regard by our family. He had come to Deer Isle from New York or Philadelphia—one of the big cities on the east coast—within the past few years, which automatically made him suspicious in the eyes of the natives. Hayes was somewhat famous for his silver sculptures and jewelry, which he sold by mail order through advertisements in national magazines. He owned a big house on Eggemoggin Reach, which he had converted into a gallery, studio, and home. He had a full head of aristocratic gray hair, swept haughtily back from his forehead, and he insisted on being called "Charles," rather than "Charlie" or "Chuck." My mother, perhaps because she, too, was "from away," had been his biggest defender right up until the day he fired her. If Cassandra was buying something from him, it constituted a significant betrayal of our family's unstated but very real vow never to do business with him again.

Elroy was still shaking and breathing hard. "What happened?" Nygerski asked. "You guys look scared to death."

Elroy and I exchanged a silent glance. "Should we tell him?" I asked. "I don't think he's gonna blab to everyone where the fort is."

"What's going on?" Nygerski's face wore a bemused expression, like he expected to be the butt of some adolescent joke and had decided reluctantly to go along with it.

"No!" Elroy said forcefully. "He'll tell your sister, and then she'll bring Betsy out here, and then our fort won't be secret anymore. Let's just go home!"

"Elroy, we gotta tell someone."

"Why?" he cried.

"Because something's out there, stupid—something I don't want to run into. Not after seeing what it did to that deer."

"What are you talking about?" Nygerski said.

"Look, he's leaving in a couple days, anyway," I told Elroy. "What does he care about our fort? Let's show him."

"Show me *what?*" Nygerski said.

Elroy looked up into Nygerski's face. "You promise not to tell *anyone* where our fort is?"

His manner was so deadly serious that Nygerski had to laugh. "Sure," he said. "I can keep a secret."

"It's not the fort," I said.

His dark eyes regarded me frankly, without concealing or revealing anything. "Well, what is it, then?"

"Come on," I said. "We'll show you."

When he saw the deer, Nygerski stared down at it in silence for several seconds. "What kinds of animals you got in these woods?" he asked at length.

"I dunno," I said. "Deer, moose, bobcats. Bears, probably. It's an island, but it's close to the mainland. We have everything they have."

Nygerski squatted down to take a closer look at the mutilated corpse, examining the ghastly wounds. "Bears don't kill like that," he said. "They maul their victims. You can tell that whatever killed this deer went right for the throat." He pointed to where half the deer's neck was missing.

"So . . . what?" I said.

"There can't be any wolves here," he said. "There aren't any wolves in the lower forty-eight, except in Minnesota."

"As far as they know," Elroy said.

"How about coyotes? You have coyotes here?"

Elroy and I shook our heads. "I don't know," I said.

"Coyotes could do that?" Elroy asked skeptically, shivering slightly as he looked at the deer. "I thought they were scavengers."

"They are," Nygerski said. "And they're too small to take down a deer, at least one-on-one. Maybe a pack of dogs did this."

Elroy began skulking around the area, examining the mud and rotted leaves and pine needles at our feet. "What are you doing?" I asked him.

"Looking for tracks," he replied. "If it was a pack of dogs, there should be tracks all over the place."

But there weren't. The footprints Elroy and I had left were quite prominent, and we could see four or five hoofprints made by this deer or another one. A patch of browned snow with holes like an old blanket nestled against the dead deer's body. A rabbit had run across it soon after it had fallen. But we searched for several minutes before Nygerski found the paw print.

It was huge—almost the size of an adult human foot, and bigger than the boot prints Elroy and I had so carelessly left. Nygerski held his sneaker out beside the unmistakably canine print in the mud, its edges sloped rather than sharp, indicating, as Elroy pointed out in a small voice, that it had been there for at least a few days. The animal's foot was almost as long and much wider.

"Maybe a big dog," Nygerski murmured.

"*Damn* big," I said.

"Any vicious dogs in the area that might've gotten loose?"

Elroy and I looked at one another and shrugged. I couldn't imagine any of the dogs I'd seen on Deer Isle inflicting the carnage I saw at my feet.

We looked around for more tracks, but there was only the one. I tried to look at the dead deer as little as possible. But it wasn't so scary with Nygerski there. The fort was a short distance away, actually within sight of the carcass through the trees, if you knew where to look for it. It had survived the winter admirably; the major boughs were still in place, and the roof had held up even under a thick blanket of snow. We went inside and replaced some of the pieces that had fallen, and Elroy brought out a bag of cookies, which we shared with our guest.

We spent the next hour or so eating the snacks we had brought and talking baseball. The dead deer was forgotten, although Elroy kept glancing nervously in its direction. Nygerski reminded us that tomorrow was Opening Day, with a game at Fenway Park between the Red Sox, the team he had rooted for since childhood, and the White Sox, the team with which he had signed. The day after that, he said, he would be leaving Maine to report to a minor-league team in Wisconsin. We asked him a ton of questions—he explained the infield fly rule, and how to calculate your batting average. He talked about how Ted Williams had hit .406 in 1941 and almost matched the mark seventeen seasons later, when he was thirty-nine years old. He told us how he'd been in the ballpark the day Tony Conigliaro, a nineteen-year-old Boston boy, hit a home run in his first game there for the Red Sox. And by the time we finished the snacks and trudged back to the house, casting a last, worried glance at the deer carcass, Elroy and I had found another common passion, one that would obsess us for most of the summer.

"Send us box scores of your games," Elroy suggested. "We'll keep track of your statistics."

I had to chuckle—it was so like Elroy, with his mind for numbers. Nygerski said he'd see what he could do, and the subject dropped. We had no inkling then of how important baseball was to become in our lives that summer. But the season was about to begin.

12.

FULL MOON

The low cloud cover of the past week had given way to April sunshine, which meant work for all of us getting Rum Runners Cove ready for summer. After lunch we went down to the Green Cabin, where we dragged the two dinghies out and put them up on sawhorses, scraped them down, and applied new coats of paint. My dad and Bob cut a few alders, and enlisted Elroy and me to haul them off to a spot at the edge of the bank. When they dried, we'd have a bonfire on the beach.

Nygerski plunged eagerly into the work, helping to get the boats ready and showing Roger how to use the caulking gun. Wendy Woolf threw open the windows in the Green Cabin and began sweeping out the cobwebs, feathers, and mouse droppings.

I was just beginning to wonder where the hell my sister was when she and Betsy Woolf showed up. Cassandra had a six-pack of cold Budweiser bottles. My father scowled when she handed one to Nygerski and another to Roger, but his face softened when she handed the next bottle to him before opening one herself. "You guys look like you're ready for a break," she said, her eyes taking in the boats, the pile of brush, and the cleared-out area by the side of the porch that was now a small field of stumps.

Looking at the two young women, you could easily tell which one had Maine blood. The day was warm by local standards. Nonetheless, short, blond Betsy Woolf wore a green turtleneck under a plaid flannel shirt, and an unzipped ski jacket over that. My sister wore blue jeans, a lightweight cotton shirt, and the red cardigan sweater. Against the skin of her bare neck the Sun glinted off a small silver five-sided star inside a circle. I noticed that Nygerski noticed it, too, and I guessed that she had bought it at Charles Hayes's gallery. I wondered if she would have dared to wear it had our mother been present.

Elroy and I sat on the upturned bottom of the aluminum canoe as the grown-ups and older kids took spots on the porch and the saw-horses or simply remained standing. I couldn't stop thinking about the mutilated deer we had seen, and I knew Elroy was thinking about it, too. Out by the mouth of the cove we saw Uncle Bill's lobster boat tied up at his dock, and several bodies moving busily around it.

"Oh, look!" Cassandra cried suddenly. "Oh, how *adorable!*"

On the ground beside the cabin were four little bundles of fur—black fur with an unmistakable white stripe running down the middle. Four baby skunks. They had emerged from underneath the cabin and were now poking around on the grass, their noses to the ground and bushy little tails in the air. They were the size of baseballs, and as cute as any litter of kittens.

"I'll be damned," said my father.

Impulsively, Cassandra moved to pick up the nearest one. She scooped it up in both hands and held it inches away from her face.

"Cassandra, I wouldn't do that if I were you," my father warned.

"They can't squirt till they get older," Elroy said. "Their glands aren't mature yet."

"How do you know that, son?" Bob Woolf asked. Everybody had gathered around Cassandra and the baby skunk, which looked back at my sister with dark, inquisitive eyes.

"I read it in a book somewhere," Elroy replied offhandedly.

"I'd still be careful," my father said.

Cassandra held the tiny skunk up to him. "He's not even afraid," she said. "I think he likes me."

It did not have the same reaction to my father. In one quick motion, the furry little thing twisted around in my sister's hands, raised its tail, and fired a squirt gun blast directly into my father's left eye.

"Aagh!" My father recoiled; the smell of ripe skunk hit us immediately. Cassandra quickly set the tiny creature down among its littermates and looked worriedly at our father for his reaction. I don't know whose face broke first, but within seconds we were all convulsed with laughter. Even my dad had to smile through the pain, though he directed a few choice words at the unrepentant animal.

"Come on, Clayton, I'll help you wash that out," Wendy Wolff said, placing an arm around his waist and guiding him gently toward the house. She was laughing with the rest of us, but it struck me that there was more than a little tenderness in her concern for my father, whose eye was still shut and stinging with skunk juice.

Perhaps alarmed by the commotion they had caused, the skunks retreated back underneath the cabin. Wendy and my father returned in a few minutes, my father in a clean shirt, and there was some discussion of what to do with the family of skunks. In the end it was decided to do nothing, for the option of extermination was shouted down by the kids, and none of the adults wanted to tackle the task of relocating them. As far as I know, the skunks lived peacefully underneath the cabin that whole summer.

Dinner was a simpler affair than the previous night's lobster fest, with just us and the Woolfs around the big table. Cassandra fidgeted with her silverware and napkin but ate very little and barely contributed to the conversation. She offered me her uneaten piece of chicken and excused herself early.

"Are you feeling all right?" my father asked her.

"Yeah, I'm . . . I'm fine," my sister said as she stood up. But she didn't look fine to me. A strand of her dark hair lay hard against her forehead, held there by faint beads of sweat I could only see because I sat right next to her. And her face was puffy and colorless, save for her lips, which seemed unusually full and red. Her left eyelid twitched rapidly.

"You didn't eat very much of your dinner, sweetheart," said Wendy Woolf, seated beside my dad. Like many of my father's female friends, Wendy fussed over Cassandra when my mom wasn't there, even though Cassandra was twenty now, and quite capable of taking care of herself.

"I'm not very hungry," Cassandra said, moving the strand of hair to one side. She looked over her shoulder into the fading day. "And I think I left something . . . down by the Green Cabin. Excuse me." She took her plate to the kitchen sink, then continued on out the door to the porch and down the path toward the shore. Long before she was out of sight, my father picked up the joke he had been telling Wendy Woolf, and Wendy laughed uproariously.

A few minutes later Betsy Woolf's gasp interrupted the conversation. We all turned to follow her eyes out the window, to where the full Moon, resplendently orange in the twilight, had just risen over the cove. The tide was three-quarters of the way in, and the Moon made a path over the water's rippled surface. You could see the trees along the opposite point, and the ocean beyond that, all bathed in moonlight.

Nygerski was the first to speak. "I believe I'll go down by the water and have a closer look," he said.

"I'll go with you," Betsy proclaimed instantly. I saw Wendy Woolf flash a quick look of disapproval, but Betsy said, "See what Cassandra's doing."

"I'm gonna go play my drums," Jim said, rising from the table.

"Oh, brother." Elroy rolled his eyes. "Can we go with you guys?" he asked Nygerski.

We both tagged along, because Elroy insisted that I come, because I didn't want to hear Jim's drumming any more than he did, and because I too was concerned that Cassandra had not come back. The four of us walked silently down to where we had worked that day on the boats. The fresh white paint on the upturned bottoms of the two dinghies, still up on sawhorses, shone in the moonlight. The Moon loomed over the cove, utterly dominating the onset of night.

"Hey! Cassandra!" Betsy called as we approached the cabin. There was no answer from inside, nor any indication that anyone was there—no light, no stirring of movement. "Cassandra!" Betsy called again.

"She's not here," Nygerski said, behind her. He nodded at a patch of flattened grass beside the two dinghies. "Look. The canoe's gone."

And so it was. You could even see the line in the grass where she had dragged it, toward the beach. We followed it to the top of the bank and looked out over the cove. There was no sign of Cassandra or the canoe.

"Where do you suppose she went?" Betsy asked.

"I don't know," I said. "But I have an idea." I looked at Nygerski. "Remember that story?" I asked him.

"You don't think . . ."

"I don't know," I said, scanning the opposite shore. "She would have landed over there someplace, by that big rock. There's a place to land in behind it. Boy, Dad'll be pissed if he finds out she took the canoe out at night, by herself."

"Why would she do that?" Betsy said.

"Unfinished business," Nygerski muttered, to no one. Then, to me, he said, "Do you think the paint's dry on that dinghy yet?"

"Why? You think we should go find her?"

Nygerski nodded in the moonlight. "The three of us can carry it down to the beach. Betsy, you stay here, in case the old folks start wondering. Better yet, wait a few minutes, then go up to the house to get a snack for Cassandra. Tell everybody she's down at the Green Cabin. I'll take Tim and Elroy with me in the boat."

It seemed so natural for him to take command like that, and none of us resented it. The same lack of hesitancy had endeared him to my father. When the time had come to help with chores, Nygerski had seen what needed to be done and pitched in immediately. He didn't waste a lot of time weighing options.

The paint had dried enough so that it did not come away on a fingertip; I wondered how it would fare in the salt water. Even the smaller of the two rowboats weighed considerably more than an aluminum canoe. It took all four of us to carry it down to the beach, lifting it over rocks and underbrush so as not to mar the new paint job. Elroy scrambled back to the stern; Nygerski took the middle seat with the oars. I removed my shoes and socks, tossed them into the boat, pushed off in the freezing, ankle-deep water, and jumped into the bow as the dinghy floated free. Nygerski dipped an oar into the water and turned the boat away from shore. He rowed expertly—you could tell he'd spent time on the water. He pulled the boat out into the middle of the cove. I drew my jacket tightly around myself in the faint but cold April breeze.

The canoe was where I had predicted it would be, behind the big rock on the far side of the cove. Cassandra had pulled it up onto a flat ledge above the high-tide line. We hoisted the dinghy out of the water next to it and tied it to a scrub pine whose roots had found purchase in a crack in the rock. I put my shoes back on, and we climbed to the top of the rock. Across the cove, we could see the lights in the big house, and the dim glow of a kerosene lantern in the Green Cabin. Betsy appeared to be doing her part. We had a little bit of time to find my sister.

We called her name several times, but there was no answer. The night was bright and silent, too early in the season for mosquitoes. I wondered what in hell Cassandra was up to now. I knew she had gone to the Hole. The path was right there, cutting across the point and coming out on the road to Dyerville, an easy walk. But why? How had she been affected by Aunt Polly's story? And what possible purpose could she have in mind?

Troubled by these thoughts, I gazed down at the water that lapped at the base of the rock. The tide was still rising; it would be higher than usual tonight, because of the full Moon. Suddenly my eyes caught the glint of moonlight off something metallic, between two smaller rocks

at the water's edge. I moved in closer to investigate, and when I saw what
the object was, I stopped breathing for several seconds. It was the silver
necklace Cassandra had been wearing that afternoon.

"Hey, guys, look at this." I approached Elroy and Nygerski, dangling
the star and silver chain from one finger.

"That's Cassandra's necklace!" Elroy exclaimed.

"Where did you find it?" Nygerski asked me.

"On the rocks, over there."

"Let me see it."

I handed the shiny pentagram to Nygerski. He examined the chain in
the moonlight. "The clasp is still fastened," he noted. "The chain's broken, like she ripped it off her neck. Or somebody else did."

"Cyrus, we have to go find her!"

Nygerski stared at the silver necklace for several seconds, saying
nothing. Then his innate decision-making skills kicked in. "You're right,"
he said. "How far is the Hole from here?"

"Less than half a mile," I said. "I'll show you the way."

"Good. Elroy, you stay here with the boat. Tim, you come with me."

"Why do I have to stay here?" Elroy moaned.

"In case Cassandra comes back for the canoe," Nygerski said. "You can
tell her we're looking for her." He pocketed the necklace. "Come on, if
we walk fast, maybe we can catch up with her."

"But I don't wanna stay here by myself!" Elroy protested.

"Somebody's gotta stay with the boat," Nygerski said. "And we won't
be gone long."

"Tim, what's going on? Why would your crazy sister be going to the
Hole, at night, without telling anyone?"

"You got me," I said. I had long ago given up trying to predict
Cassandra's behavior.

"Hurry back," Elroy called after us, with some urgency, as Nygerski
and I set out along the path. I didn't blame him for being scared. I was
a little scared myself, even with Nygerski beside me. Elroy would be

there all alone, listening to the owls and the wind through the trees and all the unknown noises of the night.

"You think she believed that story?" Nygerski asked me when we were out of earshot.

"Yeah, I think she did," I said. "She's tight with Aunt Polly. Everybody in the family thinks they're both strange."

"I'm beginning to wonder why she asked me to come up here with her in the first place."

"How come?"

"Because I feel like a fifth wheel. Except for taking me to see Aunt Polly, she's hardly spent any time with me at all. When I met her in New York, I was on my way to see my mom and sisters before the season started. Then your sister appeared, and she was scared of something, really scared. We got on the bus together—I was going to Boston—and she talked me into coming up here. Said I'd make her feel safe. But she's got you, and Betsy, and this whole extended family around. She doesn't need me."

We had been walking briskly, and we soon came to where the path ended, on the side of the road we had driven down two days earlier. We saw lights on in several of the houses in Dyerville, and the lobster boats bobbed in the moonlit water of Dyer's Inlet. Neither of us had thought to bring a flashlight, and we really didn't need one, so thoroughly did the Moon illuminate everything.

No one was outside as we walked quietly past the houses and on down the road toward the Hole. We passed Clem's cabin, and I was mildly puzzled to see the door open but no light on inside nor any sign of activity. But Clem might have gotten drunk in the early afternoon and fallen asleep with the door open. It wouldn't be the first time.

We reached the clearing by the shore and gazed out at the open water. The moonlight reflected off tiny waves lapping at the mixture of pebbles and shells at our feet. There was no sign of anyone or anything. "Well, I guess she's not here," Cyrus said after a moment.

"Thank God," I added. "What now, back to the boat?"

But before he could answer, something in the trees across the water bayed at the Moon. The throaty howl broke the silence so abruptly that Nygerski and I both jumped in our shoes.

"What the hell was *that?*" Nygerski said.

"Cyrus, I think we should go." The hair on the back of my neck was electrified, and suddenly I could feel moisture in my armpits, despite the cold night.

Another howl came from the trees to our right.

"Let's get out of here," Nygerski agreed. We were indeed already walking up the road as he said this, our footsteps crunching in the gravel. We cast long shadows ahead of us, and our strides were long in that New England way of walking without seeming to hurry but with purpose toward a destination. We passed Clem's darkened house again and marched through the trees toward Dyerville. We were almost to the field behind the town when we heard something beside us in the woods—low branches snapping, a rustling pounce, a pause, another broken twig —and I realized we were being stalked.

It stepped out into the road in front of us right where the trees ended. Nygerski stopped and threw a protective arm against my chest. The Moon was behind it, so that we could not see its face, only its canine silhouette. But it was bigger than any dog I'd ever seen, and it stood directly in our path, challenging us.

A low, keening wail came from somewhere in the back of its throat, slowly rising.

I froze in terror.

At my side, Cyrus Nygerski fished into his pocket. He pulled out my sister's silver necklace. The star caught the moonlight, reflected it. The creature growled softly once, then whirled and bounded back into the trees.

"Come on," Nygerski said, tugging my arm. I needed no urging. Our pace quickened.

"How did you know to do that?" I asked him, when saliva returned to my mouth and I was able to speak.

"I . . . don't know." I could hear the bewilderment in his voice. He looked at the necklace in his hand. "I just did, somehow. Sometimes . . . sometimes animals are scared of bright things."

"What *was* that?"

"Big dog, I guess," he said uneasily. "I didn't get a real good look at it. Didn't like its attitude, though, I'll tell you that." He laughed, but I got the feeling it was only to make me feel better.

We got back to the dinghy to find Elroy waiting anxiously for us at the water's edge. "Did you hear those howls?" he asked us. On our way back across the cove, we related our encounter with the large dog, or whatever had accosted us, and we agreed that it would be best not to alarm anyone else until Cassandra turned up. Betsy had heard nothing. We hauled the boat back up the bank, lest its brief absence be noted, and replaced it on the sawhorses.

I looked at Nygerski. "What now?" I said.

"Dunno. She's supposed to drive me to my bus in the morning."

"I hope she's all right," Betsy said.

"I hope so, too," Nygerski replied. "But what more can we do? We went and looked for her. We didn't find her. Only thing to do now is wait for her to come back."

Sure enough, Cassandra showed up at breakfast the next morning with damp hair and a gleam in her eye. Any sign that she had not been feeling well the previous evening had evaporated. Cassandra looked better than healthy; her face glowed in the sunny spring morning. She astonished us all by announcing that she had taken advantage of the weather for an early-morning swim, the first by any of us that year in the cold Maine water. If my mother had been home she would have reprimanded my sister for such a reckless act, but my father just chuckled softly to himself and shook his head.

Her simple denim shirt was open at the neck, and I could see a small welt, a spot of red, at the base of her throat where the silver star had been. There was no time for questions, though, because Nygerski had to leave. He had a Greyhound bus to catch in Stockton Springs, an hour's drive away, and my sister was to drive him there in my father's car.

Everyone got up to see him off. Even the old guys working on the shed came over to the car to wish him luck during the upcoming baseball season. Elroy gave him a lucky rock with two stripes around it; his big brother Roger put an old Yale baseball cap on the young ballplayer's head. Cyrus Nygerski had only been with us a few days, but his departure caused more of a fuss than when the Woolfs and the Grangers left at the end of the summer.

I shook his hand silently, and our eyes locked for a minute. We had not spoken of last night's adventure, and it appeared that it would remain intact as a memory, not to be eroded by the acid rain of conversation. "Have a great season," I managed finally. "Make us lefties proud."

"You have a great summer, too, Tim," he said, and that was all, though it felt like volumes remained unspoken between us. For the first time, I realized that someone important had crossed my life, and changed it in some way. I can't exactly explain this, even now, but I stood there looking up the road long after the car had disappeared around the bend and the sound of its wheels on the gravel could no longer be heard.

Nygerski's departure seemed to deflate everyone, for we were slow wrapping up breakfast and getting on with the work of the day. My dad and Bob Woolf were outside talking to the carpenters by the side of the garage, and Elroy and I were putzing around, loading board ends into cardboard boxes, when Stan Hutchinson, the game warden, arrived.

His uniform and dark, slickly parted hair looked out of place among the old buildings and unfinished projects. Hutchinson was a portly man whose job was to keep track of the local deer population. When I saw him a lump rose in my throat. He looked around before slowly approaching my father and Bob, his back erect, his thumbs in his belt loops. I nudged Elroy and whispered, "They found the deer, I bet."

"Mornin', Clayton," the game warden said to my father.

"Hello, Stan. What's up?"

"You got dogs out here, Clayton?"

"I have two Labradors," Bob Woolf volunteered. "Is there a problem?"

Elroy and I had put down our boxes and edged closer to the conversation. My father threw us a quick look over his shoulder, and then returned his attention to the game warden.

"You happen to know if those dogs were home last night?" Stan Hutchinson asked.

"Well, yeah," Bob said with some uncertainty. "Sure, they were. They're always here. They don't run off."

"Where are they now, if I may ask?"

"Uh, I think they're down by the beach, with the older kids. Either that or in the house."

In truth, Bob rarely knew where his dogs were. At night they slept in the back room off the kitchen; during the days they were usually where the most people were. Yesterday they had been down at the Green Cabin while we messed with the boats, and this morning after breakfast Roger and Betsy and some of the others had taken them clamming.

"What's going on, Stan?" my father asked.

The game warden glanced at Elroy and me. "Maybe it's best I tell you alone."

"No!" I cried, before I could stop myself. My father glared at me. "I mean, I want to know what's going on, too."

"Me too," said Elroy, at my side.

"It's okay," my father said. "Whatever you've got to tell me, they can hear it, too. Can't keep secrets around this place, anyway."

Stan Hutchinson looked at my father and sucked in his breath. "We found a man's body," he said. "Over in the woods by Dyerville. It looks like old Clem Dyer. He appears to have been the victim of some sort of animal attack."

Every blood vessel in my body froze. For a moment my eyes focused on nothing, and then they came to rest, queerly, on the yellow metal badge pinned to Stan Hutchinson's chest. Clem Dyer dead! Killed by an animal, near the place where Cyrus Nygerski and I had been accosted ourselves. My legs felt weak underneath me.

"Now, I'd like to see those dogs, if you don't mind," Hutchinson said.

Bob Woolf cleared his throat. "Elroy, would you go find Molly and Sam? I think they're at the beach with Roger."

"I'll go with you," I said.

Just then Wendy Woolf poked her head out the door. "Clayton, there's a phone call for you," she called.

"I'm kind of busy right now," my father said. "Can you find out who it is, and I'll call them back?"

"It's your daughter," Wendy said. "I think you'd better talk to her."

My father heaved an exaggerated sigh at the trials of parenthood. "I'll be right back," he said to the game warden. "You boys go get those dogs." He disappeared into the house.

Seconds later, we heard him bellow: "WHAT?"

Stan Hutchinson flicked a glance at the door of the house. Elroy and I stopped also.

"GODDAMNIT, CASSANDRA, YOU LISTEN TO ME!" my father yelled. It was an even bet that they could hear him at the beach.

Wendy Woolf came out of the house and greeted the game warden. "What happened?" her husband asked her.

She looked at him and shrugged. "I was coming out here to ask you," she said.

Bob Woolf looked at Hutchinson and back at his wife. "There was some sort of animal attack, over by Dyerville. Old Clem Dyer's dead. Stan wants to make sure our dogs didn't do it."

As if on cue, Molly, the female Lab, bounded around the corner of the house, recognized Bob, and jumped on him. "Oh, Molly, get down!" Bob cried, pushing the eager dog away. "Look at you! You're covered with mud!"

"We got a bunch of clams, though, Dad!" Jeff cried, coming around the house with full hods in both hands.

"Molly, down!" Wendy Woolf commanded, grabbing the dog's collar. "Now Stan, does this dog look like a killer?"

At that moment my father emerged from the house, his face a red sea of rage. Roger, Betsy, and Holly Woolf appeared with more clams and Sam, the other Labrador. Wendy and Bob looked at my father. "Clayton, what's wrong?" Wendy said.

My father was so mad, he couldn't get the words out on the first or second try. Cassandra had left the car in Stockton Springs. At this moment she was on a bus, on her way to New York with Cyrus Nygerski.

13.

NEW YORK, NEW YORK

"It's just so unbelievable," Nygerski said, shaking his head. "Werewolves?"

"I think so. It's the only explanation that makes any sense."

Cassandra bit her lower lip and looked away from him, out the bus window at the countryside of suburban Connecticut as it rolled by. Nygerski waited for her to continue. He had learned during the past week that asking her pointed questions usually yielded not answers but more questions. She remained as much of a mystery to him as she had been a week ago, when she had literally slammed into his life in the Port Authority bus terminal. In Maine she had relaxed, and kept her distance, but now as the Greyhound neared New York, he could see her anxiety returning. He wanted to comfort her, but did not know what to say.

"Sooner or later, my dad's going to find out I dropped out of the university," she said. "And when he finds out, he's gonna be furious."

"Why don't you just tell him?" Nygerski asked. "You're an adult; you can do what you want."

"Because when he learns the circumstances, he'll probably disown me," she said. "And he'll never send me another penny."

"Oh."

"You know, Maine is one of the most prejudiced states in the country. There aren't any Negroes there, but people hate 'em, anyway."

"And your father—"

"An enlightened man, for the most part. When we lived in Ohio, both Timmy and I had black friends, and it was never a big deal. My dad coached black kids on his football team. He's not a bigot—at least he doesn't think he is. But it was okay as long as my black friends were girls. He's got his family's attitude about interracial dating."

"I see."

"When James came to the university, it was a revelation to all those kids from Fort Kent and Machias and Brownville Junction, who'd never seen a black man up close, let alone an eloquent black man. He's brilliant. He talked about history—not just slavery and black history, but the whole history of nonviolent revolutionary movements, Jesus Christ and Ghandi and everyone in between. He had more to say in one afternoon that most of my professors do in a lifetime."

"And you and he—"

"I managed to get introduced," she said, a small smile curling her lips. "And I found out he's just as brilliant and charismatic in a one-on-one conversation as he is in public. His hero is Martin Luther King Jr. You've heard of him, right?"

"Come on," Nygerski said. "I read more of the newspaper than just the sports section."

"Well, James was going around the country, giving speeches against the war and encouraging Negroes to burn their draft cards. It sounded more exciting than sitting in a classroom. I went with him."

"And now you think he's a werewolf?"

She nodded, and brushed a strand of hair away from her eyelid. Nygerski noticed that it was twitching.

"Well, do you have any proof?"

"Just a lot of corroborating evidence," she said. "At first, he wanted me with him all the time. He seemed to like flaunting his relationship

with a white woman—it was like an act of defiance for him, an exten-
sion of his politics. But when we got to Atlanta, and James was supposed to appear at a rally that Dr. King had organized, he put me up in
a cheap hotel miles from where he and his friends were staying, and
refused to let me go with him. I was crushed. I mean, Dr. King is a great
man, and I wanted more than anything to meet him. But James wouldn't
allow it. And that same weekend there were three grisly murders, right
in the same neighborhood where James was staying. The newspapers
said they looked like animal attacks. I didn't think anything of it until a
few days later, when he took off his shirt and I saw the scars."

"What scars?" Nygerski asked.

"They looked like bite marks. Around his neck, like he'd been attacked
by a vicious dog or something. Within a couple of days they were gone."

"And from that, you concluded he was werewolf? Cassandra, that's
nuts. It could be anything."

"I'm not finished. The Moon was full that weekend in Atlanta. I
hadn't given it a second thought. But a month later we were in Baltimore, and he pulled the same disappearing act. Everything was the
same. The full Moon, the scars afterward, and four more murders."

"Okay. So did you say anything to him?"

"I did. That day in New York. The day we met, a week ago."

Nygerski fell silent and looked out the window. There really weren't
any appreciable spaces between the towns down here, Nygerski thought.
Not like Maine, or even Massachusetts west of Boston. He wondered
what Wisconsin would be like. He had never seen the Midwest.

"You know it's always the most violent people who are the most
vocal about peace," she went on. "I couldn't stop thinking about the full
Moon, and the murders, and James and his friends. One of his friends
was particularly strange. He was from Haiti, and I could barely understand a word he said. He wore necklaces of teeth and bones, and
everything he said sounded like an incantation. The night before, I'd
walked in on some kind of ceremony. James and the Haitian guy and

about four other black men were all in a circle, and they were wearing animal masks—wolf masks. It was about three days before full Moon. When the Haitian guy saw me, he screamed at the top of his lungs and brandished a knife. That's when I decided to get the hell out of there."

"And *that's* why you think he's a werewolf?" Nygerski exclaimed. "That's your evidence?"

"Ssh!" Cassandra admonished him. "This isn't something we want overheard." They had been speaking in half-whispers aboard the half-empty bus, but at Nygerski's outburst, several of their fellow passengers turned to look at them.

"All right," Nygerski said in a lower tone. "But I think you've been watching too many bad movies. You don't really believe that werewolves exist, do you?"

"I think it might be worse than that," she said after a pause. She did not elaborate.

He reached into the pocket of his jeans and pulled out the silver pentagram on its broken chain. "Does *this* have anything to do with it?" he asked her.

Cassandra's eyes widened. She took the medallion from his open palm. "Where did you find this?"

"On the rocks, on the other side of the cove," he said. "Tim and I went looking for you. We found the canoe missing, and we took one of the rowboats over. What were you doing?"

"Cyrus, I don't remember a thing about last night. Not a thing. From what I've read, that's typical. And as weird as it sounds, James did bite me. You know, during sex. He liked it rough, sometimes."

Nygerski shifted in his seat, inching away from her. "I think this is more detail than I need to hear," he said.

"Fine. But James is still in New York. There's a big march against the war tomorrow. Dr. King is speaking at the U.N. I'm sure James will be involved in some capacity."

"He's your unfinished business," Nygerski said dully.

Cassandra nodded in silence.

"What do you plan to do?"

"I know where he and his friends stay," she told him, expertly avoiding a direct answer. "We can get there easily. We can take the subway from the station . . ." She stopped, aware that Nygerski was looking at her with something akin to morbid curiosity. "What?"

"Well, I was just thinking about what Tonto said to the Lone Ranger."

"What did he say?"

"'Whaddya mean "we," white man?'"

She smiled thinly. "Cyrus, I don't want to involve you in anything dangerous against your will. You don't have to come if you don't want to."

"Why are you telling me all this?"

"Because I trust you. I watched you in Maine, with my people. Mainers can spot insincerity a mile away. I know you won't betray me. And I know that if anything happens to me, I can count on you to tell the world the truth."

"What truth? I told you, I don't believe in werewolves. Or ghosts, or vampires, or any of that shit."

"But you have an open mind. You're not afraid of things you don't understand, or people who think differently. At least that's my impression. Am I wrong?"

He had to laugh. "You know, I like you, even if you are nuts," he said. "I guess that's why I let you talk me into going to Maine. And I admit I'm curious, though I don't believe for a minute that you're a werewolf. I'll tag along until my train leaves, if only to keep you out of trouble."

"What time is your train?" she asked him.

"Nine-fifteen tonight."

"Should be time enough," she said.

They arrived in New York around noon. It was a gray day, a bit cold, but one didn't really notice the weather among the tall buildings and the crowds. Cassandra disappeared into a women's room and reemerged in a red dress that ended several inches above the knees and a white cardigan sweater she had not buttoned. "We have to get to One Hundred Twenty-fifth Street," she said. "Best bet's the subway."

Several blocks from the station she located the subway line, and they descended beneath the grimy streets into the bowels of the city. It was all a blur to Nygerski. In Boston he knew the landmarks, the accents and nuances of the people on the street, the rhythm of the days. New York just seemed big and relentless. He lost all sense of geography and the time of day. Morning, afternoon, midnight—it didn't seem to matter.

Cassandra looked grim and determined. She had not smiled at him since their arrival. Her lips pressed together in a thin line that discouraged conversation. Her makeup was spare but artfully applied. A subway train rumbled into the station, and she stepped forward to meet it. Nygerski followed.

Several minutes later she dragged him off the train into another graffiti-filled subway stop. They emerged onto a filthy street lined with old tenement buildings. Nearly every face they saw was black. Nygerski remembered the uniform whiteness of Deer Isle, and noted that Cassandra moved with the same grace and sense of purpose here as she did there. He imagined that she would walk with the same assurance down a street in Mexico or China.

She stopped in front of a building that looked decrepit even in comparison with those around it. "Here," she said.

Nygerski looked at her in disbelief. "Here? What could possibly be here?"

"James," she replied, her mouth tight. "This is where he stays when he comes to New York." She cast him a sidelong glance, and one of the corners of her mouth lifted in amusement at his stunned expression. He saw her left eyelid twitch. "He's a college graduate, with plenty of influential friends," she went on. "He could get a hotel room in any part of the city. But he prides himself on being with his people, as he says."

"Noble," Nygerski muttered. "But, Jesus, Cassandra, look at this place."

"I know. You can wait for me out here if you want."

Nygerski glanced quickly both ways down the block. Indifferent groups of black men and women regarded them from the stoops and windows of nearby buildings; most of the people on the street paid them no attention at all. "Are you kidding?" he said. "I'm sticking with you."

"Come on, then." Cassandra stepped nimbly over the broken glass and skipped up the half-dozen steps and through the open doors of the building. Hurriedly, Nygerski followed.

The hall stank of urine and urban neglect. Pieces of the grayed, once-white linoleum had broken off, revealing the cement beneath. A door down the hall opened, and a timid black female face peered curiously out at them. The face disappeared and the door closed.

"He's on the fifth floor," Cassandra said. "Apartment 543. If he's here, that's where we'll find him. It's a cinch there's no elevator that works. Come on, let's find the stairs."

The stairs were at the end of the hall, and they were even more foul-smelling. "No wonder there are riots," Cassandra said. "People have to live in some kind of dignity."

The girl took the steps at a speed that forced Nygerski to struggle to keep up. "Thought I was in shape," he panted as they passed the third-floor landing. "Cassandra, what are you planning to do? When you find him, that is. Assuming that you do."

She stopped, two steps above him, and looked at him seriously. "I'm going to kill him," she said.

"*What?*"

"Cyrus, he's killed half a dozen people, maybe more. And if someone doesn't stop him, he's going to go right on killing." She reached into her purse, and a dull metal object appeared in her hand. Nygerski gasped. It was a revolver.

"Now you know the real reason I went to see Charles Hayes in Maine," she said.

"The silversmith? I don't get it."

"A silver bullet through the heart is the only way to kill a werewolf. It's between full Moons, so the werewolf side of him is dormant, but I don't want to take any chances."

"Cassandra, what if you're wrong?"

"I'm not wrong," she said, her jaw set. "Look, I told you I'd do it alone if you didn't want to come with me. You want to wait outside? You can go back to the bus station, even. I don't care. But I'm gonna do what I have to do."

"You ever kill anyone before?"

She shook her head. "And I hope I never have to again. Look, Cyrus, I knew I had to do this the day I met you. I didn't think I could do it then. That's why I ran away. I'm not even sure I can do it now. Being with you has given me the courage to go through with it. All last week, in Maine, it's all I thought about. Facing up to what I know. And what has to be done."

"It's murder, Cassandra."

"It's self-defense," she shot back. "You think the death of one human being is the height of evil in the world? I'm doing the right thing. Now, are you gonna stand there arguing with me, or are you gonna let me get on with it while I've still got my courage up?"

She didn't wait for him to answer. She tucked the gun back into her purse and continued up the stairs. Numb with fear, Nygerski hurried after her.

There was less trash in the fifth-floor hallway, and the smell wasn't quite as bad; otherwise, it was identical to the hallway on the ground floor. Some of the numbers on the doors had fallen off, but most were there. Apartment 543, its number intact, was near the far end of the hall. Cassandra closed her eyes as if saying a silent prayer, and knocked on the door.

"Who's there?" a gruff male voice demanded.

"Cassandra."

There were several seconds of silence, and then the door opened as far as the chain on the inside would allow. A bearded black face regarded them from more than six feet above the floor. "Whatchoo want?" the face said.

"Is James here?"

"Hey, let her in, Larry," said another male voice from inside the room.

"Someone with her, man," Larry said over his shoulder.

"He's a friend," Cassandra told him. "He's okay."

The door closed, and a moment later swung all the way back into the apartment. Cassandra and Nygerski stepped inside. Two more black men sat in the small living room, one on a couch, the other in an armchair. In front of the couch, papers were spread all over a low wicker coffee table. The tall, heavyset man who had answered the door wore dungaree overalls and nothing else, but the two seated men were sharply dressed. The tall man stretched out in the armchair sported a huge Afro with accompanying sideburns, striped bell-bottom jeans, and an equally colorful shirt with billowing arms. The man on the couch was smaller than either of his two companions, but Nygerski could tell instantly that his was the most powerful presence in the room. His hair was neatly trimmed; his intelligent face was adorned with a small mustache and wire-rimmed glasses, and he wore a leather vest over a white shirt, and blue jeans that appeared new. His face broadened into a smile when he saw Cassandra.

"Hiya, babe," he greeted her. "I knew you'd come back. Have a seat."

"James, we gotta work on this," said the man in the armchair, nodding at the papers.

"In a minute. Who's your friend, babe?"

"His name doesn't matter. James, I need to have a word with you alone."

"Babe, I got a speech to deliver tomorrow, and we're just cobbling it up. You want a drink? Sit down and relax for a bit. It's good to see you."

"It can't wait, James."

"It's gonna have to."

Nygerski could see into a small kitchen, where a young woman at an ironing board had stopped what she was doing and now watched them intently. The man in overalls moved past them and into the kitchen. "We got beer, we got soda, we even got a bottle of Jack," he said.

"I didn't come to drink." And as Nygerski watched with a mixture of amazement and horror, Cassandra pulled the gun from her purse and leveled it at the man on the sofa.

"I'm not fucking around, James," she said. "I know what you are. Now you and I are going out into the hall to have a little chat. Get up."

In the kitchen, the iron dropped to the floor with a bang. James recoiled on the couch and looked at his chest. The big man in the overalls froze in the doorway between the kitchen and living room. The woman behind him screamed.

"Shut up!" the big man snapped at her.

"Good idea," Cassandra said. Nygerski didn't move. What had he gotten himself into?

James regained his cool almost immediately. "Baby, put that away," he said softly. "You know that nothing gets resolved that way. That's what we're all about here." He looked around at the papers and his companions.

"Don't any of you move," Cassandra said, her eyes darting from one face to another. "I don't want to hurt anyone. James, get up. I want you to—"

Suddenly, a large black arm grabbed Cassandra from behind, around the throat. "Drop the gun, bitch."

The man had sneaked up behind them in the hall. Nygerski flattened himself against the wall in a futile attempt to become invisible. He was sure he was going to die. The man was bigger even than the guy in overalls. He locked his arms around Cassandra's neck and squeezed. "I said drop it!" he barked in her ear. The revolver fell to the floor.

James sprang nimbly off the couch and grabbed the gun. The man loosened his hold on Cassandra so that she could breathe, but he did not let her go. James walked up to her.

"Now, you mind telling me what this is all about?" he demanded. "I don't much like being set up. Who are you working for, babe?"

"I told you, boss, assassins everywhere," said the man holding Cassandra. "Though most of 'em ain't this pretty. I say we turn her over to the pimps downstairs. Her friend we can toss in the river."

James traced a neat little circle around the pair as Nygerski tried to slide away from them along the wall, toward the door. "Don't you be thinking of going anywhere," James said to him. "I want some answers."

"Saw 'em coming a mile away," said the big man. "Couple a white kids, walkin' through Harlem, like they knew where they were goin'. Knew it couldn't be nothing but trouble."

"You post guards now, James?" Cassandra asked. "Since when are you so paranoid?"

The man in the armchair spoke up. "Girl, how many niggers you know make speeches about equal rights and live into old age? It ain't paranoia, it's self-preservation."

"What you want me to do with 'em, boss?" the big man asked. "Make 'em disappear?"

James shook his head. He handed the gun to the man in the chair. "Disarm this thing, Willie. Guns make me nervous."

The big man still had an arm around Cassandra's neck. Nygerski watched as Willie turned the gun on its side and opened the chamber. Six shiny bullets dropped, one by one, into his palm.

"Pretty fancy-looking bullets," he commented.

"They're silver," Cassandra said, looking straight at James. "They were made especially for you."

For several seconds James just stared at her. Then, abruptly, he burst into laughter. "Oh, girl, who you been talking to? What's gotten into that pretty little head of yours? Set her down on the couch over here, Nate. If she won't tell us who put her up to this, maybe her friend will."

He glanced at Nygerski, who widened his eyes and tried to look as innocent as possible. Hey guys, he would say, when they asked, I'm just along for the ride. I met this crazy chick at the bus station, and she took me to Maine and told me stories about time portals and werewolves. Not that I believe her, you understand. It's just that, well, she's got a certain way about her, you know what I mean? Look, I got a baseball team to report to, out in Wisconsin. Do what you want with her; I'll just be moseying along now. . . .

But he never got to deliver that weaseling little speech. The big man took his arm from around Cassandra's neck and guided her by the shoulders toward the couch. And Nygerski saw his opportunity. It was there for only a second, and afterward, when he had time to think about it, he would shudder in disbelief that he had summoned the necessary courage. With a rush of adrenaline, Nygerski drew back and drove a well-aimed toe into the big man's crotch.

The man made a gurgling sound and dropped to the floor, doubled over. "Run!" Nygerski shouted at Cassandra. They were out the door almost before the word had left his mouth. He heard curses behind them as they hit the stairs. James and Willie and the man in overalls came after them. They flew down the stairs and into the street.

"Come on!" Nygerski cried. He grabbed Cassandra's hand and pulled her along the street as the three black men emerged from the building. Nygerski ran as hard as he could, gulping air. A few of the men on the stoops came out of their lethargy and cheered on their pursuers as Nygerski and Cassandra dodged children and pedestrians and turned a corner. He risked a glance over his shoulder to see that the man in overalls had fallen back. But James and Willie kept pace, half a dozen steps behind them. Nygerski knocked over a trash can. James and Willie hurdled it, barely slowing down. Cassandra stumbled next to him; he pulled her arm roughly and kept her on her feet. The mouth of a subway entrance yawned half a block away. "Down there!" Nygerski shouted, and Cassandra nodded, her face gaunt with fear. They pushed through the loose clump of pedestrians and heard cries and curses. And then they were underground, the crowd pressing all around them. Nygerski felt in his pocket for the two subway tokens he'd bought for the return trip. They pushed through the turnstiles. He looked back again, sure that James and Willie were there somewhere, but he couldn't see them among the sea of black faces. Luck smiled upon them in that moment, for a subway train was in the station, and they climbed aboard. Cassandra collapsed against him on the plastic seat.

"Do you think we lost them?" he panted.

"I don't know." Cassandra gulped, and swiped tousled hair away from her sweaty face. "I didn't see them get on, did you?"

"Nope. Wasn't looking, either."

"Shit," Cassandra muttered, closing her eyes and leaning back against the window. "Shit, shit, shit."

"Cassandra, that had to be the most harebrained idea. . . . Even if you'd killed him, how did you possibly expect to get away with it? How did you even expect to get out of the neighborhood alive?"

She opened her eyes and looked at him. "I was going to take him to the basement, or somewhere secluded," she said, her voice heavy with despair. "I don't know, Cyrus, I've been so confused lately. Can you blame me? Everything I try to do turns out wrong. Maybe Aunt Polly's right. You can't mess with time."

"Cassandra, what are you talking about?"

"I don't know. I think I'm losing my mind. I never should have come back here."

"You're not making any sense," he said. And why, he thought, after spending a week with her, should I expect this beautiful, headstrong, perceptive, and irrational woman to make sense?

The train stopped at the next station and exchanged some departing passengers for fresh ones. "I've screwed everything up," Cassandra said as it rumbled on. "Cyrus, I'm sorry. I'm sorry I dragged you into this. I know you think I'm insane. You'll be well rid of me."

"It's okay," he told her. "Except for the part with the gun. That was a little unnerving, I'll admit."

She gave him a tender look and a weak smile, and he felt better. The train stopped again, and a minute later continued on. "Which way are we going, anyway?" she asked after several minutes of silence between them.

"Don't ask me. I don't know New York at all."

The train stopped again, and she peered through the window at the sign on the wall. "Oh, Christ, we're in the Bronx," she said. "We've gotta get off and go the other way. Back to Manhattan. You've got a train to catch." She stood up, but too late. The train began to move.

"It's okay," he said. "My train's not for hours. We'll get off at the next stop."

Another awkward silence passed between them. "What will you do?" he asked at length. "You finished with attempted murder?"

"I don't know. I wish . . ."

"You wish what?" he asked, when she did not continue.

"I wish I could tell you everything. The thing is, I'm starting to forget it myself."

The train ground to a halt, and they rose to disembark. Nygerski looked at the sign on the wall. It said: YANKEE STADIUM.

14.

THE NO-HITTER

"It's already the eighth inning," the ticket-taker said. "You can just go on in."

It had been Nygerski's idea. "I've never seen Yankee Stadium," he had told Cassandra as they left the subway. "Surely we've got time for a look."

"My name's Cassandra, not Shirley," she had replied, and he had taken heart at the joke, for the confrontation and the chase had drained them both. YANKEES VS. RED SOX, TODAY, 2 P.M., the marquee proclaimed, and that had cinched it—even though they were an hour and forty-five minutes late.

Like most New Englanders whose lives have been touched by baseball, Nygerski had hated the Yankees from childhood. Through 1964 they had won the American League pennant nearly every year of his life, while the Red Sox had floundered in the second division. But the mighty Yanks had fallen on hard times in recent years, and last year they had finished dead last, half a game behind the ninth-place Red Sox.

But he had to admit that the lair of the enemy was indeed magnificent, with its columns and facade and the numbers of Ruth, Gehrig, and other greats hanging on the wall beyond the outfield. As he and

Cassandra emerged into view of the playing field, he looked up at the scoreboard and saw that the Red Sox were ahead, three to nothing.

They found two empty seats on the first-base side, at field level, several rows back from the railing. Nygerski sat down next to a portly man with a salt-and-pepper mustache beneath a tan fisherman's hat. "Looks like a pretty good ball game," he said, just trying to make conversation. "We just got here."

"Hmff," the man snorted, filling his mouth with a handful of Cracker Jack. As the Boston pitcher walked to the mound, a buzz of anticipation, something more than one would expect for a 3–0 game in April, rose from the stands around them.

"What's going on?" Nygerski asked.

"Look at the scoreboard," the man replied, with typical New York gruffness.

"It's three-nothing. So what?"

"Look closer," the man said, through a new mouthful of peanuts and popcorn.

Nygerski looked. The Red Sox had three runs, seven hits, no errors. The Yankees had zeroes across the board. Understanding dawned on him. "It's the eighth inning, and the Yankees don't have a hit?"

"Shh! You don't wanna jinx it, do you?"

"Red Sox fan?" Nygerski asked hopefully.

"Naw. Yankee fan, my whole life. But I've been to a hundred ball games. Never seen a pitcher throw one."

"Who's the pitcher?" Nygerski asked.

"Some rookie left-hander I never heard of. Rohr's his name. Billy Rohr. First game in the bigs, I think."

"It's his first game? And he's pitching a no-hitter?"

"Shut up! He's gotta get six more outs—and talking about it don't help."

Nygerski was, of course, aware of the baseball superstition that to talk about a no-hitter in progress is to invite a hit. The young pitcher's teammates would not be saying a word to him in the dugout. But surely the kid knew. Everybody in the stadium knew. An outsized cheer went up as the first Yankee hitter flied out.

Nygerski turned to Cassandra. "This is amazing," he said.

A beer vendor came down the aisle; Cassandra bought two and handed one to Nygerski. He gulped it eagerly. The Yankee crowd cheered lustily as the tall, skinny pitcher retired the next two hometown hitters and left the mound. Three outs to go.

The Red Sox went quietly in the top of the ninth. Another cheer went up as Billy Rohr came out to the mound and threw his warm-up pitches. The people in the seats around them leaned forward. Nygerski had almost forgotten about the confrontation and the chase. A no-hitter! During the course of an entire baseball season there might only be one or two no-hitters. In some years there were none. And this left-handed Red Sox rookie was three outs from tossing one in his very first game.

Tom Tresh, the first Yankee hitter, smacked a drive into deep left field.

The crack of bat against ball hit Nygerski like a punch in the gut. The Boston left fielder raced after it, but even Nygerski could see that he had no chance. It was going to either hit the wall or go over for a home run. But Yastrzemski did not give up on the ball. Running headlong away from home plate, the left fielder leapt into the air, speared the ball with his glove, and came down in a full somersault in front of the wall. On his knees he held the ball triumphantly aloft, a scoop of vanilla ice cream at the very top of the webbing. The crowd went wild.

"What a catch!" Nygerski cried.

"He's gonna get it now," the man next to him exclaimed amid the noise. "He's *gotta* get it now! That's the best goddamn catch I ever saw!"

Joe Pepitone stepped in. Many of the people around them remained standing. Cassandra tugged at Nygerski's sleeve. "Look!" she hissed, her voice urgent. "Behind us, at the top of the steps. Don't be obvious about it."

Nygerski looked over his shoulder and peered through the crowd. "Where? What?"

"You don't see them?" He could hear the fear in her voice.

"No."

The crowd cheered as Pepitone took a strike.

"Up by where we came in."

And Nygerski saw them. James and Willie stood at the entrance to the stands, surveying the crowd. Cold fingers squeezed his heart. "Oh, God," he groaned.

"They must have followed us onto the subway," Cassandra said. "They must have seen us get off, and followed us. Cyrus, we've got to get out of here!"

He glanced up again. James and Willie split up, walking slowly in opposite directions, scanning the stands.

"Sit low in your seat. Maybe they won't see us."

James started down the aisle to their right.

"Oh, shit, he's coming this way," Cassandra cried softly, panic edging in. Her hands gripped the arms of her seat, the tips of her fingers whitening. She looked desperately at Nygerski. Her eyelid twitched like mad.

"Cassandra, stay where you are. What can they do in a stadium full of people?" Willie started walking down an aisle on the other side of them, his eyes roving over the seats.

"We're gonna be trapped!" she said. "We have to get out of here, now!"

On the field, Joe Pepitone lofted a lazy fly ball. The crowd cheered the easy out. Elston Howard, the Yankee catcher, was announced as the next batter. The Boston manager came out of the dugout and went to the mound. The stands throbbed with noise. The man next to Nygerski cupped his hands. "Come on, kid!" he yelled. "You can do it! One more! One more!"

One aisle over and several rows up, James heard the shout and looked toward its source.

"Oh, shit, he's seen me!" Cassandra whimpered.

James waved at Willie, and the two men began pushing through the stands, coming toward them from opposite directions. Cassandra left her seat.

"Cassandra! What are you doing?" Nygerski shouted after her.

The manager returned to the dugout. The tall, skinny, white left-hander looked in at the compact black man waving the bat slowly back and forth. He threw a pitch low and away. Howard swung and missed. The crowd screamed its approval.

Cassandra bounded down the concrete steps toward the railing separating the stands from the field, in the only direction she could flee. Nygerski was out of his seat now, but almost everyone else around him was standing, too, in anticipation of the kid finishing off his no-hitter. James and Willie closed in on her from opposite sides. Nygerski followed her into the aisle, ignoring the fans around him, whose attention was riveted on the field.

It happened very fast. Cassandra reached the railing. James reached the bottom of the stairs, a short distance away from her, at the same time Willie reached the aisle. They were seconds away from grabbing her. Nygerski felt himself moving down the aisle, toward the impending confrontation. There was nowhere for Cassandra to go. As Rohr went into his windup, Cassandra vaulted the railing and ran out onto the field.

A different kind of cry rose from the stands. There was an almost imperceptible hitch in the pitcher's motion as he threw the ball, and then Howard fell to his knees in the dirt, one hand gripping his opposite elbow, his bat and helmet on the ground. Three beefy security guards tackled Cassandra and dragged her out of sight, under the stands.

Nygerski froze. James and Willie looked at one another. Nygerski prayed they wouldn't see him. The two black men moved slowly up the next aisle over, toward the exit. Everyone else's attention was on the field, where several men in blue Yankee jackets had gathered around the hit batsman. Bill Rohr stood on the mound, his hands at his sides, gazing in at home plate.

The no-hitter was still intact, but the injury had momentarily deflated the crowd. Most people remained on their feet, their faces a mixture of concern and anticipation.

Nygerski watched out of the corner of his eye as James and Willie left the stands. He waited a moment longer before starting to make his way back to his seat. He would have to locate the security office, find out where they had taken Cassandra. He would have to do it soon, before James and Willie found her.

Elston Howard got to his feet, assisted by the Yankee trainers, and was helped off the field to the accompaniment of respectful applause. A pinch-runner was sent in to replace him at first base. The loudspeakers announced Charley Smith as the next batter, and the buzz from the stands resumed.

Nygerski passed his seat and stopped at the top of the stairs. He watched as the pitcher looked in for the sign. Would the delay break his concentration? He still needed one more out. He turned to watch as Rohr delivered the pitch.

Smith hit a routine fly ball to center field, and the crowd erupted. The centerfielder squeezed it and threw his arms triumphantly into the air. The young pitcher was mobbed by his teammates and carried off the field to a standing ovation.

The noise reverberated behind him as Nygerski turned and walked briskly into the corridor behind the stands. He knew that he had just witnessed something miraculous, a once-in-a-lifetime event. He would marvel at it later. But right now he had to find Cassandra.

It proved easier than he thought. A distracted usher gave him directions. The two cops had not even put Cassandra into a holding cell.

They sat at desks in their small office beneath the stadium, Cassandra on a couch like a dental patient kept waiting too long, as a television monitor blared the aftermath of the no-hitter from a small shelf high on the wall. Willie and James had apparently decided not to stick around and draw attention to themselves, for he hadn't seen them anywhere.

Cassandra leapt up from the couch when she saw him, and threw her arms around his neck. The two cops stiffened and sat upright in their chairs. "She's with me," Nygerski said sheepishly, over Cassandra's shoulder. He smelled her hair against his cheek, felt the contours of her body against his.

"You can't keep her off the field during a game?" one of the cops growled.

The other officer's eyes did not even move from the television, where the face of the young pitcher stared forth from behind a clump of microphones held by reporters jockeying for position. Rohr's face was calm, almost serene, as he answered their questions. "The pitch just slipped," he said. "Why would I throw at a guy with two outs in the ninth inning of a no-hitter? It just got away from me, that's all. I'm sorry he got hurt."

"Two guys were chasing her," Nygerski said to the cop. He unwrapped Cassandra's arms from around his neck, not missing the look of pure affection she gave him. "I saw the whole thing. She was pushed."

"Pushed, huh? She sure hit the ground running." The cop leaned forward and pulled a piece of paper toward him on the desk. "Well, we're just gonna give her a citation and let her go," he said. He looked at Cassandra. "Miss, you can either mail in the fine or tell your story to the judge."

Nygerski nodded at the screen. "Amazing, huh?"

"First game in the big leagues," the cop said, nodding. "Twenty-one years old. Never happened before, probably never happen again." He pushed the paper forward on the desk. "Just sign next to the X, ma'am,

and you and your friend can be on your way. And next time you come
to a game, do us all a favor and stay in the stands."

Outside the stadium, at the taxi stand, Cassandra tore up the ticket
and let the pieces scatter on the cement. She caught Nygerski's look of
surprise. "I have no intention of paying a fine or sticking around New
York to go to court," she said. "I'm going to Wisconsin with you. Happy?"

His heart soared. At that moment he thought he understood something of what Bill Rohr must be feeling. It was spring, it was April, it
was the beginning of the baseball season, when hope and promise and
youthful optimism dominate doom, and anything seems possible. He
was going to Beloit to begin his own baseball career. And if a kid barely
two years older than he could no-hit the Yankees in his very first game,
why he, Cyrus Nygerski, could do anything. Anything at all. The beautiful woman standing beside him was proof enough of that.

"Ecstatic," he said.

By the time they retrieved their belongings and made their way to the
train station, the evening papers had hit the stands, blaring from their
front pages the news of Bill Rohr's unprecedented feat. Nygerski
grabbed a paper and devoured the write-ups. Baseball historians had
unearthed the story of Bobo Holloman, the only other pitcher to throw
a no-hitter in his first big-league start. But Holloman had made relief
appearances before that. Today had been Rohr's very first appearance in
a big-league game.

The article went on to say that Holloman had been a flash in the
pan, winning a grand total of three games in his single major-league
season.

Meanwhile, the paper said, Elston Howard, the Yankee catcher, had
sustained a broken right elbow and would be out of action for six to
eight weeks.

The incident was given passing mention in print; Cassandra was iden-
tified only as "a young woman who ran out on the field." And it hadn't

affected the outcome. These were, after all, professional ballplayers, paid to ignore distractions. But Rohr was an untested rookie in an extraordinary situation, and Howard, at thirty-eight, maybe didn't have the quick reflexes he once did.

That night, Nygerski and Cassandra made hurried, furtive love in the deserted dining car of their train as it hurtled westward. They slept in their seats, her head in his lap, his arm draped protectively across her shoulders. And by the time the Sun peered through their moving window and nudged him awake, they had crossed the Appalachian Mountains into the great expanse of the American Midwest.

15.

THE BEST LEFT-HANDED SECOND BASEMAN IN WISCONSIN

May was all gloom, until my mother returned.

She came back on Memorial Day, long after the last threat of a spring snowstorm, and late enough to worry my father. It did snow, but only an inch or two, the day after the no-hitter, the day after the Woolfs left and the isolation of Rum Runners Cove pressed down like a glass inverted in water. But the snow went away quickly, and since it was a Saturday, I didn't even miss a day of school. What a gyp.

I think there were three sunny days the whole month. The carpenters finished the addition to the shed, my dad got some more alders cut and the Red Cabin painted, and one weekend he and I and Uncle Bill and his boys got the dinghies down to the water and onto the outhaul, where they would stay all summer, floating at high tide and sitting on the mud when the water went out. Fifth grade coasted toward its conclusion. My father spent many evening hours on the phone with my mother while I was upstairs doing my homework, but he never let her absence outwardly upset him, and one evening near the end of the month he entered my room and told me matter-of-factly that she was coming back.

If I was a somewhat confused kid, at least some of the responsibility lay with my parents for the indecisiveness that characterized their marriage. My dad had carved out a comfortable middle-class life that deeply dissatisfied him, and my mom had bought into an adventure she did not feel. Their ongoing conflict did not much affect my older sister, for Cassandra was always her own unique self, but it left me painfully in search of an identity. Maine was a place where roots mattered. Mine were forever being torn up and replanted. I talked differently, because I had grown up in a different part of the country, and my best friends were the kids I saw in the summer rather than the kids at school. My cousins teased me relentlessly that first autumn for showing up at school in shorts on a warm day. No one had thought to clue me in to the local customs.

My mother's frequent threats to move us back to Ohio didn't help. Jordana was a small, feisty woman with red hair and a fierce temper. She was also an adept organizer who prepared for emergencies and paid attention to details, and my father would have been lost without her. When they pulled together, things could be magnificent. When they disagreed, I felt lost at sea, in the fog, with ledges all around and no compass.

Fog swirled around Rum Runners Cove for most of May and into June. I'd walk out to the top of the road each morning to meet the school bus, barely able to see the trees on either side, until they loomed out at me from the mist. The fog never deterred the lobstermen. From the shore we could hear the horns, the pulleys, and winches, the radios broadcasting the news of the previous night's Red Sox game. It always amazed me the way sound traveled in fog, and how Uncle Bill and his fellow fishermen could pick their way through it. My father and I could get lost in the dinghy in the friendly confines of the cove. But they had an instinct handed down through generations. They could go far out into the bay in fog so thick you could barely see one end of the boat from the other, and they would not only find all their traps but return home unerringly. Uncle Bill could do it, and once in a great while he'd take me out and try to impart some of his skills—how to read a current, listen for breaking water, and trust a compass, even if you're 100 percent sure it's wrong. "The compass don't lie," he'd say. "Your mind can play tricks on you." But I noticed that he didn't look at it that often. Like I say, it's instinct, and Uncle Bill ribbed my dad about losing his when he went away.

Being ten years old was like navigating through fog, feeling for identity along familiar signposts shrouded in mystery. By the time I was ten I had swum across Rum Runners Cove and convinced myself that I could survive in the water, and I was never really afraid in a boat again. I had begun to read books for pleasure, for there was often little else to do when the fog closed in around our lonely outpost. I had seen the rings of Saturn through Elroy's telescope and knew what a light-year was, and we had wondered together about extraterrestrial civilizations. And I had discovered baseball, and knew that if you got a runner to third with less than two outs, there were numerous ways of scoring him.

But I didn't have a clue about the finite nature of opportunities, or about consequences and their costs. And I didn't learn it from my parents or my rooted cousins and schoolmates. No, that lesson would come from Cassandra and Cyrus Nygerski.

Nygerski stood in the batter's box at Fallon Field, squinting into the afternoon gloom. An angry Midwestern sky threatened rain. He was glad for the rare day game, however, for on damp spring nights the walls of the tiny dressing room beneath the stands oozed condensation, and the clammy chill permeated his bones. He had discovered that if you wanted a hot shower after the game, you had to hurry. What passed for a grounds crew consisted of kids and old drunks who couldn't be trusted with factory jobs any longer. Nygerski had lost at least three hits already by falling on the muddy base paths.

The reality of life in the low minors had quickly taken the glow off his first paying job in organized baseball, or "OB," as the players called it. The dugouts were simply patches of dirt beneath leaky metal awnings. The home dugout had a bench with a backrest—a rare luxury, for the visiting dugout and both dressing rooms had only simple wooden slabs. The lockers that had once been there for football had long ago been ripped out and taken elsewhere. Nygerski and his teammates hung their clothes on coat hooks and long, rusty nails that had been pounded into the woodwork at regular intervals along the wall. The balls were stored in a duffel bag like the one Nygerski traveled with; the bats were kept in a metal trash can.

The stands were almost as uncomfortable, and poorly fitted to the field. The infield was wedged inside a horseshoe that began near first base and ended in short left field, a few steps into fair territory. From this strange abutment ran a series of advertising billboards, arcing out into center field before they stopped at the state line and the lot full of abandoned cars beyond right. It looked like what it was: an old football facility awkwardly made over for baseball. And definitely not a left-handed hitter's park.

Still, Nygerski loved it, every minute of it. Never had his life been so full—of ball games and practices, quick meals at the house he shared with four teammates, and long nights of lovemaking at the budget motel where Cassandra had taken a room at a weekly rate. She was in the stands now as he faced the opposing pitcher with two out and two on in the eighth inning, the Turtles down by a run. The pitcher came in with a fastball, and Nygerski smacked it neatly into center, scoring both runners. He stood on first base and looked up at the cheering crowd. He had never doubted he would get a hit. Cassandra was up there somewhere. She believed in him, and that was all that mattered.

In the clubhouse, the game won, Nygerski's teammates offered subdued congratulations. Even Cliff Gillespie, the gruff, monosyllabic manager, swatted him on the butt and said, "Attaboy, Cyrus. Nice work out there." The members of the team were still feeling each other out, getting to know one another. So far they had played at home and taken two small trips to play teams in the Madison area. Tomorrow they were scheduled to leave on their first extended road trip, a three-week bus tour of several Midwestern states.

He stepped out of a lukewarm shower, wrapped a towel around his waist, and moved through the crowded room to his "locker," a space on the wall where he hung his clothes above a milk crate that held his equipment. "Hey, Nygerski!"

He turned to face one of his new roommates, a small, right-handed pitcher named John Thorne, who was already in street clothes because he hadn't played and had nabbed a spot in the showers as soon as the game ended.

"A few of us are goin' to this bar," Thorne said. "They got a rock-and-roll band. You wanna come?"

Thorne was twenty-one, in his second year with the Turtles, and probably didn't have a good enough fastball to be considered a top prospect. He was from California, somewhere south of Los Angeles, and he had the blond good looks one associated with the surf culture. His speech was peppered with words Nygerski had never heard, and his musical tastes ran to the Beach Boys, the Ventures, and some of the new music that was beginning to work its way east from San Francisco. They hadn't seen that much of one another, because Nygerski simply hadn't spent that much time at the house. But he considered Thorne a likable fellow. The other day he had actually seen Thorne reading a book—a paperback novel—a rare sight in a minor-league clubhouse where a lot of the players were challenged intellectually by the sports section in the daily paper.

"Sorry, John, maybe another time," he said, pulling on his pants. "I got a date."

"Bring her," Thorne suggested. "Where else you gonna take her in this shithole town? Besides, we gotta celebrate."

Cassandra was all for the idea, and half an hour later a group of six ballplayers and four girls gathered around two pushed-together tables watching three young men thrash out popular rock songs. Nygerski noticed that the band was fronted by a left-handed guitar player who worked on the grounds crew at the ballpark. Many of the bar's patrons were young, some almost certainly on the wrong side of the drinking age, like himself, but the blond, thirtyish waitress brought pitchers of beer and frosted mugs without so much as raising an eyebrow. Two of the girls ordered Cokes, but Cassandra matched the ballplayers beer for beer. Nygerski had already discovered that she could drink. His teammates paid a great deal of attention to her, for she was much better looking than the other three women at the table. The girl and the game-winning hit combined to make him the man of the hour, and it felt strange. He was relieved when the band took a break and the guitarist came over to talk, diverting some of the attention.

He was tall, with a shock of curly brown hair and a pair of black plastic glasses repaired on one side with electrical tape. "How'd the game go?" he asked.

"You're lookin' at the hero right here," Malcolm Wood said, clapping Nygerski on the shoulder. "This here's Cyrus Nygerski, the best left-handed second-baseman in all of Wisconsin."

"I bet you're the *only* one in Wisconsin," the guitarist said. "Gotta love your unorthodox way of turning the double play. I didn't think lefties could play second or short."

"Or catch, either, if you listen to the right-supremacists," Nygerski retorted. "It's nothing but discrimination." He swung his chin in a little arc toward the stage, where the guitarist's instrument rested against an amplifier. "I notice you're a lefty, too."

"Like Jimi Hendrix and Paul McCartney." He put out his left hand; after a moment's hesitation, Nygerski shook it with his own. "Name's Sammy Mavrogenes."

Nygerski looked him over. He had a bemused, intelligent face behind the hair and glasses, with squinty brown eyes and a lopsided grin.

"Cyrus Nygerski," he said. "I never met a professional musician before."

"And you still haven't. What I really am is a professional college student. I take as few credits as I can to stay in school and prolong the time till I graduate. Keeps out the draft, if you know what I mean. Workin' at the ballfield pays the bills. We play here every Saturday, for tips and free beer. You guys keep coming, maybe the owner'll eventually decide to pay us."

"We'll keep coming," Nygerski said.

"We're about to go on our first big road trip," John Thorne reminded him. "You get to find out what minor-league baseball is all about. Hours and hours of bus rides. Joliet, Peoria, and Kalamazoo. A three-week tour of the hot spots of the Prairie League."

"I always wanted to see the Midwest," Nygerski remarked, bringing his mug to his lips.

"You're seeing it," Mavrogenes replied. "It all looks like this."

It was late when Nygerski walked Cassandra back to her motel. When she turned on the light he saw that she had cleaned the room and packed the small silver suitcase, which stood at the foot of the bed. "What's going on?" he asked, his stomach already knotting, fearing the answer.

She encircled her arms around his neck and kissed him full on the mouth. "You're going to have a great season," she told him, smiling at him, showing him the flash of slightly crooked teeth that had taken his heart on that weird trip to Maine, a lifetime ago. Had it been only a month? So much had changed. "You're going to be a star," she said. "I just know it."

"You're leaving, aren't you?" he said to the floor.

She laughed, and touched her lips to his again, quickly, as if she had already left, the passion that had played between them already fading into memory, leaving nothing but the faint taste of tenderness. "Cyrus, what did you expect me to do when you went on the road? Sit here in Beloit, Wisconsin, and pine away for you?"

"I dunno," he mumbled. He could not bring himself to look into her eyes. He felt wretched. "Something like that, I guess."

"You're so young," she said gently. "So much to look forward to."

"Every day I look forward to being with *you*," he said. "How can you leave *now*?"

"Cyrus, have you looked at this town? I mean, really looked? I've seen a lot more of it than you have. I've walked around, while you're off in your world of baseball. I've met the people, and talked to them. And I've seen it all. The factories, the dirty river, the air that smells like rancid cheese, and the people who'll never leave. It's ugly. It's depressing. I'd go mad here."

"It'll be uglier and more depressing without you."

"You just play baseball," she said. "You keep playing the way you're playing now, and they're bound to send you someplace better. They'll have to. You've got nowhere to go but up, Cyrus. This town can't hold you. And you know it."

"You're my inspiration," he said, almost in a whisper.

"Then think of me every time you come to bat. Know that I'll be thinking of you. When you make the majors, look for me."

"But we just met, practically! Can't you stay a little longer?"

She shook her head. "I have to leave before the next full Moon," she said seriously. "I've told you why."

"Not that werewolf business again!" he cried, more angry than surprised. Nothing this woman said or did surprised him anymore, not after New York.

She nodded solemnly.

"Cassandra, that's just nonsense! You can't believe—"

"James is in San Francisco," she said. "There's another antiwar rally there next week, the biggest one yet. James'll be there. He knows people in California. I plan to be there, too."

"Oh, Cassandra, will you stop deluding yourself? You're gonna get yourself killed, or thrown in jail or a psycho ward. Don't go."

"I have to do what I have to do," she said.

"Don't you know that I'm in love with you?" he blurted.

"I'm not a good woman to fall in love with. I'm sorry."

He recovered his composure, wiping at his eyes. "Don't kill him," he said. "You don't have the gun with the silver bullets anymore. And it's wrong, even if you think he's a werewolf. It's wrong."

"No promises," she told him. "Promises lead to expectations, and expectations . . . lead to disappointment. I'm not a politician, Cyrus."

"Will I ever see you again?"

"I don't know."

Bitterness welled within him. Hadn't he stuck with her, when the cops dragged her off the field in New York? Hadn't he risked his own butt for her earlier, in the apartment? Hadn't he followed her all the way to Maine, just because she wanted him to? She had needed him then; he needed her now. And she was leaving.

"Well," he said to the floor, "it's a college town. I'm sure there are plenty of girls."

"I won't be jealous, if that's what you're thinking," Cassandra said.

"I don't care."

"I love you, too, you know."

He looked at her hard for several seconds, but when she opened her arms to him, he responded and they embraced.

They held each other for a long time. He didn't want to let her go. But eventually he became aware of the effect of gravity on bones and muscles, and they stepped apart, their fingertips lingering, curled loosely together. "The team bus leaves at six in the morning," he mumbled.

"Mine leaves in two hours." They looked at one another, the silence widening the space between them. "You're going to make it, Cyrus," she told him. "Keep the faith. You'll be playing in a big-league park someday, in front of thousands of people. And I'll be there."

16.

THE FIRE

The Grangers, the third family at Rum Runners Cove, arrived on June 15 minus their mother. Their appearance confirmed to me that nothing in this world is permanent, for while my own parents were talking about divorce, Fred and Mary Granger were actually going through with it.

Fred had the kids, two girls and two boys, for the first half of the summer, and he had hired a cute, freckled woman about Cassandra's age named Jocelyn to help him keep tabs on them. The two older boys, Alex and Andy, bracketed my age, and we played together with a sort of desperate fierceness, nothing like the easy companionship Elroy and I enjoyed. They were very athletic and competitive, and they made a great show of hating each other's guts. Asking one of them to pass the ketchup at dinner could engender a five-minute argument over who was closer to the ketchup bottle. Connie, the oldest, would gravitate toward my mother, helping her with the vegetable garden and other projects, while six-year-old Lauriann clung to her father and tagged after Jocelyn, clearly missing her own mother.

The Grangers brought something else with them that summer—a large black-and-white TV. My father's heart must have sunk when he saw it. For years he had resisted the incursion of television into his private paradise, even in winter, when the nights were sixteen hours long and ice crystals pattered at the storm windows. The Grangers were up for the summer, but the television was here to stay. Its use, my father quickly announced, would be restricted to an hour a day during the week and two hours on weekends. Though the rules would be relaxed as the pennant race tightened, he needn't have worried too much, for on Deer Isle you could get three channels with varying intensities of snow, and the Bangor stations carried baseball games infrequently. I continued to follow the Red Sox mainly on radio.

The very night the Grangers arrived, in fact, Alex and Andy and I listened to a game out in the Red Cabin. The opponent was the White Sox, and I thought of my sister's friend Cyrus, wondering how he was doing in the minors. But the game caught us up, for it went scoreless into extra innings. In the top of the eleventh, the White Sox scored a run, and when the first two Red Sox hitters made outs in the bottom of the inning, it appeared to be over. But then Joe Foy hit a single, and on a 3–2 pitch, Tony Conigliaro belted a home run to win the game. We shouted so loudly that my father came out to the cabin, alarmed that we were making so much noise. But when we told him the reason, he laughed, and went back into the house to tell the other grown-ups. The win put the Red Sox into third place, four games back.

That game marked the real beginning of the pennant race. For the rest of the summer the Red Sox provided a backdrop for everything we did, everything that happened. We kids sensed that this was to be the Last Summer, that the Grangers' divorce and my parents' battles and Uncle Bill's and my father's conflicting desires would all conspire to end the carefree days our fathers had bought with legal fees. We had all heard the arguments. The place was expensive, and generated zero income, despite my father's dreams. Bob Woolf wanted to rent it out to wealthy families by the week or weekend instead of running a full-fledged camp. Uncle Bill wanted his lobster pound. Fred and Mary

Granger each wanted their share of the property in the divorce. But the baseball season distracted us from that. During long stretches of that summer of discontent, the only thing that held us together, it seemed, was rooting for the Red Sox.

Then, in late June, old Clem Dyer's shack burned to the ground.

We were coming back from Stonington—my parents, Alex and Andy and I—when we saw the smoke. It was evening, and the Moon had just risen; a few of the brighter stars were out. "Looks like there's a fire in Dyerville," my father said. He exchanged an assenting glance with my mother across the front seat of the car as he made the turn. The fire truck had not arrived when we pulled up behind several other cars on the side of the road a short distance from the burning shack that had been Clem Dyer's home. Most of the men from Dyerville were there, and they had formed a bucket brigade from the shack to the shore. Even from a distance the heat was staggering.

My father jumped out of the car. "You boys stay here," he shot back, over his shoulder, as he went to join the bucket line. Already the building was a total loss. The men poured water around the periphery, as close as they could get to the blistering heat, trying to keep the fire from spreading. They shouted to one another to be heard above the roar of the flames.

I gulped as we watched a wall of the shack come crumbling down, scattering embers the men chased down and doused with buckets of seawater. We had been there less than a minute.

"Wow!" Andy said, beside me. "That happened fast."

"You have four minutes," my mother said, "to get out of a burning house. That's why you don't stop to grab anything. You just get out."

"Clem's dead, Mom," I reminded her. "I wonder who started the fire."

"It could have been an accident. Exposed electrical wiring, a gas leak near a pilot light, something like that."

"Or some kids in there smoking," Alex suggested.

In the distance we heard sirens. Soon the Deer Isle volunteer fire department was on the scene with two trucks, breaking up the bucket brigade. The men retreated to the sidelines as the firemen contained the blaze. My father rejoined us.

"Well, that's some excitement for the evening," he said.

"Any idea how it started?" my mother asked him.

He shook his head. "Nope. Just a freak thing, apparently."

We went home and had a late supper. Uncle Bill came over to drink beers with my dad. The Red Sox were on TV, one of the rare midweek games broadcast by the Bangor station. Fred Granger diddled with the antenna until the picture came clearly enough to follow the path of the ball. "They've got a decent team this year," he said to my father. "For a change."

"Decent," my dad acknowledged. "Not great."

"We'll see how they hold up through July and August," Uncle Bill chimed in, echoing the famed Maine skepticism.

"They're doing okay," Fred said. "They're hitting like crazy. If the pitching holds up, they could make a run."

"That's a big if," Uncle Bill replied.

"What happened to that kid who pitched the no-hitter against the Yankees?" Fred asked. "Haven't heard much about him lately."

"Got sent to the minors," I mumbled.

"Yeah?"

"Uh-huh. Idiots." Bill Rohr's demotion had been a bitter blow.

"Son, he didn't do a thing after his first two games," my father reminded me gently. "The no-hitter, another good game after that, and then nothing. Couldn't get anybody out."

"Still, they should've given him another chance."

"He'll be back. He's just a kid. Right now that manager wants to win some ball games."

"Usually they're already out of it by this point in the season," Fred Granger said.

And so it went. I was almost asleep by the time the game, in Kansas City, ended in a Red Sox victory. In the middle of the postgame interview (with Conigliaro, who had contributed to the win with another homer), the phone rang. My parents looked at one another. It was eleven o'clock at night. Who could it possibly be? My father went to answer it, and my attention returned to the screen.

"*San Francisco?*" we heard him shout. "What the *hell* are you doing *there?*"

A minute later he reappeared in the living room, his lips tight and pulled down at the corners in a don't-fuck-with-me expression. He looked at my mother and jerked a thumb toward the kitchen. "Your daughter wants to talk to you."

Cassandra! It had been two months since we had heard from her. I jumped to my feet and followed my mom. "Let me talk to her," I pleaded.

"In a minute, Timmy," she said, and picked up the receiver. "Hello, darling. Is everything all right?"

I shifted impatiently from foot to foot as my mother mostly listened, interjecting occasionally with short acknowledgments and comments like, "Your father is very concerned," and, "Why haven't you written?" I could hear my father in the other room, venting to Fred and Uncle Bill, cursing fate for giving him such a willful daughter. Fred Granger told his sons to go to bed. I kept maneuvering into my mother's sight as she turned, wrapping the cord around herself. Finally, she said, "Timmy wants to say hello," and handed me the phone.

"Hi, sis," I said.

"Staying out of trouble, little brother?" It wasn't a great connection—it sounded as if someone were pouring milk over Rice Krispies close to the phone—but the affection in her voice was evident, and my heart swelled.

"Trying to," I replied.

"Mom's back," she said. "That should mellow Daddy out a little bit."

"Clem Dyer's house burned down," I told her.

"Oh, no!" she said. "Poor Clem."

"Cassandra, Clem died," I told her. I don't know why I was surprised she didn't know. She had left that very morning, before we found out, and we had had no communication with her since.

Briefly, I filled her in. She asked a few questions, but mostly she listened.

Cassandra didn't say anything for several seconds. For a moment I thought we'd been disconnected. Then she said, "Timmy, is the Moon out?"

"Yeah. It's a beautiful night. It's full."

"It just came up out here a while ago. You can see it reflecting off the bay. It's beautiful."

"What's it like in California?" I was genuinely curious. No one I knew had ever been there. It might as well have been Timbuktu, for all I knew about it.

Cassandra laughed. "Well, it's big. It's a huge state. I've been to Los Angeles, and Big Sur . . . it's beautiful. It's just as pretty as Maine. Except there are mountains. And lots of people. More people than you'd meet in five years back there. Young people, like me, from all over the place. And always something happening. It's a whole different culture. It's a different world."

"You hear from Cyrus?" I asked.

She paused. "No. I imagine he's doing well."

"Are you coming home ever?"

There was another pause on her end of the line. "I don't know, Timmy," she said seriously. "New England seems so small and limiting. Plus, I think Daddy's kind of upset with me."

"Since when has he not been?" I said, and we both laughed.

"He'd be even more upset if I told him I was living in a big house with nine other people, most of 'em long-haired musicians," she said. "Timmy, when you're older, you've simply *got* to come to California. It'll blow your mind."

"You seen the Golden Gate Bridge yet?"

"I walked across it last week."

"Cool! You can walk across it?"

"Uh-huh. It's like the Deer Isle bridge, only about ten times as big."

"Cool!" I said again.

"Time for bed, Tim," my mother interjected. "Cassandra can tell you all about California when she comes home."

If she comes home, I thought. "Mom wants me to get off the phone," I said.

"I'm glad Mom's back," Cassandra said.

"Yeah, me too. Take care of yourself, sis."

"You know I always do."

As I walked out to the Red Cabin, I looked up at the Moon and glowed with the knowledge that Cassandra was looking at it, too. An invisible string went up from Deer Isle, wrapped around the Moon, and came down on the other side of the continent, and if she pulled her end of the string I could feel it here. We would always be connected, my sister and I. No matter what.

The next morning no one talked about the fire. The Woolfs were due to arrive in a matter of days, and we set about getting the place ready. School was out, the weather was warm, my parents were happy, and the Red Sox were playing good ball. If this was indeed going to be the Last Summer, I wanted it to be a great one.

17.

HOME RUN FOR THE MONEY

The Turtles lost twelve of fifteen games on their road trip, and Nygerski managed just two hits. They returned to southern Wisconsin with empty beer bottles rolling up and down beneath the seats of the bus. The players engaged in meaningless card games and even more pointless epics of sexual exploits, most of which had taken place only in their imaginations. A last-place attitude had already settled over the team like a blanket. Nygerski imagined that this must have been what it was like to play for the Red Sox over the past decade, except that the Red Sox had nicer accommodations.

They got into Beloit just before sunset, two hours before another night game. The city that had held such promise a few weeks ago now looked dirty, Midwestern, and old. Cassandra had made its ugliness possible to ignore. Now she was gone, and the loneliness and long odds of minor-league life pressed down upon him.

But there was mail at the ballpark. Nygerski set aside the letter from his mother and eagerly grabbed the postcard with a picture of the Golden Gate Bridge on it. On the back was a single sentence: *Cyrus, Keep the faith. Love, Cassandra.*

That was it—no return address, nothing. But she had made it to San

Francisco, and she was thinking of him. He must have been grinning when he went out for infield practice, for Sammy Mavrogenes, raking the dirt behind second base, gave him a big smile and a hand-slap and said, "Look out, world—the best left-handed second baseman in Wisconsin has returned!"

And in his first at bat, Nygerski ripped a double into the gap in right-center, and came around to score the first of five runs in the inning. The Turtles won the game, Nygerski got three hits, and after the game he and several other players went to the bar to watch Sammy's band perform. The team split six games over the following week, but Nygerski continued to hit. His ground balls began finding holes between infielders; his soft line drives started dropping in. Since it was still early in the season, a couple of good games could do wonders for one's batting average. And as his average rose, so did his confidence. He made only one error in the field all week, on a behind-the-back throw that would have nailed the runner at second had the shortstop been expecting it.

The team left town on another road trip, ten days this time, and Nygerski returned with a batting average well over .300. Opponents noted his unorthodox fielding style, but their comments were usually made under their breath as they trotted back to the dugout. Nygerski kept the postcard from Cassandra taped to the wall in the clubhouse where he changed, as a reminder of his inspiration.

Necessity had turned him into a night owl, for minor-league baseball was mostly night baseball, and after the games he either went out with some of the players or hung out with Mavrogenes and his musician buddies. The friendship with Sammy filled some of the void Cassandra's departure had left, and provided a life away from baseball. Sammy taught him some chords and took him to parties. Many nights he didn't drag himself home until dawn.

Only Sundays were different. The team counted on Sunday double-headers to boost revenue. Attendance was usually better on Sunday, because fans got two games for the price of one, and vague religious stirrings kept a lot of men out of the bars. They could still get drunk at the ballpark, though, with the added bonus of being able to bring their families along. The opportunity for promotional gimmicks was not lost on the team's cash-strapped management. They gave away hats, T-shirts, coloring books, and tickets to poorly attended midweek games. Sometimes they staged on-field contests: Throw a ball through a hoop and win free tickets; run the bases faster than the team mascot (who wore a bulky turtle suit) and get a free hot dog and Coke from the concession stand. It was all very rinky-dink and low-budget, as befitted a team three rungs below the majors.

One of the most popular promotions was "home run for the money," sponsored by a local department store. Each fan, upon entering the ballpark, was assigned an inning and a player's name. If that player hit a home run in the specified inning, the store would award a hundred-dollar gift certificate to the fan whose number was drawn from the winning ticket stubs. It was good publicity for the department store, and it didn't cost much, because the Turtles weren't exactly the '61 Yankees.

But in the second inning of the second game on the second Sunday in June, Nygerski sent a deep drive into left center field. The ball cleared a billboard advertising Big Red chewing tobacco. Three runs scored on the homer, and the Turtles went on to a sweep of the twin bill. More significantly, as things unfolded, Nygerski got to have his picture taken at home plate with the sponsoring store's owner and the contest's lucky winner.

The Turtles' games were broadcast on a local radio station, and Hiram Reese, the young, awkward, not-too-bright announcer who could not pronounce Nygerski's name, doubled as team photographer. He was equally inept at both jobs. Nygerski imagined he had been the kid who was always picked last at school for team sports and the butt of cruel physical jokes. He wore thick glasses, and his shiny, jet-black hair needed shampooing. As he fiddled with his tripod and camera, he kept up a steady stream of banter, as though still broadcasting. Almost everyone had deserted the ballpark seconds after the final out. Most of Nygerski's teammates had raced for the showers, but a few of the ballplayers lingered near the dugout to check out the contest winner, a not-unattractive redhead of thirty or so in a tight blue dress that did not quite conceal a small bulge at her midsection and showed off her two best features just above it. Nygerski wondered if she was wearing a push-up bra as he tried to keep his eyes on her face when they were introduced. It was a pretty face, not striking, but knowing and bemused, and she smiled warmly at him as he took her hand. She wore her hair in a flip, like the Elizabeth Montgomery character on the TV show *Bewitched*.

"Cyrus Ny-jerski, Rhonda Whittingham," Hiram Reese said. "Congratulations, Mrs. Whittingham, you're our first home run for the money winner this season." The announcer beamed as though he expected her to hug him.

"I owe it all to this young man here," the woman said, grabbing Nygerski's arm. "Honey, thanks to you, I can go and get those new shoes Ed won't buy me."

"Yeah, and you can rotate 'em with the other twenty-seven pairs," growled a portly man standing on the third-base line. He was bald, unshaven, and overweight, and looked bored out of his mind with the whole deal. Nygerski took him to be the woman's husband.

"Come on, Ed, be happy for me," the woman pouted. "I've never won anything before in my life. Have you, Cyrus?"

"Well, maybe a few baseball games, here and there," he said.

Rhonda Whittingham laughed in pleased surprise. "The only thing Ed's ever won is football bets," she said. "And he spends 'em right there at the bar. As you can see, his athletic days are behind him."

The husband's scowl deepened. Rhonda prattled obliviously on. "Sunday's the only day I can get him out to the ballpark. I've been a Turtles fan for years. Beats sitting at home waiting for Ed to drag his belly home from the bar. Of course they've never had anybody who amounted to anything. Maybe you'll be the first."

"Okay, let's get the three of you to move closer together," Reese instructed, after adjusting the camera for the fourth or fifth time. The store owner was as fat as Ed, but better dressed and groomed. A tie bearing the store logo dangled beneath the lowest of several chins. His thick gray hair was held in place by either glue or Brylcreem, Nygerski couldn't decide which.

"I hope you'll come by our store sometime," he said to Nygerski. "We have a ten percent discount on our suits for all players on the team." He smiled woodenly, as though reciting the words for a TV commercial.

Rhonda stood between them, just over five feet tall in her heels. Reese had Nygerski hold his bat out in front of him, and the store owner brandished an oversized cardboard gift certificate. "Smile, everybody, this is for the local paper," Reese said, and hunched behind the camera.

"Might help if you took the lens cap off," Nygerski told him.

"Oh, yeah." The photographer-announcer stood up and bumped the tripod, nearly knocking the whole operation over. "Shit," he muttered, and set about adjusting it all over again. Ed Whittingham shook his head and pawed at the chalk foul line with his toe.

The store owner didn't move, but Rhonda sidled even closer to Nygerski and placed a hand provocatively against the small of his back. "I admire the way you play the game," she said. "You're a natural."

"Can we get this over with?" Ed growled from the sideline as Hiram Reese continued to fumble with the camera.

"What's the matter, Ed?" Rhonda snapped at him. "Afraid you'll miss something important on TV, like championship bowling?" Nygerski shifted nervously. The woman was still touching him, perhaps in a deliberate attempt to provoke her husband. Ed heaved a sigh and looked into the empty stands. The storekeeper remained as motionless as his hair.

"Just another couple of seconds here," Reese mumbled. "There! Okay, now, squeeze together and smile." He clicked off one photo, then another. "Hold that certificate up, Mr. Fowler. Okay, Cyrus, move the bat forward just a little bit . . . that's good." He managed to take two more shots before bumping the camera and knocking it off target. "Shit," he muttered again, and bent to tighten the screw that held the camera to the tripod. "Just let me get a couple more, and then we'll be done."

"Christ, are they paying you by the hour?" Ed growled.

"Oh, give it a rest, Ed," Rhonda shot back at him. "You're just jealous because my picture's gonna be in the paper. So, what's your batting average, Cyrus?"

"Um . . . as of right now, it's .351," he said, with a quick glance over at Ed. There was no doubt about it. She was deliberately flirting with him.

"You *are* a star," she said, beaming. "I'm gonna clip this picture, and when you make the big leagues I'm gonna frame it and show it to all my friends. And Mr. Foster will display it in his store."

"You never know," the store owner said, with all the emotion of a mannequin.

Reese took several more pictures and narrowly missed tripping over the tripod as he moved to shake hands with Rhonda, Nygerski, and the store owner and thank them for their patience. The announcer grabbed Ed's reluctant hand and said, "I hope we'll see you out here again real soon, Mr. Whittingham."

Ed grunted in reply. "Come on, Rhonda, let's get out of here. Your shoes are getting lonely." He turned and began walking toward the exit.

"Just a minute," his wife said. "Thank you for the certificate, Mr. Fowler. You'll see me in your store real soon. There's a darling little dress I've had my eye on."

"It's our pleasure doing business with you, Mrs. Whittingham," the fat man oozed.

Nygerski kept his face impassive, though the man's smarmy insincerity made him want to vomit. As he turned to go, Rhonda touched him lightly on the arm. She nodded at the retreating figure of Ed, moving through the stands toward the exit. "Can you imagine fifteen years with that guy?" she said. "He's hard to take for fifteen minutes."

Nygerski didn't know what to say. "I'm glad you won," he managed.

Rhonda fished into her purse and produced a scrap of paper and a pen. She scribbled something quickly and thrust the paper into his palm. He looked at her face. She wore too much mascara, but otherwise she wasn't bad-looking at all. Her rude, slovenly husband could do a lot worse.

"Call me sometime," she said. "I'm usually home in the afternoons."

And without waiting for a reply, she turned and walked briskly after her husband.

18.

HECTOR FALLS

July brought summer's full onslaught to Rum Runners Cove. All three families were there, in various combinations. The two small sailboats were in the water, the buildings were painted, the alders were beaten back, and the raspberries ripened. There were no more reports of marauding animals attacking deer or humans. Elroy and I went out to check on our fort, but we still did not dare to spend a night there. With Jim, Alex, and Andy we set up camp in the Red Cabin, three sets of bunk beds at one end and all our recreational junk, including Jim's drum set, at the other. We didn't let him play at night, because not only was it annoying as hell, but I owned the clock radio, and if there was a baseball game, we all wanted to listen to it. By midmonth Jim no longer argued.

It couldn't last, this three-family arrangement that had given me the only sense of belonging I had ever known. There were too many tensions, too many differences left unresolved for too long. Had the Red Sox lingered near last place that year, as they had every summer in recent memory, I believe that things would have fallen apart long before they did. Baseball was the glue that held us together.

Even my skeptical father got caught up in it. On one beautiful

Sunday, with sails filling the bay beyond the ledge and the grass practically squeaking as it grew, we all sat in the living room around the Grangers' black-and-white TV and watched the Red Sox take a doubleheader from Cleveland. The wins were their ninth and tenth in a row. By the end of July they were in second place, a game behind Chicago.

Every day, Elroy and I grabbed the sports section and pored over the box scores. We made up fantasy lineups for the Red Sox and various opponents, and played out nine-inning games on the baseball dartboard in the Red Cabin. We cut out pictures from the newspaper and taped them to the walls.

Baseball mania gripped the entire area. We'd stop at the store for milk and bread and get into a conversation with the clerk about the pennant race. Uncle Bill kept the radio in his lobster boat tuned to the official Red Sox station, and when there wasn't a day game he and his sons listened to sports call-in shows and shouted baseball news across the water to the other boats. At night we'd gather around the radio in the kitchen, because most of the games weren't on TV. When the Red Sox played on the west coast, and the games started at ten o'clock at night, Jim and Alex and Andy and Elroy and I would try to keep each other awake as long as we could, lying in our bunks in the dark listening to the voices of Ken Coleman and Ned Martin as they beamed the play-by-play back to New England.

I kept after my father to take us to a ball game in Boston, especially after Fred Granger left the cove at the end of July and his estranged wife arrived. There was a lot of shuffling back and forth that summer, due to the Grangers' impending divorce. Some of the older kids got summer jobs and stayed behind. But most of the kids were in Maine most of the time. Fred had taken a place in Boston, and once the subject of actually attending a ball game came up, I would not let go of it.

My father hated cities. He'd returned to Maine to get away from them. He saw little reason to leave the Maine coast, where there were boats to row and clams to dig and trees to cut, during the height of summer. But the pennant race and the Grangers' divorce conspired to change his mind. My mother obviously sympathized with Mary Granger, which could not have sat well with my dad, since he and Fred were old friends. Bob Woolf was away on business for two weeks, leaving my father as the only adult male in residence. And the Red Sox were his team, too, though he was a football fan first, and old enough to be cautious. Elroy and I had no such reticence. We were convinced that they were going to win the pennant, and we wanted more than anything to witness a part of it in person. Just one game.

Finally, my father relented, and on Friday, August 18, Jim, Elroy, Alex, Andy, and I piled into my father's station wagon for the six-hour drive to Boston and the pilgrimage to Fenway Park.

Fred put us all up for the weekend, and all seven of us went to the game. It was still daylight when we arrived. I was awed by my first sight of a big-league ballpark. Unlike most modern baseball stadiums, Fenway Park sits in the heart of the city, surrounded by street life instead of parking lots. We took the subway to Kenmore Square and negotiated our way through the hot dog vendors and the newspaper boys and the people who had simply come out to share in the Red Sox resurgence. Fred said that the area around Fenway had been dead in recent years, but it had come alive again in the summer of 1967. We pushed through the turnstiles and came into the ballpark itself from underneath an overhanging balcony. My first impression was of an emerald expanse of grass. The lumpy lawn at Rum Runners Cove never looked that good, not even from a distance.

And I could not help but be impressed by the towering left-field wall, a drabber green than the outfield grass, with the manually operated scoreboard at its base and the red neon Citgo triangle above it. This was the Green Monster, over which right-handed power hitters pulled home runs and off which Carl Yastrzemski expertly played caroms and threw out runners at second base. It looked far more imposing in person than it ever had in still pictures or on TV. The seats were wooden and uncomfortable, and a few of them—not ours, fortunately— were situated behind stone pillars that partially obstructed the view of the field. Our seats were on the third-base side, about halfway up the lower section and a little ways into the outfield. Our fathers bought us hot dogs, and we settled in to watch the grounds crew prepare the infield as the players milled about on the grass in front of the dugouts.

It was *so* cool, all of it: the food, the smells, the crowd streaming in, the players down on the field, hanging out talking to one another just like the carpenters at Rum Runners Cove before they got down to work. I sat between Elroy and my father, and couldn't quite believe that we were here, in the middle of the pennant race, in the presence of heroes.

Finally the field was readied, the starting lineups were announced, and we rose for the national anthem. The opposing team was the California Angels. Elroy, budding statistician that he was, wrote out the starting lineups on the scorecard in the back of the program as I looked over his shoulder. The Red Sox took the field to a thundering ovation, and the game began.

For three innings Boston's Gary Bell and California's Jack Hamilton gave up no runs, although there were a couple of hits for each team, which Elroy dutifully recorded. Darkness fell, and the lights came on. Bell retired the visitors in the top of the fourth. We were still settling into the game, riding the excitement of just being there, waiting for something to happen, for one team to make a statement. The crowd buzzed around us in a shared sense of expectation.

George Scott, the large, black Boston first baseman, led off the home half of the fourth with a base hit between two outfielders. The crowd roared as he steamed around first base, trying to stretch the hit into a double, then groaned as the throw beat his slide into second. Head down, Scott jogged back to the dugout.

Somewhere out near the Green Monster, a fan threw a smoke bomb onto the field. Smoke billowed into the air from the grass in front of the Angel left fielder.

"Idiots," my father said, shaking his head, quick to disapprove. "For some people, coming out to see a ball game isn't enough," he said. "They just have to show off."

The umpires called time, and the grounds crew materialized on the field to clean it up. There wasn't much they could do but wait for the thick white smoke to clear. It took ten minutes. My dad flagged a vendor in the stands and bought us more Cracker Jack. We fidgeted in our seats, waiting for the game to resume.

Reggie Smith was the next batter. He hit a long fly ball to straightaway center. The crowd oohed in expectation, thinking it might go, and sighed as the centerfielder settled under it for the second out.

Tony Conigliaro stepped to the plate.

"C'mon, Tony, hit one outta heah!" cried a man in the stands somewhere behind us.

The noise level rose as the young slugger readied himself. He stood over the plate, waving his bat easily back and forth, daring the pitcher to try to throw a fastball past him.

On the mound, Jack Hamilton stared back, reading the sign from his catcher. With two out and nobody on, it was not a moment of particularly high tension. Still, the crowd stirred restlessly, expectantly. We knew that at any time and against any pitcher, Tony C. could go deep. He was a presence at the plate, a coiled force, like the cocked fist of a young boxer waiting for an opening. Hamilton went into his windup.

The pitch sailed in on Conigliaro, high and tight. His bat flew in one direction, his helmet in another. He threw his hands up, too late, toward his face. And then the sound—the most horrifying sound I've ever heard, halfway between a rifle shot and an orange being hurled against a fence—reverberated in the night air. The ball dribbled out partway into the infield. Conigliaro dropped in the dirt and did not move.

There may have been a collective gasp, an involuntary sucking in of breath, and then a deep and awful silence overwhelmed the ballpark.

The sharp and squishy sound of a baseball colliding with a human head remained in our ears for long, terrible seconds. No one said a word. We sat there, stunned in its echo, as players and team personnel ran from the dugout and gathered around the fallen warrior.

In my ten years I had been exposed to very little violence or serious injury. I had seen Alex fall on the rocks in Maine and sprain his ankle, but all he did was cry a little bit and lean on my shoulder as he limped back to the house. This was different. It reached down into instinct, into the reptilian core where we keep our compulsion to survive. Suddenly I felt small and alone. I looked over at my father's face. It was ashen.

"Is he gonna get up?" I asked weakly.

"I don't know, son." We leaned forward, like rubberneckers at an auto wreck, but we were too far away. I couldn't see Conigliaro at all; he was completely surrounded by teammates and people in street clothes whom I took to be team doctors. In baseball everyone wears a uniform. The appearance on the field of men in regular clothes heralded something serious, something beyond the game. I felt the sting of tears. Beside me, Elroy made a little choking sound and bit his lip.

Finally, a few people in the stands began to boo the pitcher, who had taken a few steps toward home plate and stood, arms folded across his chest, looking in at the crowd around the fallen figure in the batter's box. But they were nervous boos, meant to chase away the silence, to wash away the imprint of that awful sound of ball against bone.

"He's just lying there!" Elroy cried. His voice was pinched and small. He still had the program and pencil in either hand, but he did not look at them. Nor was he looking at home plate. His eyes were somewhere else, unfocused, seeing something they did not want to see.

"It's going to be okay," said Fred Granger, unconvincingly, a stab at comfort. "He's going to be all right."

"In the head," Elroy said, to no one. "It hit him in the head."

"He's gonna be okay," said Jim, his older brother. His gentle tone surprised me.

"My friend Steve's uncle got hit in the head by a metal beam at a construction site," Elroy said, his eyes moist. "He died."

"He's not going to die," my father snapped. But the tone of his voice frightened me. He was as unnerved as the rest of us.

Long minutes passed as a stretcher was brought out from somewhere and Conigliaro was lifted onto it and carried off the field. We still had not seen him move. Hamilton took the ball from his catcher and readied himself on the mound to renewed boos from the stands. It was strange how people found so little to say to one another. We were all too stunned, too individually faced with our separate frailties. Words were hollow and insufficient at a time like this.

Reserve outfielder José Tartabull was announced as a pinch-runner for Conigliaro, and took his spot at first base. The scorecard hung loosely from Elroy's hands; he was still staring lifelessly at a spot somewhere in the outfield. "Aren't you going to write that down?" I prodded him.

"Oh. Oh, yeah." And I watched as he carefully penciled in the name in the space below Conigliaro's: T-A-R-T-A-B-U-L-L. Rico Petrocelli followed with a base hit, and I had to remind Elroy to record that, too. I desperately wanted to get back to normal, to take solace in the hits and outs of an ordinary baseball game, though I knew already that this game, my first in a big-league ballpark, would never be normal. Elroy didn't care anymore. He had retreated into a protective shell of indifference from which he would not emerge, not ever. The Red Sox scored two runs in the inning, but Elroy did not record them, and the cheers of the crowd were perfunctory. The terrible silence that had come crashing down in the seconds after Conigliaro had been hit never lifted entirely. The rest of the game, a 3–2 win for the Red Sox, was played in the mournful fugue of a funeral. Elroy left the unfinished scorecard under his seat as we filed solemnly out of the stadium. I had expected victory to feel different.

There had been no public address announcement about Conigliaro during the game. But people on the street outside the park had transistor radios, and from them we learned that he had been taken to a hospital in Cambridge, and that he had a fractured cheekbone and damage to his left eye. It was likely, the announcer said, that he would miss the remainder of the season.

The next morning's newspaper featured a ghastly front-page photo of Conigliaro's face, his left eye blackened and swollen shut. The ball had hit him near the temple, just below the eye socket. One doctor said that if the ball had hit just a couple inches higher, Conigliaro might indeed have died. The name of Ray Chapman, the only player in big-league history to be killed by a pitched ball, was invoked. Conigliaro, the paper said, was resting comfortably in the hospital and would watch Saturday's game on television.

We watched it on Fred's new color TV—all of us, that is, except Elroy, who found a book on the planets and disappeared with it into the backyard. I don't think Elroy ever watched a baseball game again. He became one of those rare American males unaffected by professional sports, skipping that section of the newspaper entirely and ignoring the increasingly commercial festivities surrounding championship contests. "It's only a game," he would say throughout the remainder of our adolescence whenever the subject of baseball came up. But Elroy *liked* games—chess, Parcheesi, poker. He was small, like me, but he excelled at contests of the mind. He could have been an astute baseball fan, an intellectual aficionado in the mold of George Will or Roger Kahn. Seeing Conigliaro go down ruined it for him. I think he was unprepared for the sudden look at the face of mortality.

But the Red Sox scored a dozen runs without Conigliaro in the lineup, and hung on to win the game by the score of 12 to 11. Afterward, we did some tourist stuff around Boston—saw the U.S.S. *Constitution*, Old North Church, and the site of the Boston Massacre, where a black man named Crispus Attucks was shot by British troops in 1770. Everywhere we went we somehow got drawn into conversations with total strangers about the Red Sox and what had happened to Conigliaro. By

Sunday morning, when my dad drove us all out to the famous historical sites at Lexington and Concord, the questions had shifted from
Conigliaro's health to whether or not the Red Sox could win the pennant without him. My father didn't think so. "They played on adrenaline yesterday," he told an older man by the bridge at Minute Man
Park in Concord. "Pretty soon reality will come crashing down.
They're young and streaky. They're bound to have a letdown."

"The Americans were underdogs against the British, too," asserted
the man's small wife, a silver-haired woman with round wire glasses and
a pleasant, lined face. "And yet, here we are."

It was a tiny little bridge over a piddling creek, surrounded by perhaps a dozen people who had, like us, come to stand on the spot of the
Revolutionary War's first official battle. The elderly couple was from
Burlington, Vermont, they told us, where pennant fever had broken out
as severely as it had in Maine. The Red Sox had become conversation
topic number one throughout New England.

There was another family there, a mom and dad and about seven
kids, dressed like they had just come from church. The father, a baby in
his arms, stood near the end of the bridge opposite the Minute Man
statue, reading aloud from a plaque about the historic battle. None of the
kids seemed to be paying much attention to him. Jim went up to one of
the boys. "Didja hear about Tony Conigliaro?" he said.

The boy nodded, his eyes wide. "I'd like to punch that Jack Hamilton
right in the nose."

"We were there," Jim told him. "We went to the game that night."

"*Really?*" The boy's eyes widened further. "Hey, Ethan!" he called to
his brother. "These guys saw Conigliaro get hit. They were at the game!"

Ethan and the rest of his siblings gathered around us like iron filings
pulled to a magnet, wanting to know all about the game and the beaning, what we had seen, heard, and felt. The father looked up from the
plaque and stopped reading.

It was extraordinary. Here we were at one of our country's most important historical sites, where the what-ifs of time extended linearly forward to the present, discussing the American League pennant race. To those of us gathered there that morning, it was more important than the American Revolution, although at one point I heard Elroy mumble, "It's only a game."

We drove back to Maine that afternoon. The Red Sox and Angels wrapped up their series with a doubleheader, and we listened to both games, switching radio stations along the way. By the time we made Brunswick and got off the interstate highway, the Red Sox had won the first game, 12–2.

At Bath we had to wait for the drawbridge. We sat there for half an hour, with the engine idling and the radio playing, as the Angels scored six runs in the second inning of the second game.

"Ah, well, can't win 'em all," my father said.

"It's early yet," Jim Woolf, in the front seat beside him, piped up.

"It's only a game," said Elroy. I glared at him.

By the fourth inning the Angels had added two more runs, and we decided to stop at a roadside diner that served batter-fried seafood. When we got back into the car, the Red Sox were coming up in the sixth, and the score was 8 to 4. They had cut the Angels' lead in half.

The ensuing rally took us all the way through Camden. My father did well to keep the car on the road. It was a beautiful day on Penobscot Bay, and things were looking up in Boston, too. We could hear the crescendo of crowd noise over the car radio. Dalton Jones doubled in two runs to make it 8 to 6. José Tartabull hit a sacrifice fly to bring the Red Sox within one. All of us except Elroy erupted into cheers as, moments later, Jerry Adair tied the game with a single.

As we neared home, conversation in the car died. We glued our ears to the radio. We had reached the turnoff and were approaching the Deer Isle bridge when Adair came up in the eighth with the score still tied. My dad rounded the curve and gunned the car up onto the bridge at the same moment the crack of the bat came over the radio, followed by the announcer's voice, shrill with excitement. "There's a long drive to left . . . way back . . . GONE! HOME RUN! THE RED SOX LEAD!" All of us except Elroy went nuts. It wasn't the first time a car had bounced up and down on that bridge, but this time nature had nothing to do with it.

There was still the ninth inning to be played, and the last twelve miles of rural road to negotiate. The game ended just before the trip did. The Angels loaded the bases, but José Santiago got the final out on a ground ball. Minutes later, we pulled up in front of the house. My mother and Wendy Woolf rushed out to greet us. "Were you *listening* to that *game?*" Wendy cried.

A weekend that had begun in tragedy had ended in triumph. The Red Sox had responded to the loss of Conigliaro by winning three in a row, the last one a heart-stopping rally from eight runs down when a weaker team would have simply given up. They had looked into the face of death and emerged stronger than they had been before. And I knew that Elroy was wrong to tell me it was only a game. The Red Sox mattered, perhaps more than anything in the world at that moment. I loved them with my heart and soul. If they could win the pennant, everything else could work out, too. My father threw his arms around my mother, lifted her off her feet, twirled her around, and kissed her on the lips.

They were still in second place, still a game behind the White Sox. Minnesota and Detroit were tied for third, two games back. Next weekend the team I loved would travel to Chicago for a big five-game series. I suddenly thought of Cyrus Nygerski, the Boston-bred second baseman apprenticing for the White Sox in Wisconsin. I knew he had to be following the pennant race. I did not know that he would soon play a pivotal part in it.

19.

NINE DAYS IN AUGUST

Only nine days passed between Conigliaro's beaning, on August 18, and Tartabull's throw, on the twenty-seventh. But they were days of hope and optimism—true summer, with fair winds and clear skies punctuated by the sounds of wood, horsehide, and leather. Nygerski supposed there were people who lived to ski and welcomed winter's first snowfall, and football players who exulted in the first autumnal chill and fall foliage, but he could not imagine the sense of ongoing joy with which he woke each day attached to any other sport or season.

He was playing the best baseball of his life. Some days it seemed like a dream. He'd leap at a line drive, and the ball would find his glove. He'd look for an outside pitch to drive the opposite way, and there it would be. The Turtles had risen to third place—not that anyone really cared about the standings, except maybe the manager. The players were all very much aware that they were interchangeable goods, all of them headed for someplace else. Already, during the season, players had been moved to higher leagues, cut, and traded, often as throw-ins to complete deals made in faraway offices by men in suits who had never seen them play. Life in the low minors was all about individual survival, not team unity. But Nygerski's .380 average was tops on the

team, and his play had won him the respect and admiration of his teammates.

It wasn't just baseball, either. Life was good all over. He spent most
afternoons in the arms of the well-endowed Rhonda Whittingham, who
taught him sexual pleasures he'd never imagined. At night after the
games he hung out with Mavrogenes and his musician friends. He still
thought about Cassandra, but only in brief, fleeting moments—usually
while he was standing on second base after driving in two runs.

Removed by a thousand miles from New England's Red Sox mania,
Nygerski had nonetheless followed his favorite team in the newspapers.
He had been stunned by Conigliaro's tragedy, and proud that the young
team continued to win in its aftermath. Privately, he was thrilled at
their run for first place. But he had to keep his excitement to himself,
because like his lust for Rhonda and her ample chest, it could get him
into serious trouble. All his teammates were pulling for Chicago. The
White Sox signed his paycheck, after all, and had been in first place
since April. His teammates cheered upon hearing the news of a Boston
defeat. Yet Nygerski couldn't help but glow inwardly as he followed his
favorite team's steady rise in the standings.

Anything seemed possible during those nine glorious days—anything
at all. Mavrogenes had encouraged him to enroll at the local college when
the season was over, as shelter from the long shadow of Vietnam. Nygerski had said he'd think about it. In truth, he had no idea what he would
do when the season was over. He could go back to Boston and get a job
and join the frenzied throngs at Fenway for the September stretch. Or he
could hitchhike out to San Francisco and look for Cassandra. Or he could
stay right here and try his hand at college. Or he could go play winter ball
in Puerto Rico, if the big club wanted him to. The future was wide open.

"What'cha readin' there, Cy?" The voice belonged to Lucius DeBartolo, the team's starting catcher, a big, affable kid with dark curly hair,
broad features, and a thick New York accent. He sat down next to Nygerski. The simple wooden bench sagged with his weight.

"Sports," Nygerski replied.

DeBartolo slapped the paper in mock anger. "I know dat, ya putz. Says it right on da front of da section. But what? Ya readin' about da big club?"

Nygerski shook his head. "Nah, I'm seeing how the women's field hockey team is shaping up for next year's Olympics."

The big catcher laughed good-naturedly. He was far from the smartest player on the team, and sometimes jokes went right over his head, but you couldn't fault him on friendliness. Even when a joke was on him, he would laugh at it. DeBartolo probably lost thirty points in his batting average because he was so slow getting to first base, and his reflexes behind the plate were only marginally faster than the backstop's. But his home runs, when he hit them, were prodigious shots that left everyone on both benches gaping in admiration. And on close plays at the plate he was a wall of granite. Runners would sometimes slide so far out of the way to avoid a collision that they missed the plate entirely, and DeBartolo would simply grin, pick up the ball, and tag them out.

"Ya know, with a name like Cy, ya should've been a pitcher," he said. This was an old joke, one Nygerski had heard at least fifty times since the beginning of the season, but it was always new to DeBartolo.

"Yeah, right. I'd fool a lot of hitters with my sixty-mile-an-hour heater."

"Then ya oughtta change your name," DeBartolo said. "A star like you oughtta have a catchy nickname. Like Tiger, or somethin'."

Nygerski laughed. A picture formed in his head, of Rhonda, naked on her bedsheets, holding up her arms to him and saying, "Come here, Tiger." With an effort, he brought his mind back to the locker room and the paper in his hands. "Here's something you should be interested in, Lucius," he said. "The Yankees are gonna be looking for a catcher. You might want to talk to the skipper about swinging a trade."

"Trade? Whaddya mean?"

"Look here. Elston Howard announced his retirement yesterday."

"He did?"

"Yup." Nygerski knew that DeBartolo liked the Yankees, but he didn't hold it against him. He began reading from the article. "'Elston Howard, the first black man to play for the Yankees and an institution behind the plate in the Bronx, announced his retirement yesterday at the age of thirty-eight, opting to spend more time with his family rather than ride the Yankee bench. Howard, a nine-time all-star and the American League's Most Valuable Player in nineteen sixty-three, never recovered from the broken elbow he suffered in the third game of the season. After missing two months, Howard was unable to regain his hitting stroke, batting a paltry .175 in fifty games. The Yankees, looking to rebuild, had lately relegated him to pinch-hitting and late-inning defense.'"

"Wow," DeBartolo said. "First Whitey Ford, now Howard. Who's next, Mickey Mantle? Dere goes da dynasty."

"I hate to burst your bubble, DeBartolo, but the Yankee dynasty's been dead for a few years now. They finished tenth last year, dead last, if you didn't notice. Even the Red Sox beat 'em."

"Well, dere's a first time for everything."

Nygerski read on. "'Howard was hit by a pitch thrown by Boston pitcher Bill Rohr with two out in the final inning of a no-hitter at Yankee Stadium on April fourteenth. He returned to the lineup on June seventeenth, and struck out four times.'" He stopped reading. "I was at that game, you know. The no-hitter. It was right before I came out here."

"Yeah, you told me. About a hundred times."

"It says the Yankees had been trying to trade him, but no teams were interested."

"What good's a catcher who can't hit?"

"You tell me, DeBartolo." Nygerski looked at him and winked.

"Up yours, Nygerski." The big catcher rose from the bench. "Da Show's got no use for no left-handed second baseman, neither." He wandered off.

Nygerski watched him go, and chuckled softly. He liked DeBartolo.

But one did not invest much emotion in baseball friendships. He would probably never see him again after the season ended. He had seen people come and go all summer. His own fate remained a mystery. Certainly he had never expected the level of success he had achieved, and at times he thought it all must be some kind of cosmic joke. He wasn't really this good, was he? He knew that baseball was an exacting game, a humbling game, with a smaller margin separating the winners from the losers than any other sport. Great players went through slumps during which they couldn't buy a base hit. He hadn't had a slump like that all year—except that brief period right after Cassandra left. What had made him so lucky?

Deciding that to question his success was perhaps to jinx it, Nygerski banished the thought from his mind, and finished getting dressed. He would have been surprised to learn that he was, indeed, being watched by officials from the big club. Beloit may have been low in the White Sox farm system, but it was also only ninety miles from Chicago on the interstate. The White Sox had great pitching but they couldn't hit, and with three other teams breathing down their necks, they were looking for anyone who could help spark the offense. A left-handed second base-man was unusual enough to attract attention anywhere, even in the wastes of southern Wisconsin, and a left-handed second baseman with a batting average near .400 merited a closer look.

Despite the differences that were tearing our three families apart, a spirit of harmony prevailed over Rum Runners Cove as the Red Sox continued to win in the wake of the Conigliaro tragedy. Our schedule during those days revolved around the games. If the Sox played a day game, we'd stop doing chores around noon and then take the transistor radio to the beach, where we would often end up in a tight circle, hanging on the final few outs. Night games were occasions for everyone to gather in the kitchen after an early supper; we were allowed to stay up past our bedtimes if the game was close.

And they kept winning. That was the remarkable thing—that they could suffer such a blow as losing their best power hitter and keep pace with the three other teams which all the sportswriters said would eventually obliterate them. We all got caught up in it—my dad, my mom, the other grown-ups, and all the kids except Elroy. I think they lost one game that whole week, and they came back to sweep a doubleheader the next day. Dick Williams used several different players in place of Conigliaro in right, and they all contributed. On Thursday, August 24, a rookie right fielder named Jim Landis saved the last game of the home stand by making a running catch with the bases loaded. The next day, the Sox announced that they had signed Ken Harrelson, an outfielder who could hit for power, to replace Conigliaro. Harrelson, however, would not join the team until the following Monday in New York. On Friday the team flew to Chicago, where they would play five games in three days against the White Sox—an epic battle for first place.

The Red Sox weren't the only thing happening in our lives, though we could scarcely go an hour without someone talking about them—a storekeeper, a hitchhiker we'd pick up on the way back from town, Uncle Bill's fellow fishermen, even our neighbor Kevin Hodge and his pot-smoking friends. Cassandra called from San Francisco to tell us that she was sick of California and was heading home, and my dad didn't even get mad at her. We dropped in on Aunt Polly, and *she* talked about the pennant race, though she was more guarded in her optimism than even my dad, the original pessimist. "Watch out for Chicago," she said. "That Stanky—I don't trust him. He's got something up his sleeve."

As usual, Aunt Polly was in the minority. We all wanted to believe that the Red Sox could pull it off. And yet there was, unspoken among us, a sense of too-good-to-be-true, a knowledge that this brief period of God's benevolent grace could not possibly last. The differences between and within the families at Rum Runners Cove really were too deep to be resolved, and would descend again as surely as the fog that periodically shrouds Maine's magnificent coast and makes it a dangerous place for boaters. The string of sunny days would end, as would that summer and our childhood innocence. The Red Sox could not keep winning forever; without Conigliaro and better starting pitching behind Lonborg they could not possibly win the pennant. The war in Vietnam would not be over anytime soon, nor would the race riots in American cities. I don't doubt that there were body bags sent home during those nine days, and outrages against humanity on the streets of New York, Chicago, and Los Angeles. There were bar fights and domestic battles and car accidents and drug overdoses and all the other horrors, large and small, we live with every day. They didn't stop; they never have. But for nine glorious days in August, 1967, almost everybody I knew stopped thinking about them.

20.

In rhonda's room

"Are you getting tired of me, Cyrus?"

The young man beside her propped himself up on one elbow against the pink pillowcase. He ran the first two fingers of his other hand gently down her neck and along her collarbone. "Tired of you? What makes you say a thing like that?"

Rhonda Whittingham leaned her face against his hand and pulled the flowered sheets over her breasts. "You haven't been by but a couple of times this week," she said. "And if I hadn't left that note with your roommate, I don't think you would have come see me today, either."

"I'm taking a chance, coming here on a Saturday." His hand reached her shoulder and snaked beneath the covers. She scrunched her arms more tightly against her chest, temporarily frustrating his explorations.

"Oh, don't worry about Ed coming home anytime soon. He'll be at the bar for hours."

"You know his habits pretty well, don't you?"

"Honey, after thirteen years, there ain't much mystery left. The Packers and Bears are playing a preseason game today, and all his buddies have bets on it. He'll use any excuse to get out of the house. He mowed the lawn this morning. As far as he's concerned, he's done his domestic duty for the week."

"Does he still fuck you?"

She loved that about him: his directness, his utter lack of guile. "He tries, when the spirit moves him," she said. "It doesn't happen very often." She sighed as the young man's index finger reached her nipple and began slowly tracing circles around it. She loved the way he touched her—gently, teasingly, almost shyly. She relaxed her arms and let his fingers caress first one breast, then the other. Her husband never touched her like that. On those rare occasions when he did desire her, it was all wham-bam thank-you-ma'am, and five minutes after it had begun he would be snoring. She had taken her first young lover five years ago. She viewed their inexperience as an asset; they took their time, and were willing to be shown how to please her. They always left eventually, but that was part of the price Rhonda paid.

"Cyrus, you're gonna make me want you again."

He flicked his tongue lightly across her lips. "Then I'll be too weak for my game," he said softly.

"Bullshit," she chuckled. "Remember that day a couple weeks ago, when I made you come three times? You went four-for-four that night."

"Yeah, but no one can keep that up for a whole season."

She didn't want to ask him whether he was referring to sex or baseball. Rhonda knew that the summer of love was almost over, that her young star would move on without regrets. Housewives were not his future.

"I'd say so far this season you've done a pretty good job of keeping it up," she cooed as she ducked her head beneath the covers.

Later, she lolled back contentedly against the pillows and watched him pull on his pants. "One leg at a time, just like the ordinary players," she murmured. "I'm gonna miss you when you go."

"Go where?" he said distractedly, looking out the window. His mind was already elsewhere.

"Honey, nobody stays in Beloit for very long. At least not anyone who's any good at anything. This is a dead-end factory town, where men grow old in bars and women grow old waiting up for them. It's no place for a star like you."

"It's been a fun summer," he said, reaching for his shirt. He wouldn't look at her.

"I've enjoyed it, too, Cyrus. More than you know." She felt a pang in her chest at the sudden emotional chasm that he had crossed, that yawned between them. It was a feeling akin to panic, and so profoundly lonely that she almost cried. She wanted to tie him to her bedpost and feast on his lovely young body until there was nothing left of it. The thought that their afternoons together were numbered was almost too much to bear. She had felt this way before, with other young lovers, but never this acutely, and she realized that it was because there was something about Cyrus Nygerski that was not boyish, and had never been.

He moved to the bureau against the far wall to retrieve his watch. She thought it was cute that he always stripped entirely naked when they made love, and she had taken to removing her wedding band when they were together—something she had never done in her previous affairs. She didn't want anything at all to come between them.

"Cyrus, do you think I'm pretty?"

He half-turned. "I think you're beautiful," he told her. But she caught the defensive tone in his voice. He did up two buttons on his shirt as he said it.

"Come here," she said.

He took two tentative, awkward steps toward the bed, his hands fumbling at his shirt. "Rhonda, I've got a game—"

"I just want you to kiss me good-bye." She folded the sheet down past her belly button, exposing her whole upper body to him. "Don't I at least deserve a kiss good-bye?"

He bent down and kissed her quickly on the mouth.

"Kiss me like you mean it," she said. "Even if you don't."

He kissed her hard this time, and ran his hands along the outsides of her breasts and down her flanks. She encircled his neck with her arms. His thumbs found her nipples; he slid out of her embrace and kissed each one in turn.

"Oh, Cyrus," she moaned.

He started to draw away. "I've really gotta go," he said.

From outside the window came the sound of tires in the driveway, followed by the slamming of a car door.

Rhonda bolted upright in bed. "Shit! It's Ed! What the hell is he doing home so early?" She shot a glance at the bedside alarm clock. Four-thirty. Early, but not *that* early. The time had gotten away from her.

The front door of the house crashed open, followed by heavy footsteps. Rhonda heard her husband's voice. "Fuckin' buncha candy-asses," he mumbled.

She turned to look at Cyrus. He cowered against the wall nearest the door, his shirt half open and his shoes in his hand, with a look on his face the likes of which she had never seen. He was actually afraid. It looked unnatural on him.

She leapt out of bed. "You've got to get out of here!" she whispered.

She heard Ed stomp across the kitchen floor and open the refrigerator. He continued to mumble. "Forty-two to six. Forty-fucking-two to six! They looked like dogs. Dogs!" This pronouncement was punctuated by the unmistakable sound of a flip-top being cranked off a can of beer.

"He's drunk," Rhonda hissed. "And it sounds like the game went badly. Quick, you can go out the window." Still stark naked, she stalked over to the window that faced out onto the side yard, grateful for the one-story ranch house design of suburbia. "Hurry up! You can put on your shoes later."

She bent down and raised the window. "Oh, shit, it's got a screen!"

"Rhonda!" her husband hollered.

"Shit!" she hissed.

"Rhonda!" Ed hollered again, and then she heard his footsteps, heading down the hall.

"Here." Nygerski materialized behind her, and he reached around her to undo the two clasps that held the screen in place. He pushed it outward, and it fell onto the grass.

Ed's clumsy steps pounded closer. She prayed that he was heading for the bathroom, off the side of the hall; she hoped that he had rented enough beer from Al's Tap to want to return some of it; she counted on the pattern of years holding true. She held her breath, and then she heard him push the bathroom door open.

Relief poured out of her. "Go, go now!" she said to Nygerski. He had one foot on the windowsill; she placed a hand on his back to push him the rest of the way out. "And Cyrus . . . I love you."

"Rhonda, what the hell is this?" Ed's voice bellowed through the wall.

She froze, remembering what was in the bathroom.

Her second baseman had been sweaty when he'd first arrived. It was a three-mile uphill walk, he told her, though no hill in or around Beloit was really all that strenuous, especially for a nineteen-year-old athlete. But it was a warm August day, and he had walked briskly and worked up a sweat. She had made him take a shower. She had helped him undress, and followed him into the bathroom, where he had run his hands up underneath her summer dress and she had taken off her panties for him. They were still there, she saw in her mind, draped across the toilet seat. Come to think of it, the dress was in there, too.

Outside the window, on the threshold of escape, Cyrus turned to look at her, perhaps in shock that she had said she loved him. Their eyes locked.

"Go!" she spat at him.

Behind her, the bedroom door crashed open. Rhonda turned to face her husband. The panties were in his clenched fist. Her nakedness momentarily staggered him—she saw him falter backward. Then dawning comprehension seeped into his drunken features. "Fucking hell!" he roared, and charged at the window.

Rhonda skittered along the near wall, out of his reach. Ed leaned out the window, and she dove for the bedsheet, wrapping it completely around herself. "Come back here, you little shit!" he bellowed. "I'll come after you, you bastard! I'll get you! I'll tear your fuckin' legs off!"

Rhonda flashed a glance at the hall door just as Ed turned back into the room. Had he not seen her in that instant, she might have made a run for it, for he was shitfaced drunk, and he had been violent with her while in that condition more than once, with far less provocation.

"It's that little prick from the baseball game," he said, leveling his eyes at her. "The guy who hit the home run. Isn't it?"

She held the sheet tightly around herself, her arms crossed across her breasts. She trembled as he took a step forward. "Ed, listen to me—"

"ISN'T IT?" he roared at her.

"Ed, please, it's not what it looks like—"

"You fucking SLUT!" he roared again, advancing on her.

She cringed away from him. "Ed, I was . . . I was . . . masturbating," she babbled desperately. "I miss you, you know, when you're away on the weekend . . . and . . . and . . . he must have been outside the window watching, I don't know . . . and . . . Ed, please—"

His fist crashed into her nose. Suddenly she was on the floor, her head slumped against the side of the bed. She felt warm blood trickling down her chin; licking her upper lip, she tasted its unmistakable saltiness. The blow had momentarily knocked her out.

Ed bent down and grabbed a handful of her hair. The mildewy smell of stale beer washed over her as he brought his face close to hers. "He was carrying his SHOES, you lying bitch." With his free hand, he slapped her face, hard. She saw her own blood fly through the air. She screamed, and tried to curl herself into a ball.

He pushed her roughly away, and she fell heavily against her dresser. Dazed and bleeding, she tried to get to her feet but stumbled over the bedsheet. She screamed again as he advanced on her.

"You fucking WHORE!" He raised his arm to backhand her, but she managed to fend off the blow with her arms.

"Ed, stop!" she pleaded with him, backing toward the corner of the room. He kicked her brutally in the ribs. She cried out in pain, but to her alarm she was unable to scream, for his foot had driven the air from her lungs. Ed closed on her with silent fury. She clutched at the sheet and balled herself as best she could against the next blow. Please don't let him kick me in the head, she prayed, hoping that even in his drunkenness his anger would stop short of murder. She could not expect the neighbors to save her, not in the nuclear family mind-your-own-business anonymity of New Beloit. Perhaps somebody a few houses away had heard her first scream over the television, but she would not be able to scream like that again. Terrified, she realized that Ed could kill her here in complete privacy if he wanted to.

His booted foot slammed into her back, near one of her kidneys, and sent pain shrieking along her spine. She whimpered and rolled herself tighter. She could hear him breathing heavily. "Fucking slut," he growled, low in his throat. He grabbed her hair again, and she threw up her hands to ward him off. He slapped her face again, and she reeled backward. The sheet fell partially off of her. She stumbled and collapsed to the floor. Then he kicked her again, for the last time.

For several seconds she could not breathe or make a sound. The room swirled around her in blurred images of pain: the warmth of her own blood, the fine strands of carpet an inch from her eyes, the taste of bile in the back of her throat, the sick and violated feeling in her stomach, where his final kick had landed. She did not remember vomiting, but there it was, yellow-green on the beige carpet—her cheek was actually lying in it. She retched again, trying to manage a full breath, and coughed up a mouthful of puke and blood. From the driveway she heard the sound of Ed's car starting, followed by the squeal of tires. He was going after Nygerski. She hoped the kid would have the sense to hide from him.

She couldn't move. The first sound she managed was a low sob. Breathing returned slowly. She tried to lift an arm and gasped in pain. She wondered if Ed had broken one or more of her ribs.

She lay there on the carpet for what seemed like a long time. The bed-sheet stank of blood and vomit, and she turned her head to face the open window through which Cyrus had made his escape. Slowly, the room came back into focus. She glanced at the phone, on the floor near the bedside table, its receiver lying on the carpet a short distance away. Grimacing against the stabbing in her ribs, she worked herself into a half-sitting position and dragged herself toward it.

She crawled to where she could reach the phone, stopping twice because of dizziness and the feeling that she was going to puke again. Who should she call? The cops? The hospital? A friend? She was hurt, she needed help. Ed was still out there, and if he did not find Cyrus, he would be back to take things up again with her. She had to get out, and if she couldn't do it under her own power, she needed to contact some-one who could help her. But the phone was not buzzing as it should have been if the receiver had simply been knocked off the hook. With an effort she pushed down the button and held the receiver up to her ear. No dial tone. Her eyes followed the phone cord. It ended in shiny gold ends of frayed wire.

"No!" she sobbed, and lowered her head to the floor. On her hands and knees she rocked slowly back and forth, holding the sheet around her naked body. How could one woman's body go through such extremes of pleasure and pain in a single afternoon? She felt like one big bruise.

It was over—not just the affair with Cyrus but the whole life she had known. Was this the price she had to pay, for the sin of looking for love outside a loveless marriage? Would Ed come back and punish her some more, with additional and more severe beatings? Or would he simply leave her, an unfit, adulterous wife, taking everything they owned with him? What would she do then?

Real tears came now, tears not of physical pain but emotional anguish, and fear. Rhonda Whittingham curled herself into a ball against the wall of her bedroom, wrapped the soiled sheet around herself, and cried and cried and cried.

21.

LAST GAME IN BELOIT

He wasn't thinking about Rhonda as he stood in with two out in the eighth, the Turtles down by a run, to face the new pitcher. The kid had an amazing fastball; Nygerski had watched the inning's first two batters go down on strikes, flailing helplessly at balls up around their chests. The next guy had been more patient, and drawn a walk, for the kid was wild, and a little bit scary, too. Twilight engulfed the ballpark, making the blurs even harder to see.

Nygerski took a strike, a ball, and another strike. In his opinion, the umpire was being a bit generous, for the last pitch missed the outside of the plate by several inches. Then again, maybe he couldn't see the ball any better than the batters could. A lot of minor-league hitters improve their averages when they get called up to the Show, because they're accustomed to the substandard lighting in backwaters like Beloit.

He stepped out and looked down at the third-base coach for the sign—unnecessary, really, because all he could be expected to do was put bat on ball if the pitch was near the plate and get out of the way if it wasn't. The coach swiped his right hand across the letters of his uniform, which meant: hit away, and good luck.

He was looking at the coach when a sudden glimmer of light atop the abutment of stands behind third base caught his eye. At first Nygerski didn't know what it was, but in another couple of seconds it became clear to him—the limb of the full Moon rising over the ballpark. He stood and watched it grow. The long shadow of the oddly shaped seating section materialized on the outfield grass.

"C'mon, play ball," the umpire growled behind his mask. But Nygerski could not take his eyes off the rising Moon. It was beautiful.

And then, someone in the stands behind third base howled. The sound was wordless and wonderful, the voice female and familiar. The hairs on the back of Nygerski's neck prickled.

"Get in there," the umpire said. On the mound, the pitcher stared in at him with silent menace. Nygerski pulled his eyes away from the rising Moon and glared back at him. Slowly, deliberately, he fixed his grip on the bat, tapped it on home plate, and readied himself. The pitch sailed high over his head, and Nygerski hit the dirt. There were a few scattered boos from the stands as the runner trotted to second and the catcher retrieved the ball.

Nygerski dusted himself off and shot daggers with his eyes at the pitcher. The son of a bitch didn't even have good enough control to throw a decent brushback pitch. Deliberately, he took his sweet time getting back into the batter's box. The Moon was halfway out of the stands now, its glow flooding the ballpark. *Protect the plate*, he told himself. The noise of the crowd died down in anticipation of the next pitch. And the woman in the stands howled again.

It was a *great* howl, and Nygerski smiled to himself in admiration. He wasn't the least bit nervous. He waved the bat easily back and forth, awaiting the pitcher's next offering. It was a fastball, of course, and on the outside half the plate. Nygerski swung.

The ball rose toward left field and the rising Moon. Nygerski knew that he had undercut it, but he hoped it had the distance to reach the abutment of stands. He dropped the bat and watched the left fielder go to the wall, reach into the seats with his glove, and come up empty. He jumped in place, clapped his hands once, and went into his home run trot as the cheers erupted. And somewhere in the noise, he heard that howl again.

The home run won the game. Jim Thorne pitched a scoreless ninth to nail down the victory, and the cramped locker room was a happy place as Nygerski stepped out of the lukewarm shower. He had his pants on and was buttoning his shirt when he heard the door to the manager's office open. "Nygerski!" Cliff Gillespie bellowed. "Get in here!"

"What's up, boss?" Nygerski said as he closed the door of the closet-sized room behind him. He had the feeling that the crusty, old-school manager still didn't like him much, but as his batting average had steadily risen over the past two months, Gillespie had grown almost congenial.

Now the chiseled face broke into a real rarity—an actual smile. Gillespie reached into a drawer and pulled out an envelope. He handed it to Nygerski across the desk. "Here," he said. "I guess you've earned this."

"What is it?" Nygerski asked, accepting the envelope.

"Bus ticket to Chicago," Gillespie said. "Apparently Stanky wants a hot left-handed bat off the bench, and you're it. You're supposed to report to Comiskey Park in time for tomorrow's doubleheader." Lowering his voice, he added, "Congratulations."

Nygerski let the envelope dangle from his fingertips. He leaned against the wall, momentarily unsure of his balance. "I've been called up? By the White Sox?"

"That's right," Gillespie said, his smile broadening. "First time I can remember that anyone's gone right from Beloit to the Show. Then again, I never saw anyone have a season like the one you've had here. You don't belong in this league."

"The White Sox," Nygerski said, working his mouth around the words as if uttering them for the first time. "The Chicago White Sox. I don't believe it."

"Believe it," Gillespie said. "Now go on, get out of here. Oh, I almost forgot." Gillespie reached into the desk drawer again and pulled out a single sheet of paper, folded once. "Someone handed this to one of the guys in the dugout to give to you."

Nygerski unfolded the paper. On it was written a single sentence. He recognized the handwriting. It read: *I knew you'd keep the faith.*

Cassandra! She was here! She had returned, at the very moment of his glory, just as she had said she would. And in that instant Nygerski knew that she had been responsible for his success. Had he not met her and fallen in love with her, he would have lacked the inspiration that had made his stellar season possible.

His legs felt weak underneath him. He looked up from the note and saw Gillespie staring at him strangely, his smile fading. "Thank you," he managed to whisper.

"Something wrong?" the manager asked.

"No . . . no. Something right."

Gillespie rose and offered his hand. Nygerski took it. "Knock 'em dead in Chicago," Gillespie said. "Make us proud."

Of course Jim Thorne asked him what Gillespie had wanted to see him about, and of course Nygerski had to tell him, and there was a lot of hullaballoo about someone from their lowly level getting called up to the big leagues. Nygerski accepted his teammates' congratulations in a daze. All he could think about was Cassandra. Where was she? Would she be waiting for him outside? He was supposed to meet Sammy after the game. Every player on the team wanted to shake his hand and clap him on the back, as though touching him would bring them some of his good fortune. Most of an hour passed before he got out of there, carrying a large duffel bag containing all of his baseball possessions.

He spotted Sammy's van across the moonlit parking lot. Sammy stood beside it, talking with Cassandra. She turned her head, and their eyes locked.

It struck him that he did not own a photograph of her and had not missed owning one. He remembered her exactly. She was dressed in blue jeans and a black pullover sweater that matched the color of her hair. She had augmented this simple outfit with two strands of turquoise beads that called out the color of her eyes. Nygerski dropped the duffel bag as they fell into each other's arms.

The feel of her body against his sent an electric thrill through Nygerski. She smelled of patchouli. He remembered the last time he had held her, in the motel room out by the freeway, when she had told him she was leaving. Now he had become a big-league ballplayer. What had she done, who had she become, since then?

Nygerski disentangled himself from Cassandra's arms, held her by the shoulders, and looked at her. "I'm going to the major leagues," he said.

She beamed at him, the same crooked smile. "I told you I'd be back when that happened, didn't I?" The news didn't seem to surprise her at all.

He turned to Mavrogenes. "They want me in Chicago for tomorrow's doubleheader," he said. "Against the Red Sox, no less."

"Cyrus, I want an autographed copy of your first bubblegum card." The guitarist grasped Nygerski's hand in both of his and shook it vigorously. "I mean that sincerely. I am in the presence of greatness."

"This calls for a drink," Cassandra proposed. "Don't you think so, Sammy?"

"Absolutely." Mavrogenes opened the van's sliding door and produced three cans of beer from the cooler. He handed them around. Nygerski looked at Cassandra and raised his can. The light of the Moon reflected off her dark hair. It was only then that he remembered.

"It's full Moon!" he exclaimed. "And you're *here!*"

"Wouldn't have missed it," Cassandra said, smiling that odd, alluring smile.

"But . . . but . . . how is that possible?"

"Anything's possible," she told him. "The Universe is crammed with possibilities."

She hadn't lost her penchant for baffling pronouncements, Nygerski noted. "Does this mean you're cured, then?"

"I was never ill," she said, casting a sidelong glance at Mavrogenes.

"But what about all that business in New York? And what you told me when you left?"

"I was wrong," she told him. "It's that simple. I discovered that I'd been wrong all along. And here I am. In the flesh. Only me."

"Did you have to—"

She shook her head vigorously, discouraging further questions. "I didn't have to do anything. It wasn't necessary."

Mavrogenes raised his beer can. "I don't know what you're talking about," he said, "but here's to Cyrus Nygerski, the greatest hitter since Ted Williams."

"Moondog," Cassandra said.

"What?" said both young men in unison.

"If you're going to be a star, you're going to need a nickname," Cassandra said. "And I'm going to call you Moondog. In honor of the home run you hit at moonrise."

"Cyrus 'Moondog' Nygerski," Mavrogenes said slowly. "I like it. Has a nice ring to it."

"So, Moondog, what are your plans?" Cassandra asked him, mimicking a sports announcer.

"Got a bus ticket to Chicago," he said, patting his pocket.

"A bus?" Mavrogenes snorted. "Stars don't ride buses. We'll drive you."

"Damn right," Cassandra said. She lifted her face skyward and howled at the Moon, a long, melodious sound. After a moment Mavrogenes, and then Nygerski, joined in.

Life, thought Cyrus "Moondog" Nygerski, is very, very good.

22.

TARTABULL'S THROW—II

Nygerski saw Tartabull's throw from the White Sox dugout. Dick Williams, the Boston manager, argued so vociferously that he was thrown out of the game, but from where Nygerski sat it was clear that the ump had made the right call. The throw was high, and the runner slid in around the tag. The White Sox had tied the game.

The White Sox—his team! He was wearing their uniform, though he had done nothing all game but sit at the end of the dugout and watch the strangers who were now his teammates. Twenty-four hours ago he had been a nameless minor-leaguer having an affair with a lonely sports widow. Now he was here.

Cassandra was here, too, in the stands, among the thousands of people, many times more people than had ever watched Nygerski play a baseball game in his life. Sammy Mavrogenes was with her. They had driven down from Beloit during the night. Cassandra had brought some potent weed from San Francisco, and they had all gotten stoned and gone swimming in Lake Michigan. After a big breakfast at an all-night diner, they had shown up at the ballpark at eight in the morning, where a disbelieving security guard had at first refused to let Nygerski in.

"Look, you idiot," Cassandra had said to the obstinate guard, "this is

Cyrus 'Moondog' Nygerski, and he's come to help you guys win the pennant."

"Even though he's from Boston," Mavrogenes put in.

"By way of Beloit, Wisconsin," Cassandra added.

The security guard remained unmoved.

"Didn't they tell you he was coming?" Cassandra demanded. "You'd better let him in. If you don't, and they lose, it'll be on your head."

Cassandra had finally convinced the guard to make a phone call, after which Cyrus Nygerski, newly minted member of the Chicago White Sox, had been allowed inside. But before he parted company with his friends, he made sure they were given passes to the double-header. "If nothing else, you can watch me take batting practice," he said.

"Oh, you'll do more than that," Cassandra had assured him. "They didn't call you up to sit on the bench."

"That's what rookies usually do," he had told her.

But Cassandra shook her head. "Not you. You're touched by destiny. I can feel it." She had embraced him then, and run her tongue around the edge of his ear. "Moments come when they come," she whispered. "You have to seize them."

Then she had turned to Mavrogenes. "Let's go find the public address booth. Make sure they pronounce his name right."

But the announcer had not, through nine innings, pronounced his name at all, because throughout the first game of the doubleheader Nygerski had done precisely what he had predicted he would do—sit on the bench.

"We'll meet you back out here after the second game," Cassandra had told him as the guard swung the chain-link gate closed, separating Nygerski from his friends. "Knock 'em dead, Moondog."

After that, he had descended into the maelstrom of major-league baseball. The equipment manager, a short, balding, nervous little guy named Norm Radke, had fussed over him with a tape measure, asked his shoe size, and issued him a crisp, black-on-white home uniform bearing the number 13. "It's a good uniform," the small man said in clipped, rapid-fire syllables. "The lower the number, the better your chances of sticking with the team. No one's worn thirteen in years." He stopped and looked Nygerski in the eye. "You're not superstitious, are you?"

Moondog was too wired from lack of sleep and too excited at being in the Show to care. Any number was a good number, if it was attached to a big-league uniform. "No," he said.

After fitting him, Radke ushered Nygerski to his locker and introduced him to Harvey, the clubhouse manager, and three players who were just arriving. Harvey seized his elbow and guided him to the side of the room. He was young, probably on the near side of thirty, too small and gawky to be an athlete. He blinked at Nygerski. "You met Stanky yet?" he asked him.

"Uh-uh." Nygerski shook his head.

"How about the big boss?"

"I just got into town this morning," Nygerski said.

"You got a place to stay?"

"Nope. Some friends drove me down from Wisconsin."

Harvey took a step backward, and looked Nygerski over. "You that lefty second baseman everybody's been talking about?"

"I guess so." He had no idea that anybody had been talking about him. Then again, he was here, wasn't he?

"We leave for Kansas City and then the coast after Wednesday night's game," Harvey said. "You ever been to California?"

Nygerski shook his head, and the clubhouse man laughed. "Pinocchio, you're a real boy now."

The meeting with Stanky had been short and to the point. "I never met a left-handed second baseman before," the manager said. "But they tell me you can hit."

Nygerski nodded. He knew of the feisty little manager's reputation for scrappiness. As a player, he had earned the respect of opponents and teammates despite limited skills. He would do anything to win, and he had carried that attitude into his managerial career. "Our infield's solid," he growled at Nygerski, "but we could use a left-handed bat off the bench."

Moondog recognized a few of his teammates' names: Hoyt Wilhelm, the aging knuckleballer, Gary Peters, a big left-hander who would start the second game, and Joe Horlen, the staff ace. Smokey Burgess was on the team, and Rocky Colavito, the closest thing the light-hitting White Sox had to a slugger. Everyone was friendly but distant—the team had been in first place most of the year, and they had done it without him. He was a newcomer who would have to prove himself. He understood this. It is the way of team sports everywhere. He was willing to wait for his chance.

It appeared that it could be a long wait. Stanky hadn't so much as looked at him the whole game. Already he had used two pinch-hitters: Burgess in the sixth, and Duane Josephson, who had just hit the sacrifice fly to tie the game.

And so the game went into extra innings. The teams dueled scorelessly through the tenth, eleventh, and twelfth. The tension grew with every batter. Still, Nygerski watched. Nobody in the dugout said much. These were professionals doing a job, Nygerski thought. Their job was to play this ball game, to win it if they could, and to play the game after that. There was no outward show of nervousness. But first place was on the line, and the special significance of this game hung in the air like the sucked-in breath of an approaching storm. The stands seethed with quiet expectation.

Through it all, Stanky watched the action on the field with unbroken concentration, conferring occasionally with one of his coaches or players. Watching him, Nygerski had the impression that the manager missed nothing on the field. A reporter could ask him a question about a particular pitch to a particular batter in the fourth inning, and Stanky would doubtlessly remember it.

The pitcher's spot came up again in the bottom of the thirteenth. It was now after four o'clock, and shadows from the grandstand crept toward the infield. And there was still a second game to be played. Nygerski realized that darkness would fall before it ended. He thought of Cassandra and Sammy, somewhere in the stands. Already it had been a long day for them. But the payoff was finally at hand, for Stanky had run out of players. The manager cast his intense eyes toward the end of the dugout.

"You, Nygerski, grab a bat," Stanky barked, and gave a little jerk of his head toward the field. "You're up next."

And that was all, except for Gary Peters swatting him on the ass with his glove as Nygerski walked by, and muttering, "Go get 'em, Moon-dog." He had revealed his newly minted nickname to his new team-mates in the brief pregame introductions, giving them no hint that he hadn't had the name for years. Moondog. He rolled the sound of it around in his mind. Every ballplayer needs a nickname if he is going to tilt at stardom, and Cassandra had come up with one that was just about perfect for him.

He watched from the on-deck circle as the hitter ahead of him fouled off several pitches and then grounded weakly to shortstop. The ball went quickly around the infield as he walked to the plate.

He was not nervous. The worst he could do was make an out, the second out of the inning, and both teams had been making outs with assembly-line regularity since the ninth. There had been a couple of hits on both sides, but the Red Sox had mounted the only threat, get-ting a man to third in the eleventh. If he got a hit, well, that would be an auspicious beginning to a major-league career. If not, nobody really expected him to succeed right away. He was a rookie, after all. His pri-mary thought as he stepped to the plate was only that he did not want to embarrass himself in front of Cassandra.

"Your attention, please," the public address announcer intoned. "Now batting for the pitcher Smith, number thirteen, Cyrus 'Moondog' Nygerski!"

There was some applause within the hollow sound of unrecognition from the stands. Nygerski chuckled to himself. Cassandra had found the PA booth, all right. That girl could do anything. He hefted his bat confidently and took a practice swing.

But his first at bat would have to wait a couple more minutes. For one of the Boston coaches, managing in Williams's stead, walked out toward the mound and waved to the bullpen, summoning a new pitcher.

When he heard the announcement, Nygerski couldn't believe it. For the new pitcher was none other than Billy Rohr, the kid he had watched those many months ago in Yankee Stadium. Recalled from the minors, he was being brought in now, a left-hander to face a left-handed batter.

Nygerski retreated to the on-deck circle to watch him take his warm-ups. Rohr was tall and thin, all arms and legs, with a flailing motion that made his pitches hard to follow. Several of his practice pitches were well off the plate; Nygerski noticed that the catcher bobbed and weaved on the balls of his feet, not quite sure where the ball was going. As long as he doesn't hit me, Nygerski thought, remembering the Yankee Stadium game. He had been hit by pitches several times during the season, and it always hurt.

Rohr finished his warm-ups, and Nygerski stood in. How things change, he thought. A few months ago, as an unknown minor leaguer yet to report for his first full season, Nygerski had watched Rohr become the first pitcher in history to throw a no-hitter in his first big-league game. Now they faced each other as equals in late August, in the heat of a pennant race.

The first pitch was in the dirt for ball one.

The crowd buzzed restlessly. Nygerski still couldn't believe how big a crowd it was. Since the tying play in the ninth inning, however, it had been subdued, waiting for something to happen. Nygerski focused his attention on the pitcher and tried not to think about Cassandra, somewhere up there in that humming wall of humanity.

He swung at the next pitch, a fastball that jammed him, and got only air. "Welcome to the big leagues, kid," said the catcher behind him as he threw the ball back. Nygerski stepped out and did not give him the satisfaction of a look.

The next pitch was a foot outside, bringing the count to 2 and 1. Rohr missed high with another fastball, and then, with Nygerski taking all the way, blazed one down the middle to make it 3 and 2.

He's going to throw me a curve, Nygerski thought. It's my first game, and he's gonna try to freeze me with the yellow hammer. He set himself for the pitch. Rohr threw. Nygerski swung.

The ball came flying off his bat toward right field, arcing toward the setting Sun. Nygerski dropped the bat and legged it as hard as he could, rounding first without slowing down. He knew he'd hit it pretty well; if the right fielder didn't catch up with it, he could get to second, at least. Out of the corner of his eye he saw Tartabull run toward the right-field wall. A moment later the roar of the crowd told him it had gone over.

His White Sox teammates poured out of the dugout as he crossed the plate with the winning run. They slapped him on the helmet, the shoulders, the buttocks, the thighs. In the midst of the celebration he chanced to look over in time to see Rohr, head down, walking alone to the Red Sox dugout. The other players filed swiftly and solitarily off the field, and for the flash of an instant Nygerski's heart went out to them.

They had needed this game. All over his native New England, Red Sox fans who hadn't known a winning team in a generation had been rooting them home. A year ago, a month ago—a *week* ago, he would have been one of them. And now he, Cyrus "Moondog" Nygerski, one of Boston's own, had dealt a bitter blow to a season that had held such promise. The pennant race was far from over, but for the Red Sox and their fans this was a devastating loss. The looks on the players' faces as they left the field said it all.

The moment passed. The crowd cheered wildly, and his teammates jostled around him, giddy as little boys. He was a hero, a goddamn hero, and tomorrow the whole baseball world would know his name. He looked up into the cheering crowd for Cassandra.

Of course he couldn't see her—there were thirty thousand people in the stands. And there was still the second game to be played. Nygerski's heroic home run had not immediately elevated his standing—he didn't play in the second game at all, a dreary, 1–0 White Sox victory. He could see that the fight had gone out of the Red Sox, for they mounted few threats, and Peters handled them easily. The doubleheader sweep put the White Sox solidly back in first place. The mood in the locker room after the game was upbeat but subdued. As though the players had expected nothing less. There was a great spread of cheese and cold cuts in the locker room, and players in various stages of dress and undress attacked it eagerly. But before Nygerski could get to his food, Harvey the clubhouse man grabbed his elbow. "I'm supposed to take you up to the radio booth," he said. "They want to interview you on the postgame show."

"Hey, the star of the day!" a player nearby, one of the regulars, shouted happily. He hoisted a frothing can of beer. The foam ran down his upraised arm.

"Don't knock it, you get a free shaving kit," said a player next to him.

"Way to go, Moondog!" somebody else yelled.

Harvey tugged at Nygerski's arm. "Come on, they want you on the air in two minutes."

Nygerski's head was spinning. When would this wild, crazy ride end? He had jumped out of Rhonda's bedroom window onto a speeding train of people and events that accelerated around each new turn. It was insane how fast it had all happened—since yesterday! People all over Chicago tonight—and New England, too, with different inflection— were pronouncing his name. Cyrus "Moondog" Nygerski. Twenty-four hours ago he had been just Cyrus.

Of course the radio guys asked him how he got the name. "I like to howl at the Moon sometimes," he said. "It unnerves the opposition."

Nygerski thought briefly of fumbling Hiram Reese back in Beloit as he sat behind the microphone with the two White Sox announcers. He didn't know until the moment the interview started that he possessed the gift of gab, that he could be spontaneously witty, that he could make his hosts laugh and keep a listening audience entertained. When the interview concluded, he didn't remember a tenth of what he'd said, but the announcers assured him he'd been great. Then he let Harvey lead him back to the locker room.

Many of the players had dressed and gone. But those who remained got a big laugh out of Nygerski's double take at the present that had been left for him. His locker was sealed shut, floor to ceiling, with hundreds of small pieces of white athletic tape.

He groaned. But he made sure to put a big smile on his face as he began picking off the pieces of tape. He recognized this prank as his welcome to the team. He was lucky it wasn't worse, given the starring role he'd played.

"Hey, Moondog, what the hell is the curse of the Bambino?"

He looked up to see two players standing near him. "What?" he said, with something less than brilliance.

"The curse of the Bambino. We heard you talkin' about it on the radio."

"Oh, that." A snatch of the interview came back to him. "Supposedly there's a curse on the Red Sox for selling Babe Ruth to the Yankees in nineteen twenty. The Red Sox won't win until the curse is removed."

The two players looked at one another and then cracked up. "A curse, huh?" said one.

"So that's why we won!" his buddy chimed in. "And I thought we just kicked the shit out of 'em, plain and simple." They collapsed into renewed laughter.

"Hey, Moondog, are you as bad a second baseman as you are a hitter?"

He sat there and shot the breeze with them for a while, and when they offered him a beer, Nygerski gratefully accepted. They asked him where he was staying, and he told them that Harvey the clubhouse man had already made reservations for him at a cheap hotel near the ballpark, and that would do at least until the team left on its road trip three days hence. All the while they were talking, Nygerski kept peeling little pieces of tape off the front of his locker; by the time he finally got it open, most of his teammates had left or were leaving. Nygerski swelled with warmth at being admitted into the major-league brotherhood.

He hoped that Sammy and Cassandra were still waiting for him, for he wanted to share the glory of this day with someone he had known for more than hours. Mostly, he wanted to share it with Cassandra, for it had been she who had assured him all along that it would come.

It was dark when he emerged from a small doorway underneath the stadium; it had been dark, in fact, since the seventh inning of the second game. The full Moon rode high in the sky above the expansive stadium parking lot, now nearly devoid of vehicles and littered with refuse from the day's festivities—beer bottles, crumpled cigarette packages, half-eaten hot dogs, programs that had been scanned and then discarded. But there was the van, a strong outfielder's throw away, parked next to one of the islands of small trees that had been planted to separate the huge parking lot into smaller sections. Sammy and Cassandra leaned against it, beers in hand. Nygerski waved, and Sammy lifted his can in recognition. God, it was good to have friends.

Cassandra waved both hands over her head, making sure he saw her. How could he not? He was looking at nothing else.

He certainly wasn't paying any attention to the low row of hedge to his right, nor to the vehicle parked behind it. There was no warning— no slam of a car door, no glint of moonlight off metal, nothing that registered in Nygerski's senses—until the man popped out from behind the hedge and confronted him.

But Moondog knew fear in that instant, for he recognized the face. It was the same face that had yelled threats of bloody retribution at him from a bedroom window ninety miles ago, and only yesterday. And though Nygerski's whole life had changed in the intervening hours, the hatred in Ed Whittingham's eyes had not. "A real hero, ain'tcha?" Ed Whittingham snarled. His bulk blocked Nygerski's way to the van. "Well, you're no hero to me."

Ed's hand came up, and too late, Nygerski saw the object in it. From somewhere miles away he heard Cassandra scream, "Cyrus!" And then Whittingham's arm came down in a blur, and Nygerski felt nothing but pain as the knife plunged into his chest.

He fell onto the pavement, looking up into Ed Whittingham's twisted face. "Won't be boffing anybody else's wife, willya?" the big man snarled. Nygerski's ribs exploded with the impact of Ed's foot. The world became a swirling carousel of agony.

He heard the knife clatter to the pavement, and Ed's footsteps as he ran away. Then other footsteps—his friends, he realized. His friends had seen it all. The bulbs of the streetlamps and the full Moon circled and bobbed in the purple sky above him; somewhere far away, a car engine roared into life and tires squealed. And then suddenly Cassandra was there, cradling his face in her arms, blood—his blood—soaking her jeans and shirt. Her face contorted and would not stay in focus.

He heard Sammy's footsteps as the guitarist ran up to them, panting. "He's gone, the fucker. Blue and white car, like a Dodge or something. Didn't see the license plate."

"Find a phone!" Cassandra cried, her voice high-pitched with panic. "Get an ambulance!" She turned back to Nygerski. "Hold on, Cyrus, help is coming. You're going to be okay."

But Nygerski knew he was dying. Cassandra grabbed his hand and squeezed hard. Already he felt cold, numb—and strangely, the pain was not so terrible. It was as though he was observing it from outside himself; yes, that hurt, but wasn't that interesting? He tasted warm wetness at the back of his mouth. He knew he was leaving his body.

The sky turned from deep blue to oscillating patterns of black, white, and red. Peripheral vision faded and was gone. Cassandra leaned close to him, pressed her hands against the awful wound in his chest, her face inches from his. He managed to smile at her.

"At least . . ." He tried to cough, but produced only a thick gurgle. In another minute he wouldn't be able to talk at all.

"Sssh. It's going to be okay."

"At least I . . . I went out . . . like . . . Ted Williams."

Cassandra lay a bloody hand against his cheek, shook her head. "Hang on, love," she pleaded. "Sammy's gone to get help. You've got to hang on!"

But he knew it was too late. The abstract patterns of brilliant reds swallowed the sky, the trees, and the parking lot. Nygerski could see a stream of his own blood flowing away from him along a crack in the parking lot's surface. He saw his own hands spread out on the asphalt at the ends of his arms, hands that would never hold a baseball bat—or a woman—again. He saw his whole life, as it had been, and as it could have been.

And then all he could see was Cassandra.

23.

THE END OF THE DREAM

I saw the throw on TV. I remember that day with stark clarity, for it was the end of summer, and of my childhood.

The fog had been in that morning when I woke, dressed, and walked to the main house for breakfast. I could barely make out the sloped roofline of the Near Cabin against the shrouded trees; the Far Cabin, up at the bend in the road, was invisible. Out on the bay I could hear the sonorous moan of a foghorn and the chiming of the bell buoy beyond the ledge. Uncle Bill and most of the lobstermen had stayed in, because it was Sunday, and the televised doubleheader provided extra disincentive to work. Fog never deterred them, but religion and baseball did.

By early afternoon it had cleared enough so that the point and the nearby islands were visible. But no one thought of work or outdoor recreation. The wind had backed around to the east, a direction it never blew unless we were going to have bad weather. It was the one direction from which the cove was not protected. Uncle Bill's boat bobbed on its mooring as angry green waves, chopped into irregular pieces by the ledges, washed ashore. The fog never left entirely, but lingered about a mile off, behind the nearby islands, a portent of unrest.

Wendy Woolf went out to the Far Cabin to paint, and my mom and

Mary Granger prepared Sunday dinner in the kitchen. Elroy went out to the shed, where he was working on a miniature wooden sailboat he planned to launch before the end of the summer. The rest of us watched the game.

"They're playing scared," my father said, just before the ninth inning. "They're playing not to lose." I looked at him crossly. I was equally annoyed with Elroy, who had steeled himself against pain by erecting a wall of indifference. What was wrong, I thought, in all my righteous ten-year-old innocence, with hope for its own sake? Even if that hope were eventually to be cruelly dashed, wouldn't something of its memory shine on, to be taken out later, dusted off, and admired? Wasn't it better to dream than to plan? Never mind that dreams do not come true. There is something pure in the dreams themselves that outlasts anything reality can dish out. Or so I thought in August of 1967.

My father went out to the kitchen to get a beer. When he came back, he didn't sit down, but stood in the doorway, shifting his weight from one foot to the other. We all saw the play. A fly ball to Tartabull in right, the runner breaking from third at the instant of the catch. The throw to the plate—too high, too high! Catcher Mike Ryan stretching up to get it. The sweeping tag, a split second too late. The runner sliding in. The umpire's safe call.

"No!" Jim and Alex and Andy and I were on our feet in front of the television, leaning in, as if our disbelief could travel faster than the speed of light and change the outcome of the play. On the screen, Dick Williams was in the umpire's face, and the White Sox were celebrating.

"Ah, Christ," my father said.

The replay was inconclusive. They didn't have a zillion cameras in the ballpark, like they do these days, and you couldn't see whether or not the catcher had made the tag in time. But I clung to my indignation. "He was out by a *mile*," I said.

"Son, the throw was high," my father said in a maddeningly adult voice. "Tartabull's throw was high. A good throw would've gotten him."

"Stupid ump," I mumbled bitterly. How could my father be so calm? The Red Sox *needed* this game. It was an outrage to have it ripped away by one lousy call.

My father shook his head and looked at the floor. I knew he wanted the Red Sox to win, too, but I hated him at that moment for being such a pessimist, and for being right. He had jinxed the game with his predictions of doom. When the Red Sox went down in order in the top of the tenth, he left the room and went outside, without a word to anyone.

The fog had edged back in a little, so that no islands were visible beyond the point. I could see the top of the apple tree outside the living room window dancing in the wind, and a few leaves came off and flew away.

In the eleventh inning the first few drops of rain spattered against the windows, and the wind rattled the loosely fitting door on the side of the house facing the cove. Wisps of fog scooted across the field in front of us, wrestling with smoke from the chimney pushed toward the ground by the downdrafts. The door on the other side of the house banged open and closed, and Elroy, his face like a ghost's, appeared in the living room.

He hadn't come from the shed, for droplets of water glistened atop his short, curly hair, and he was breathing hard, like he had just been running. He came directly over to my chair, pulled on my sleeve. "Timmy, I've got to tell you something."

"What?" I had been annoyed with him lately, for abandoning our mutual passion for the Red Sox and the pennant race. We didn't keep statistics anymore, and if I wanted to play a game of baseball darts I had to cajole Andy or Alex, neither of whom were as good or as enthusiastic as Elroy had been. At least they didn't tell me it was only a game, or turn disdainfully to a book when we tuned in the broadcasts in the Red Cabin. I had hoped he would get over it, but it had been a week now since we'd returned from Boston, and he continued to ignore baseball almost completely, even as everybody else jumped aboard the band-wagon.

His eyes had a wild, haunted look, and he was clearly agitated, shifting his weight from foot to foot. "Not here," he said in a fierce whisper, and tugged at my sleeve again.

I stayed in my chair and flashed him a look of exasperation. "What's wrong with you?" I snapped at him.

"Come on outside for a minute," he said urgently, in that same quiet, too intense voice. A quick sweep of his dark eyes took in everybody else in the room, like a cat calculating an efficient escape. "It's important."

"So's this game," I replied, nodding at the television. The White Sox were batting in the bottom of the eleventh; two out, nobody on.

"I know," Elroy said, surprising me with the acknowledgment. "But not as important as what's out in the Far Cabin." He whispered this last bit of information through his teeth, and flicked his eyes toward his older brother, desperate to make certain that he had not been over-heard. Jim stared at the TV screen, oblivious to Elroy's presence. Nobody else paid any attention to him, either.

But he was scared, I realized suddenly. I remembered April, and the deer in the woods by our fort. Had he seen another deer? Or something worse, perhaps? As upset as I was with him, he was still my best friend, he had seen something that had profoundly disturbed him, and he had come to me. I owed him my loyalty. Heaving a sigh, I got up out of the chair and let him lead me into the dining room, where the rattling door led to the outside.

A blast of wind rattled the chandelier as he opened it. My mom peered out from the kitchen. "Is the game over?" she asked.

"Nope," I said quickly. "Still tied."

"Where are you boys going? It's raining out."

"It's just sprinkling," I said as Elroy grabbed my sleeve and pulled me out the door.

"Well, don't be gone long. Food's almost ready."

"This better be good," I said to Elroy as I followed him around the side of the house. "What's going on? What's in the Far Cabin?"

He turned, stopped, and looked at me seriously. "Your dad," he said. "And my mom."

Somewhere in the distance I heard the faint rumbling of thunder.

"They're in the Far Cabin," I said. "So what?"

"*Together,*" Elroy said meaningfully. Heavy drops of rain, real drops, began to fall. Elroy led me down the dirt road toward the cabin. I became aware that the hair on my arms was standing on end. "Listen, I saw your dad go up there. I was bored with working on my boat, anyway, so I went for a walk. When I passed the Far Cabin, I could hear them . . ."

There was a flash of lightning somewhere out over the water. "What do you mean, you could hear them?" I asked.

Elroy's face was pained. "That cot squeaks." He paused. "And I could hear them, you know, moaning."

Another clap of thunder, this one much closer. The rain intensified. We were past the Near Cabin by now. I stared at my friend in horror. "You mean, they were . . . ?"

Elroy bit his lower lip and nodded.

"Bullshit!" I cried. "You drag me away from a tie game, out into the rain, to tell me *this*? My dad's having sex with your mom? Fuck you, Elroy! Get away from me!" I turned to go back to the house. Water dripped from my hair.

He grabbed my arm. "Don't believe me? Go look. I did."

"Don't touch me!" I yanked my arm away savagely.

"Your dad's not watching the game, is he?"

"No," I said, looking at the muddy ground at my feet.

"Go ahead. Look."

We were steps from the cabin now. Elroy led me through the bushes around toward the back. Another bolt of lightning lit the gray sky. "One, two," I counted, before the crack of thunder. The storm was nearly on top of us now. I was soaked, but I didn't care. We crouched by the back of the cabin. Slowly, I raised my head to one of the gaps in the wall.

My father was sitting on the side of the cot, buttoning his shirt. He had his pants on, but he was barefoot. Wendy Woolf lay in the bed, the dark green blanket pulled up to her chin. Her clothes were draped over the back of the rocking chair. A cigarette burned in the ashtray on the bedside table. Wendy propped herself up on her elbows and reached out a bare arm for it. I could see the rounded side of her breast above the edge of the blanket. "My goodness," she said. "That storm's getting closer."

"What did I tell you?" Elroy whispered beside me.

There was another clap of thunder. My father and Elroy's mother looked at one another, and silent laughter passed between them. I wished that the next bolt of lightning would strike the cabin and burn it the ground, with them in it. "I'd better go," my father said.

Water ran freely from the back of my neck as I lowered myself from the side of the cabin. Elroy was soaked, too. "Let's get out of here," I said. Shivering, he nodded.

We clawed through the low bushes behind the cabin back to the road. Lightning lit the sky as we started to run toward the house.

Suddenly my mother appeared on the doorstep. "Tim! Elroy!" she called. Then, spotting us: "What on Earth are you doing out here? Get out of the rain and come eat!"

She ducked back inside the house, and Elroy and I looked at each other with something close to relief, and slowed to a jog. But a moment later she was back, underneath a yellow rain slicker with a hood, walking purposefully to meet us.

"Where have you boys *been* in this weather?" she said crossly as she approached us. "And what've you been up to? I can tell by your faces you've been up to something."

"It's nothing, Mrs. Paine," Elroy said, and that was a mistake. The kids always called the grown-ups at the cove by their first names. Only in moments of distress did we revert to formality.

"We just went to check on our fort," I said. But Mom wasn't buying it. She was never one to take comfort in ignorance. She looked from one to the other of us, there in the rain, knowing that we were hiding something from her. I felt like someone standing onshore watching a sailboat plow toward a reef, too far away to yell out a warning. This was it, I thought. This was the end of summer. Of all summers. With all of my will I avoided glancing over my shoulder at the Far Cabin.

But the rain had abated a little, just enough for all of us to hear the door to the Far Cabin open and close. And my mother looked beyond us and we turned, and there was my father on the path, head down, buttoning the top buttons of his flannel shirt against the wind and the wet. He hadn't seen us.

My mother put a hand on each of our shoulders and gently pushed us apart. She stepped between us, then took a few more steps up the road, to meet my father. There was nothing Elroy and I could do but stand helplessly to the side. "Clayton!" she called. He was close enough now that she did not have to yell. "What are you doing?"

He saw her and he stopped. Just stopped. Had he blurted out a confession right then and there it would not have more clearly telegraphed his guilt. My mother stopped, too, and looked at her husband, and at the cabin where Wendy Woolf practiced her art. A bolt of lightning split the sky somewhere behind them, and a few seconds later the accompanying thunder rolled in. The storm was moving off, but it had already done its damage.

My mother turned to Elroy and me. "You boys go back to the house. Everybody else is eating. And put on some dry clothes. I need to have a word with your father."

"Let's all go eat," my father suggested, too easily, as he walked up to us. "Jordana, listen—"

My mother whirled on him. "Don't you move," she said. "I want to talk to you out here. Tim, Elroy, go. You're soaked."

"It's raining," my father said inanely. He was hardly wet at all.

"Go!" my mother said to us. We knew she meant it. We went. As we hurried toward the shelter of the house, though, I looked back and saw my mother leading my father back to the Far Cabin. My father seemed to be hanging back a little bit.

"What do you think's gonna happen?" Elroy asked me.

"Dunno. Maybe she'll kill them both." I felt miserable. I suspected Elroy didn't feel any better, but he never said he was sorry for showing me what he'd shown me. I had no clear idea what ramifications this afternoon would have, what it would mean for the direction of our lives. But I knew that things had irrevocably changed, and not for the better.

The thunderstorm had knocked out the electricity—probably a tree limb had crashed across a power line or something. That happened a lot on Deer Isle. Everyone had moved into the big dining room to eat, and Mary Granger had lit candles and a kerosene lantern against the dark, stormy sky outside. There was no more thunder, but it continued to rain softly, and the wind hummed through the trees and the gaps in the old house. It was not loud enough to cover the sound of my mother's voice, audible all the way from the Far Cabin through closed doors and windows as she screamed at my father and Wendy, though we could not make out more than a few of the words. We spoke very little. No one mentioned the baseball game.

In a few minutes Wendy Woolf came in and went directly upstairs to her bedroom. My mother came in as we were finishing supper and took Mary Granger aside. By this time it had stopped raining, and the clouds were moving off. The power had not come back on. Mary enlisted her older daughter's help cleaning the kitchen and suggested that we boys go down to the beach to check on the boats. They would need bailing, at least, she said, after the downpour. We recognized it for what it was—a ploy to get us out of the house—but we also knew that it was more than a suggestion. My father had not returned at all.

When we got back, my mother had two suitcases by the door. She walked with me, alone, to the Red Cabin and kissed me on the fore-head. "I'm going to go visit your grandparents for a few days," she said. "Mary will drive me to the airport. Your father's over at Uncle Bill's, but he'll be back this evening. Be good, and do what he says."

"Are you coming back, Mom?" I was trying like hell not to cry.

"Yes, I'll be back," she said, kneeling down and holding me by the shoulders. "Your father and I have some decisions to make. I love you, Tim."

She wrapped her arms around me and held me for a long time. And despite my attempt at bravery, I felt the tears like big marbles rolling down my cheeks, onto my mother's shirt. Neither of us tried to stop them.

The power remained off all night. It wasn't until the next morning that we learned that the Red Sox had lost both games of the double-header, and that Cyrus Nygerski was dead.

24.

THE FALL

Ted Williams hit a home run in his last at-bat. Hoyt Wilhelm, the famed knuckleball pitcher, homered the first time he came to the plate in a big-league game, played for twenty more years, and never hit another one. But Cyrus "Moondog" Nygerski is the only man in baseball history to hit a home run in his first, last, and *only* plate appearance.

I suppose it would mean more today had the White Sox won the American League pennant in 1967. But they didn't. Detroit backed in on the season's final day when the Red Sox knocked off Minnesota. I didn't even watch the World Series.

My mother didn't return from Ohio. She filed for divorce and custody, and after Christmas I went to live with her. The Woolfs also got a divorce, as did the Grangers. Three for three.

My father and Bob Woolf sold out their shares of Rum Runners Cove to Mary Granger, who won her husband's share of the property in their divorce in exchange for joint custody of the kids. Her name isn't Mary Granger anymore. She remarried a man with an unpronounceable Russian name, and they now spend half their time in Europe. The cove is mostly rental property, although they go there occasionally. Uncle Bill built his lobster pound. It thrived for a while, but a few years ago Bill Jr., filed for bankruptcy. The Green Cabin was finally torn down, like the Near and Far Cabins before it. You can't see the water from the ledge anymore.

I don't get back to Maine much. My dad moved his law practice to Ellsworth, forty-odd miles from Deer Isle, and bought a modest place with a view of a small lake. He's retired now, though he still takes on a case occasionally, as a favor to a friend. He got married, divorced, and married again. His third wife died two years ago. My mom's remarried and still lives in Ohio.

But all that lay far in the future on the day my sister Cassandra returned to Rum Runners Cove following the death of Cyrus Nygerski, or "Moondog," as the papers were calling him. The Grangers had left and the Woolfs were leaving. Things were pretty awkward among the adults. Bob Woolf was back. I don't know if he knew about my dad and Wendy—I don't know if he ever found out, actually—but my dad and Wendy knew, and that kind of guilt is hard to keep away from the dinner table once you've invited it in to eat. There weren't any more songs at night, and the gatherings around the radio in the kitchen became unenthusiastic affairs that petered out early. The Red Sox went into a losing streak from which they never recovered.

My sister's arrival was the punctuation on a sentence of sadness—for the pennant race, for the young man murdered in front of her, for the summer now ending, and for our lives that would never be quite so idyllic. For my childhood. She spoke very little and no one really knew what to say to her. She moved her few belongings into the Green Cabin. She took long, solitary walks along the shore. She told my father she would return to the university.

And on her second day home, a day after the Woolfs' long and somewhat strained departure, Cassandra announced that she wanted to see Aunt Polly.

Of course I went with her. It was too lonely at the cove, too strange. The three of us—me in the Red Cabin, my father alone in that drafty and echoing house, Cassandra down by the shore in the Green Cabin with her candles and tapestries—had all slept badly. An autumn wind had kicked up from the northwest, moaning through ill-fitting boards and the creeping trees. I had tried to fall asleep to the Red Sox game, an excruciating loss that dropped them three games out of first and didn't end until midnight, but sleep would not come. My father had bags under his eyes and hadn't combed his hair. Cassandra looked like she hadn't slept in days.

Aunt Polly welcomed my sister and me with cocoa and cookies. She didn't have a phone, and we never announced our visits beforehand, but she never reacted with surprise when we showed up. I had seen her only a couple of times all summer, and we hadn't really talked since that day in April when Cyrus Nygerski had been among us.

"Well, Cassandra, what will your father do now?" Aunt Polly said after we were settled in her living room.

"I don't know," my sister said, gazing out to sea. The stiff offshore wind had cleared away any vestige of translucent moisture; you could see all the way to the horizon between the islands. "I don't think he even knows."

"He's certainly made a mess of things, hasn't he?"

"Yes. He has."

Aunt Polly rocked back and forth twice, the runners squeaking on the hardwood floor. "And he's not the only one. Is he?"

Cassandra stared into the bottom of her cup. "No," she murmured, barely audible.

"I'm sorry," Aunt Polly said, after another long pause, "about your young man."

Cassandra didn't raise her eyes. "Me, too," she whispered.

Aunt Polly got to her feet and moved to take Cassandra's cup, and mine. She moved slowly but without the painful stiffness one associates with old people; she seemed to get around the small house quite easily. "More cocoa?" she said to me.

"Please," I replied, handing her my cup. I wanted to say something about

Nygerski, too, that I was also sorry that he was dead, and that his death had hurt my sister, perhaps dealing her a wound from which she would not recover. But I couldn't find the words. And words were all I had. Aunt Polly and Cassandra seemed to be able to communicate on a deeper level, a level that was and would forever be beyond me. The years have taught me that language, as versatile and descriptive as it is, can be limiting.

"What will you do?" Aunt Polly asked Cassandra as we sipped our fresh cocoa. She pushed gently on the floor with her foot, rocking the chair slowly back and forth.

I looked from one woman to the other, expecting Cassandra to tell Aunt Polly, as she had told my father, that she would return to the university to complete her degree. But that wasn't what Aunt Polly meant, and Cassandra knew it.

My sister looked up from the mug of hot chocolate at my aunt, who rocked easily in her chair, waiting for an answer. "Do?" my sister said.

Aunt Polly nodded. "You realize that you have a choice. With all its attendant costs."

It was as though I was no longer in the room. Their eyes locked—my sister's crystalline, shattered-glass blue that seemed to shine with a light of their own, and Aunt Polly's, the roiled, ever-changing aquamarine shade of the Maine sea. "I do," Cassandra said. Some sort of silent affirmation passed between them, and then Cassandra abruptly stood up, cup in hand, and walked to the big window.

"The world is so beautiful," she said, looking out at the harbor, the birds, and the wind-driven whitecaps between the islands. "So beautiful, and so sad."

"We make our own worlds," Aunt Polly said. "The trouble is, we then have to live in them."

School started the following week. The weather remained clear but autumn-chilly. I moved most of my things out of the Red Cabin and took up residence in the house, in the Grangers' room. I had lived in the

Woolfs' room the previous winter, but somehow, now, that seemed too painful. My father didn't say a word about my choice.

The fall semester started at the University of Maine, but Cassandra did not enroll. My father asked her about it once at dinner, but she said, "Maybe in the winter, Daddy. Right now I just need some time." He didn't pressure her. Something inside him had changed, too.

We got the newspaper every day, and sometimes in the evenings my father and I watched the news on TV. We followed the escalation of the war in Vietnam, the racial unrest in the cities, and the slow fade of the Red Sox from the top of the standings. Cassandra didn't seem to care about any of it. She went to see Aunt Polly several times a week, and when she was home she mostly kept to herself, taking long walks or holing up in the Green Cabin. My father suggested several times that she move into the house, as the nights were growing cold and the Green Cabin had no heat and it was getting near time to haul the boats besides, but my sister put him off. She wanted her space.

I worried about her. The spirited, headstrong sister who had left in April had returned as a much older woman struck stone-cold by grief. Nygerski's death weighed heavily upon her, as if she somehow had been responsible. She drank beer by herself down in her cabin, bagged up the cans meticulously, and brought them up to the house to be thrown away. She helped with the chores and kept the cabin clean. We talked on occasion, and she told me about her summer, but only in anecdotes, in detached vignettes that could have been told in the third person, so stripped were they of emotion. This worried me most of all, for my sister Cassandra lived in a world of emotion. Something inside her, something that made her who she was, had died with Cyrus Nygerski in that parking lot in Chicago.

A storm blew in on the autumnal equinox, bringing rain and tearing one of the small sailboats loose from the outhaul and driving it up on the rocks. My father examined the damage to the hull and told Cassandra that it was past time to get the boats out of the water, and that she would have to abandon the Green Cabin that week. Cassandra accepted the news without protest; her rebelliousness, too, had fallen victim to the jealous husband's knife.

Clear, cold air moved in behind the storm. I didn't see how Cassandra could stand it down there in the Green Cabin, but she piled on extra blankets and said she would sleep there until we hauled the boats that weekend. The tides would help us, because Friday night was full Moon.

When I got out of school on Friday, I helped Cassandra haul her stuff up to the house and put it in the Woolfs' room. She had already taken down most of the decorations in the Green Cabin, and I was a little surprised—usually the tapestries stayed up over the winter, surrounding the boats. But Cassandra told me she didn't plan to sleep there again. "Don't tell Daddy, but I'm going back to San Francisco," she said.

"You are?" I was stunned. "I thought you were going back to school."

"I'll go in California, if I go," she said. "I can't bear it here, with all the ghosts."

"So you're going to leave, just like that?" I cried. "For good?" Suddenly Rum Runners Cove had grown several orders of magnitude more lonely. "What about your family?"

"If you haven't noticed, the family's disintegrating. All three families." Her eyes swept the empty cabin. "Daddy's dreams—they're just that. They're not gonna happen."

Silence fell between us. "When will you go?" I asked her.

"Next week. As soon as I can get on a bus." She smiled at me thinly, compassionately. "Look, Timmy, I'll write; I'll call. You and Mom can visit me. Dad'll never leave Maine, we both know that. He's in love with his illusions. Mom couldn't take it. Neither can I."

"It's so far away," I said. "California."

Cassandra laughed and touched my shoulder. How I loved her! "It's only far away if you think it is," she said. "The Moon's a lot farther, and people are going to go there soon. We have our lives to live, Timmy."

And then she did something that both shocked and delighted me. She put her arms around me and held me to her for a long moment. I returned the embrace, fiercely. I couldn't remember the last time she had hugged me. I knew this hug would have to last a long time.

"Promise me one thing," she said when she let me go.

"What?"

Her crystal eyes stared intently into mine. "Stay inside tonight. Don't go out, no matter what happens."

"What? Why?"

"I can't tell you," she said. Her hands were on my shoulders; her eyes would not let me go. "Just promise me you won't go out, okay?"

I tried to look away, but her eyes pulled me back. "It's important, Tim. Promise me you'll stay inside. Please."

"Okay," I said. "I promise."

PART THREE

SEPTEMBER

25.

MENDOCINO, CALIFORNIA, 1995

The cabin sat back from the cliffs, surrounded by trees, out of sight but within earshot of the pounding surf. A mailbox painted blue with a yellow crescent Moon and a handful of stars marked the head of the long dirt driveway that had led him there. The woman was tending a small herb garden in back, bent from the waist in her green jeans and red-plaid flannel shirt, a loose strand of dark hair hanging down outside the ponytail into which she had gathered it. She looked up when she heard his footsteps, and he saw that her face had aged but the eyes were the same. He saw recognition and knowledge in them, but not surprise. She straightened slowly, brushing the wayward hair aside with a gloved hand, and waited for him to come to her.

"Cyrus 'Moondog' Nygerski," she said softly. "I always knew you'd come walking down that road someday." They had not seen each other for twenty-eight years.

"Hello, Cassandra," he replied, and waited for her to invite him in.

She made herb tea and served it to him in a red-patterned china cup at the square table in the cabin's kitchen. The place was small and sparsely furnished, with beamed wooden ceilings and hardwood floors. A long string of garlic hung beside the refrigerator. The walls were ringed with dried herbs, and the place smelled of wood smoke and sage. It was a warm day, but little sunlight penetrated the cabin between the trees. In the main room, above the fireplace, Nygerski noted a Winslow Homer painting depicting a slickered fisherman in a dory on the green Atlantic. The built-in shelves were filled with hardcover volumes and a few figurines; a spherical crystal the size of a grapefruit, mounted on a metal stand, seemed to have a prominent place. The door to the bedroom was open; he saw that the double bed had been neatly made up that morning.

"It took me three years to find you," he said.

"And twenty-five to start looking," she answered him, looking into his eyes. She wore glasses now, oval wire-rims with one lens much thicker than the other. But the eyes were the same shattered-crystal blue he remembered. He would have recognized them anywhere.

"Your name's not Cassandra Paine anymore."

"No." She looked down into her tea, swirled it around in the bottom of her cup, a twin to his. "I've had a lot of names," she said. "Tom is my fourth husband."

"You're married," he said.

She nodded.

"Where is he? At work?"

She nodded again. "He's a forest ranger," she said. "He's away for days, sometimes weeks at a time. Right now he's up in Oregon. He makes good money. I keep the house, and when he comes home I cook for him and take care of his needs. It's a pretty good arrangement." She looked up at him and smiled. "I'm hard on men on a daily basis."

She was still pretty, though age had worked some erosion around the edges. The long dark hair was streaked with white; if she kept it long, in old age she could wear it in silvery braids that much younger women would envy. She was skinnier than he remembered, though the simple woodsy clothes she wore were not designed to show off curves. There were lines around her eyes and mouth. Her teeth were still spectacularly crooked, and the smile showed flashes of its former brilliance, though she did not smile as widely or as readily.

"Do you know why I started looking for you?" he asked.

"Are you going to make me guess?"

He laid his hands on the table, palms down. He had long, aristocratic fingers, kept nimble by playing a guitar. The index fingers were almost as long as the middle digits, and the fingernail on his right index finger was entirely black. A bluish bruise was visible beneath the corresponding fingernail on his left hand.

"Oh, no," she whispered.

He looked into her crystalline eyes, held them with his own, watched for the subtle change of color that would betray her emotions. He had never seen eyes like hers. They were blue kaleidescopes, a thousand shifting pieces of nuance more mysterious than the evening sky. He saw pain in them now as she stared back at him.

"Cyrus, how did it happen?"

"There was some trouble a few years ago," he told her. "In a small town near where I lived, in the southern part of the state. People turning up dead on the full Moon. Dead in horrible ways. I tried to help."

She digested this information in silence for several seconds. "And you knew what it was, of course," she murmured. "Because of what happened in nineteen sixty-seven."

"I didn't believe you," he said. "But now I know that you always told me the truth, even when you contradicted yourself. He bit me, Cassandra. And anyone who is bitten by a werewolf and lives—"

"Becomes a werewolf." She laid her hands out on the table, inches from his. Both fingernails on her index fingers were black, and the fingers themselves were actually longer than either the ring or middle finger. Nygerski noticed that she was not wearing a wedding ring.

He placed his hands over hers. "You're still . . . after all this time . . . Cassandra, is there no way to remove the curse? Are we stuck with this forever?"

She withdrew her hands from his, pushed back her chair, and went to the stove to pour more tea. "Do you want some?" she asked.

"No, I'm fine. Cassandra—"

"It rains here a lot," she said, returning to her chair. "I'm not affected every month. And there aren't a lot of people around."

"But you tried," he said. "You tried to undo the curse. And if I hadn't gotten in the way, you might have succeeded."

Cassandra sipped her tea. "Yes, but at what cost? Everything costs something." Her eyes studied his face. "How much do you remember?"

"Some," he said. "Most of it, I think. But it's bits and pieces, and I'm not sure after all this time what's memory and what's imagination. Do you remember the baseball game we went to?"

"Which one?" she asked over the rim of her mug.

"The one in Chicago. You gave me a tab of acid."

She smiled thinly, her lips closed, and nodded.

"Do you still take LSD?"

"I don't do *any* drugs," she said. "I don't need to."

"There was a play at the plate," he said. "Somehow, everything revolves around that. José Tartabull, a reserve outfielder who never did anything else at all noteworthy in his career, threw out the tying run at home to end the game. Elston Howard was the catcher. He'd come over from the Yankees a few weeks earlier. Tartabull's throw was high, but Elston Howard blocked the plate and made the tag."

Cassandra sat silently, listening to him.

"But that's not what I remember," Nygerski said, leaning forward. "I mean, that's what I remember *now*, because that's the way it happened. Diehard Red Sox fans *still* talk about it. But I was *there*, Cassandra. And Elston Howard wasn't the catcher. And the runner was safe."

"Go on," she said.

"Well . . . if Elston Howard doesn't make the play, and the runner scores, the Red Sox don't win the game. They don't win the pennant. The storybook season doesn't have its storybook ending. And . . ."

"Yes?" she prodded him when he hesitated.

"And a lot of other stuff doesn't happen."

"A lot of other stuff," she agreed.

"But maybe that's not such a bad thing," he said emotionally. He grabbed her hands in his own, ran his thumbs over the blackened fingernails on the elongated fingers. "Maybe *this* didn't have to happen."

She made no move to pull her hands away. "It's way too late," she said softly. "It was already too late, even then. I wish I'd known that. I wish"—she shook her head and looked away—"No. What's done is done. I've made peace with it, Moondog. You should try to."

"But you could have changed it," he insisted. "You knew how. You could have spared yourself all this." His eyes made a quick tour of the cabin. "This reclusive existence, hiding from the full Moon. You could have lived a normal life, if not for me. It would have been hard on Red Sox fans like that old man next to us at the game. No pennant on the last day of the season, no wonderful memories . . . but was it worth it? To you?"

"It's not such a bad life," she said. "And I didn't do it for the Red Sox."

Another curtain of silence fell between them. He parted it and stepped through. "Do you ever go back to Maine?" he asked her.

"No. Not for years. This is my home now."

"I think about Alaska," he said. "All that emptiness."

She sipped her tea. "Tell me," she said. "What do your friends call you? Do they call you Moondog?"

"Most of them, yeah."

"And do you ever tell them how you got the name?"

"No."

"Why not?"

"It's lost in the mists of time," he said, grinning uncomfortably. He looked down into his empty cup. "And besides, I doubt that any of them would believe me. I'm not sure I believe it, myself. I mean, it wasn't real."

"Oh, yes it was. You remember it. Why else would you have come?"

He stared into his cup and shook his head. "It was so long ago," he said. "It seems almost surreal now. I forgot for years and years and years. Until . . . this." He held up the hand with the black fingernail. "Then the dreams started. Only they didn't seem like dreams. . . ."

She pushed back her chair and stood up. "Let's walk down by the water," she said. "There's a bench there, at the top of the cliffs. We can talk some more. We have a lot of catching up to do."

The waves crashed far below them, against rocks that had fallen to the base of the cliff several earthquakes ago. Dwarf spruce trees, their tops flattened by the wind, surrounded the tiny grassy area and the bench someone had constructed there of silvered limbs that had once belonged to the forest behind them before becoming driftwood. The tall trees that surrounded Cassandra's cabin shied back from this small point, and they could see a little ways up and down the rocky coast, as well as out to sea, to the Earth's horizon. The Sun was in the west, on their faces, and they were warm despite the wind.

"Do you remember the day we met?" she asked him.

"In the Beloit bus station—"

"The morning of the game," she affirmed.

"Yes," he said. "We were strangers. But we weren't, really. I had the overpowering feeling that we'd met before, that we'd . . . interacted. Because we had, hadn't we?"

She nodded. "Yes," she replied. "But not in this life."

"What do you mean?"

"We *had* met before. In another time line."

He stared out into the empty Pacific, trying to fathom this. "That baseball game. . ."

Cassandra laughed gently. "You were quite the baseball player once," she said. "It was poetry, the way you played."

"Oh, come off it, Cassandra. I sucked. I got released after less than one full season."

She shook her head but kept the shadow of the smile. "All you lacked was belief in yourself," she said.

"That and about a hundred and fifty points in my batting average."

"You used to tell me how exacting a game baseball is," she countered. "You talked about the thin line that separates success from failure. About how baseball needs hundreds of games to determine who the best teams are. And how the best team doesn't always win."

"That's true," he acknowledged. "Like the seventy-eight Red Sox. Cassandra, don't you ever miss Maine? I mean, this is a pretty spot, right here, but compared to where you're from—"

"Every day," she said seriously. "I miss it every day. But there's such a thing as fate, Cyrus, even though we sometimes have the power to change it. I've accepted mine. You need to accept yours."

"You're talking in riddles," he told her.

"Complicated questions don't have simple answers."

"So you never think about going back?"

"And reliving my past? I did that once, and it didn't turn out the way I wanted. The cost proved to be too high."

"There was another game," he said. "In New York, at the beginning of the season."

Cassandra nodded. "The no-hitter," she said.

"Except it wasn't. Elston Howard singled with two out in the ninth to break it up. It's too bad, because it would have been a great story. Kid throws no-hitter in first big-league game. But it didn't happen."

Cassandra looked out at the ocean and said nothing.

"And that means everything else I think I remember is faulty, too," he continued. "No trip to Maine, no chase through the streets of New York, no stellar season. No love affair. None of it really happened."

"Oh, yes it did," Cassandra said.

"Your aunt's story about the hole in the ocean—"

"Real," Cassandra asserted. "It really is a time portal. I know; I went through it."

"Come on, Cassandra. Time travel is—"

"I know," she said, holding up her hand. "Impossible, because of the paradoxes. You can go back and change history into something you then couldn't go back and change. But that's a linear, logical way of looking at it. Maybe it's not the right way. Do you know anything about quantum physics?"

He drew a short distance away from her on the bench and studied her face. "Do *you?*"

Her crooked teeth gleamed in the sunlight. "I've been doing some reading," she said. "Don't look at me like that. I've got lots of time to read. And why shouldn't I read about quantum physics, if the subject interests me?"

"It's just that I never thought of you as a scientist," he said.

"We were prejudiced against science back then," she said, "because science was coming up with new and better ways to ravage North Vietnam. Our parents' generation invented the atomic bomb. So we rebelled against it. Rejected math and science in favor of music and mysticism. Even the Moon landing, probably the greatest thing this country's ever done, was tainted by that attitude."

"So how does quantum physics relate to what happened to us in nineteen sixty-seven?"

"Two ways," she said. "You're familiar with the big bang theory of creation?"

"A bit, yeah."

"So you know that scientists are trying to explain the first milliseconds of the Universe, when all the matter in all the galaxies was supposedly compressed into a space smaller than the head of a pin?"

"I've heard something about it, yeah."

"Okay," Cassandra said, warming to the subject. "Now ask yourself how that can happen. Supposedly matter is made up of fundamental particles. People used to think the basic unit of matter was the atom. Then someone discovered that atoms are made up of electrons orbiting a tiny nucleus, with mostly empty space in between. If you strip away the electrons and smash all the nuclei together, you get incredibly dense material. A spoonful of it can weigh as much as a mountain. And astronomers have found stars, compressed by gravity, made up of this stuff. They're called neutron stars. If you compress a neutron star still further, you get a black hole, which is so dense, not even light can escape from it."

"Okay, but I still don't see what this has to do with—"

"I'm getting there," Cassandra interrupted him. "Some scientists think they've traced the beginning of the Universe back to ten to the minus forty-third of a second after the big bang. That's a decimal point, followed by forty-two zeroes, followed by a one."

"I know what it is," he said, astounded that he was getting a science lecture, here, on this bench overlooking the Pacific, from this woman.

"Okay, now think about this. What can happen in ten to the minus forty-third of a second? That isn't even enough time for light to travel the width of an atomic nucleus. What is time, really? It's a human invention, to measure the change in matter. The Earth revolves around the Sun and makes a year. It turns and creates a day. We divide the day into hours and minutes and fractions of a second to measure things that happen faster, like sports events and explosions. But if nothing changes, time becomes meaningless. Now they've discovered more fundamental units of matter within the atomic nucleus, but essentially, when you talk about a ray of light crossing the nucleus of an atom, you're talking about the fastest thing in the Universe interacting with the smallest thing in the Universe. What can change in that amount of time? Nothing."

"Okay," he said. "So what?"

"So it's wrong to think of time like a number line," she said. "You can't go infinitely dividing a second, adding more and more zeroes behind the decimal point, just like you can't infinitely divide an atom. Eventually you'll get down to electrons and quarks. If there's a basic unit of matter, doesn't there have to be a basic unit of time? Call it the moment, for lack of a better word. And if, at the beginning, all the matter in the Universe was gathered together, well, all moments had to be there, too."

Nygerski stared at her in silence for several million of those singular moments, too astonished to say anything as birds wheeled in the sky above them and waves crashed on the rocks.

Cassandra went on. "Now, in those poorly understood first few moments after the big bang, all kinds of exotic subatomic things were created. One of the things that should have happened is the formation of a whole bunch of tiny black holes—tiny in terms of the space they take up, but massive enough to distort space and time around them. And there's nothing to stop one of those little atom-sized black holes from flying around the Universe for billions of years, until it collides with something—like the Earth."

"The Hole," Nygerski murmured.

"Exactly! We used to speculate about how it got there—a two hundred-foot spot in a shallow tidal inlet. Do you remember my brother, Tim, thinking it was created by a meteorite? I didn't know or care anything about this stuff back then, but the more I think about it, the more I think my brother had the right idea. Only it wasn't a piece of rock and metal that hit Earth in that spot—it was a quantum black hole."

"And that would explain the time distortion," Nygerski said.

"Right! According to Einstein, any large mass curves space-time around it. So two moments that are normally months apart can be folded right next to each other."

Nygerski sat back on the bench and watched the birds, letting this sink in. "You've thought about this a lot, haven't you?" he said.

She laughed. "I've had a lot of time."

"But I still don't understand why what I seem to remember conflicts with what actually happened. I mean, if all these moments exist, folded around quantum black holes or not, doesn't Elston Howard *always* get the hit to break up the no-hitter? Isn't he *always* there, later in the season, after being traded to the Red Sox, to make the play at the plate on Tartabull's throw? The guy is either safe or out. He can't be both."

Cassandra shook her head. "Nothing is predetermined," she said. "How can it be? We're free people."

"But then how can both moments exist at the same time?"

"Well, there's another part of quantum physics that deals with that," she said. "Have you ever heard of the uncertainty principle?"

"You mean the theory that by observing something, we change what we observe?"

Cassandra nodded. "It turns out that you can precisely measure the position or velocity of an electron in its atomic orbit, but not both. Pinpoint the position, and you can't tell the velocity, and vice versa. Just by looking at it, we change where it is, or how fast it's moving."

"I've seen stuff about that," Nygerski said. "But it always seemed sort of pointless. Like the tree falling in the forest."

"Okay, put it another way. How is Elston Howard like an electron?"

Nygerski stared out to sea for several seconds. "Are you trying to tell me," he said, finally, "that what happened in nineteen sixty-seven depends on whether or not I observed it?"

"On *how* you observed it," Cassandra said. "On where you observed it from. On your point of view. It was all real, Moondog. Everything that happened, happened. What seems like a contradiction is only an alternative."

"But what about consequences? You change the past, you change the present and future as well. If Elston Howard doesn't get that hit, if you run out on the field and distract the pitcher so that he hits Howard instead, the Red Sox never trade for him, and he isn't there, later in the season, to catch Tartabull's throw. The kid can get his no-hitter, but it will cost his team the pennant."

"Among other things," she said quietly, and looked away.

Nygerski swallowed hard. "Your brother . . ."

Cassandra turned back to him and smiled, but there was pain in her eyes. "Aunt Polly used to tell me that everything has a cost. We pay for everything. Nothing comes cheap. Especially not our lives. Do your dreams tell you that, Moondog?"

"It was my fault, what happened to him."

"No. It was my choice. And choices have consequences."

"But . . . why?"

"Because I loved you," she said simply. Her hand reached for his along the bench; their fingers intertwined. For a long minute they stared out to sea, saying nothing.

"You killed Rhonda's husband," he remembered. "But in the other time line, he found out that I was screwing his wife. He followed us to Chicago, came after me with a knife . . ." Sudden recollection flooded Nygerski's mind. He clapped his hands over his mouth. "Oh, my God!"

"Yes," she said.

"In the other time . . . *he* killed *me*."

She managed a feral grin. "That, at least, should teach you not to mess around with married women."

"You came back to Beloit the night of my last game there, and the Moon was full. And you weren't a werewolf anymore."

"I know," she said.

"The man in San Francisco—"

She shook her head. "I was wrong about him. It was me all along."

"You went through the Hole. Like that sailor."

"Yes."

"To a time before you became a werewolf."

"It's very confusing," she said. "Do you remember Aunt Polly telling us about Jake Weed's excape from the Hole? He swam to the dinghy, she said. And you asked how he could do that, since he'd learned how to swim in the other time line, which hadn't happened yet. A good question, but it assumes that time is linear, that the laws of cause and effect are absolute. They aren't. Some things carry over from one time line to another. Like your name, Moondog."

"You're right," he said after a moment. "It is very confusing."

"You followed me to Deer Isle. Do you remember what happened there?"

He drew his hand away from hers and looked at the ground. "I've tried not to," he said.

"I've thought about you every day for twenty-eight years, Cyrus. I've wondered if there's another alternative time line in which we could have been together. But you died. You died, and I couldn't bear the thought that I had caused your death. That's why I went back through the Hole. It's enough for me, knowing that I gave you back your life."

"But at what cost, Cassandra?"

She smiled weakly. "One can never know that until after the fact," she said. She stood up. "Let's go back to the cabin. We still haven't talked about the rest of the story."

CHAPTER 26.

METAMORPHOSIS

On a breezy afternoon in late September 1967, Cyrus "Moondog" Nygerski steered the 1959 Ford Falcon he had bought with the last of his baseball money onto an unmarked rural road on Deer Isle, Maine, six miles past the bridge. He had never been to Deer Isle before, except by boat, yet he felt certain that this road was the right one. On the seat beside him was a map of Maine. The road wasn't on it.

He had been driving since morning, with a stop for lunch, and now maybe two hours of daylight remained. His mother had expressed mild surprise at his sudden departure and his destination, but they both knew it was time for him to get out of the house for a while. He had received a letter from the draft board earlier that week.

And he had to find her. He had to find out what the hell was going on. Why her face kept haunting his dreams, and why he woke up suddenly in the middle of the night, thinking in those first few seconds of wakefulness that he had to get down to the ballpark, that important people would be watching him. At other times he awoke in terror, envisioning the glint of moonlight off a silver knife blade. None of this had happened before he met the girl.

He remembered the name of the place—Rum Runners Cove. It

wasn't on any road map. He'd found it, finally, on a nautical chart at the Boston Public Library. It was on the eastern edge of Deer Isle, and if any road would lead him there, it had to be this one.

He'd listened to the Red Sox game on the way up, an 11–7 win in Baltimore. With a week left in the season, the team was tied for first place, and Boston was crazed, just crazed. He'd gone out to Fenway twice during his time at home and hadn't believed the change. Usually this time of year the team was battling for last, not first, and you could play Frisbee in the bleachers without hurting anyone. Now the old ballpark was packed to the rafters daily. He'd caught snatches of the game when he'd stopped for gas in Brunswick and again for a sandwich and a Coke outside of Camden. Pennant fever had penetrated to the hinterlands. Maybe Cassandra was right. Maybe they really were going to win.

The trees were resplendent in their autumn colors. Many of the fiery leaves had already fallen, and others were falling around him, for it was a windy day, with wisps of cirrus clouds in the cobalt blue. The road crossed a causeway with the ocean on either side. He knew he was close now. He would not need to ask for directions. His subconscious mind was leading him to her. He recognized everything. As though he had been here before, in another life.

It was the same with the dirt road, and the cabins, and finally the house, big and red and looking deserted. The Sun hovered over the trees behind him as he rounded the final curve. There was a station wagon parked next to a shed, and a newer cabin, painted red to match the house, beyond that. But he could see no sign of human activity. He parked the Falcon behind the station wagon and went to the door.

He paused. Would Cassandra answer the door herself? Would she be glad to see him? (Had she summoned him, somehow?) Or would he be met by a mother or a father, to whom he would have to explain himself? Nygerski sucked in his breath. He had made the drive, after all. And this had to be the place. It felt *right*. He knocked.

The door opened, and a boy of about ten or twelve peered out at him. "Hi," Nygerski said. "I'm looking for Cassandra Paine."

The boy stared at him. "She's probably down at the Green Cabin," he said. "That's where she spends most of her time since she got back. Who are you?"

"My name's Cyrus. And you must be . . . Cassandra's little brother."

"Tim," the kid said.

"Well, Tim, I need to find your sister. Can you show me the way to the Green Cabin?"

The kid frowned and looked over Nygerski's shoulder, into the Sun. "Cassandra made me promise I wouldn't go out tonight."

"Why?"

"She didn't say. She made it sound like it was important, though."

I'm sure she did, Nygerski thought. The same way she left me at the baseball game. Like it was matter of life and death. "Are your parents around?" he asked the kid.

The boy laughed shortly and bitterly. "My mom's in Ohio," he said. "My dad's over at Uncle Bill's, on the other side of the cove. He goes over there a lot, since my mom left."

Nygerski looked around at the trees and buildings. "It's still daylight," he said. "Show me the way to the Green Cabin."

"I'm not supposed to go out." The kid was still looking at him queerly, as if he was not sure Nygerski was really there. For a moment, Moondog wasn't sure of it, either.

"I think I could find it, if I had to," Nygerski said. "But it would be faster if you showed me."

The kid considered this for a moment, then said, "Okay. Let me grab a sweater. Here, you might as well come through the house." He moved away from the open door, and Nygerski stepped inside.

The kid led him through the small front room into a dining room dominated by a huge wooden table. There seemed to be no one else in the house. Windows looked out onto a field that sloped gently downward toward a row of spruce trees at the water's edge. A worn footpath ran down the center of the field, which needed mowing.

"Wait here," the kid said, and bounded up a set of stairs and out of sight.

It all seemed oddly familiar to Nygerski and, he had to concede to himself, just a tad frightening. He looked out the windows at the waning day and laughed nervously.

The kid reappeared, wearing a thick, off-white wool sweater. Nygerski had on a denim jacket with a lining, for it was late September and the New England evenings had grown cold. "Okay," he said, opening the door leading to the field. "Come on."

"Are you the only one here?" Moondog asked. "Cassandra told me there were a lot of kids around."

"The other two families are only here in the summer," Tim explained. "It's pretty busy around here for a couple of months. And then . . ." He swept his hand, dramatically taking in the scene around them, lit by the slanted rays of day's end. A few birds called to one another as they flew home to their roosts. "Most of the time it's pretty deserted. Right now it's just me and my Dad and Cassandra. And she's kept to herself a lot since she came back."

They ducked between two rows of trees and turned a shallow corner, emerging into a small field overlooking the cove. The cabin, slightly bowed in the middle and in need of a fresh coat of green paint after a summer's worth of sun, sat back from the bank against a clump of alders. The raspberry bushes that pushed up through the cracks in the porch had been cut back and needed to be cut back again. On the lumpy grass in front of the cabin lay a large rowing dinghy and two small fiberglass sailboats, their masts and rigging laid out beside them. The cabin's screen door flapped open and closed in the evening wind.

"Cassandra!" Tim called out as they approached.

There was no answer. They stepped up onto the porch and through the open door. The interior of the cabin was dim and spare. The windows were dusty, and the Sun by now had sunk behind the trees. Cassandra was not inside. Nygerski surveyed the small room. Several empty drawers had been pulled from a dresser and now lay on the floor. The small bookshelf had likewise been partially emptied. Books lay on the bed and the small table; a couple of them had also fallen to the floor. A wine bottle covered with dripping wax of many colors with a red candle thrust into its neck lay on its side on the bedside table. Next to the far wall an easel and a set of paints had not been put away. The picture clipped to the easel was not finished; the background of trees and water needed to be filled in, and the full Moon was still only a sketched circle. But Nygerski had no trouble recognizing the painting's central figure. It was a wolf.

"She didn't tell me she painted," Nygerski remarked. "That's rather lifelike."

"She just took it up," Tim replied. "When she came back."

"She's pretty good," Nygerski said.

Tim shrugged. "My sister can do a lot of things."

"She's not here," Nygerski said, stating the obvious. "Where do you think she went?"

"I think I know," Tim said quietly.

Nygerski looked at the kid in the darkening cabin. He seemed a lot older than ten. "Tell me," he said.

"I think she went to the Hole."

"What's the Hole?"

"It's something no one in my family talks about very much," Tim said. "Except for Aunt Polly, and everyone thinks she's crazy."

"Tim, you talk in riddles, just like your sister," Nygerski said. "Who is Aunt Polly, and what is the Hole?"

"It's a time portal," the kid said with absolute seriousness. "At least that's what Aunt Polly says."

Nygerski stared at the boy, evaluating this outlandish pronouncement. "Tim, your sister ever slip you any drugs?"

The boy shook his head. "Uh-uh," he said. "I caught her smoking pot one time, but she wouldn't let me try it."

"I think we need to find her," Nygerski said. "What's the fastest way to get to this Hole? Can we drive there?"

"Yeah," Tim said. "But Cassandra made me promise I wouldn't go out tonight."

This just gets weirder and weirder, Moondog thought. Aloud, he said, "It's obvious that *she* went out. And I didn't drive all the way up here from Boston not to talk to her. You'll be safe with me. Come on, let's get in my car."

"Just a minute." Tim left the cabin and walked the few steps to the bank overlooking the cove. Nygerski followed at a short distance.

Tim scanned the water in the gathering twilight. "She went to the Hole, all right," he said, pointing. "The canoe's on the far shore."

"But you said we could drive there, right?"

"Uh-huh. It's longer by land than it is by water, but we'll get there quicker."

"Then let's go," Nygerski said.

Nygerski saw a cloud of reluctance cross Tim's face, but he turned and began walking briskly back toward the house, and Tim followed. When they reached the car, the boy pulled back. "I did promise . . . ," he said.

"Your sister owes us both some answers," Nygerski said. "Come on, get in."

Tim got in and closed the door, and Nygerski bucketed the car up the dirt road, driving perhaps a little faster than was prudent.

"Turn here," Tim said when they reached the road to Dyerville. Nygerski had already started the turn. How did he know his way around so well if he had never been here before? Was he being led here, by some force beyond his control? And where was Cassandra?

The car rumbled through a small settlement of old houses and stacks of lobster traps. Nygerski continued on; the road curved into the woods and then back toward the water. He slowed as they approached a small tarpaper shack with an array of outboard motor parts splayed out around a halfway disassembled motor propped up against a sawhorse in the dirt out front. The door was partially opened, and Nygerski peered at it curiously. "Who lives here?" he asked.

"An old geezer named Clem," the boy replied.

"And this hole of yours—"

"Right up here," Tim said, nodding at the patch of water Nygerski could see just up ahead, where the road emerged from the trees into a grassy area by the side of the water. Nygerski stopped the car, and they got out. The tide was down, and the wind rippled the water beyond the mudflats. He scanned the area, but saw no one except a lone clammer, far out by the water's edge. Nygerski turned and began walking up the road, toward the shack.

"Where are you going?" Tim called after him.

"Gonna ask the old man if he's seen her."

The kid hurried to keep up with him as he strode purposefully up the road. Nygerski looked around before knocking on the open door and poking his head through.

Cassandra looked up from lighting the last candle in a tight circle of cork floats in the middle of the cabin floor. Inside the circle, in chalk, she had drawn a five-pointed star. Nygerski felt in his pocket for the necklace she had given him. Her eyes locked on his. The lit match in her had trembled and went out. "Oh, no," she said.

"I had to find you," he replied.

Her eyes widened as she looked beyond him. "Timmy! I told you to stay inside!"

The boy stood just inside the door. He swung his chin in a small arc toward Nygerski. "He needed me to show him the way," he said. "Cassandra, what's going on? Where's Clem?"

"Oh my God, you've got to get out of here right now!" The girl was clearly agitated. She stood up and began pushing her brother toward the door. "He's clamming, but he'll be back! You can't be here! I've got to take care of him myself. Go!" She pushed Tim through the door toward the sawhorse and the outboard motor.

"Cassandra, what's going on?" Moondog asked, following them outside. "What's with the star, and the candles? What is all this?"

She whirled on him. "There's no time! You're going to ruin everything!"

"I just want some answers," he said.

"Answers? Answers! You're going to get more answers than you ever wanted if you don't get out of here in five minutes! For Christ's sake, if Clem comes back and—"

"What are you doing? And what's the hurry?"

Cassandra cast an agitated glance toward the water. "Moonrise, you idiot! Ah, God, you weren't supposed to know about this! You've got to get him out of here!"

"Cassandra . . ."

"Listen to me! You take that boy, and get in the car, and drive the hell away from here! You're not going to want to be around when the Moon rises."

"Come on, Cassandra! What the hell's going on here?"

"Get out of here, both of you!" She pushed her brother toward the car.

"All right!" he cried. "We'll go. But I want to know what this is all about. The circle of candles. The star. This." He pulled the silver necklace from his pocket and dangled the pentagram in front of Cassandra's face.

She threw up her arms and recoiled from him. He looked back and forth from her face to the five-sided star inside the circle.

"Why did you give this to me?" he asked her.

"Put it away!" she cried. "Please, I'm begging you, get away from here before the Moon rises. Before it's too late!"

"Who *are* you?" He held out the necklace, and she backed away.

"Timmy!" she gasped. "Get to the car, inside the car! Go, now!"

Bewildered, the boy looked back and forth between Nygerski and his sister. Moondog heard squishy footsteps and looked up to see an old man in yellow hip boots, carrying two hods full of clams and a small pitchfork, emerge from the shore onto the grassy area beside the car. He walked bowleggedly toward them.

"Shit, it's Clem!" Cassandra hissed. Nygerski could see beads of sweat on her forehead. "God help us all."

Nygerski looked at her as Clem approached. He suddenly wondered if she was ill, for her face looked drawn; the skin tight over jaw and cheekbones, and the whites of her eyes had taken on an ugly, yellowish hue. As the old man approached them Nygerski noticed that he did not look well, either. Several days' worth of white stubble covered his reddened face, and his walk looked forced and uncomfortable. He set down the clams beside a gas can near the pile of motor parts and stared at them. A gust of wind whipped the trees overhead. Clem opened his mouth. "I warn't expecting no company," he said.

The man was missing his front teeth on top, and his other teeth were crooked and yellow. He and Cassandra stared at each other.

"I wasn't, either, Clem," she said. "It was supposed to be our private ritual."

"Huh?" The guttural emerged as a growl, for the old man was as agitated as the girl. He, too, was sweating, despite the cool of the evening, and Nygerski saw that his hands, freed from the handles of the clam hods, were shaking.

"Timmy, GO!" Cassandra cried, her eyes not leaving Clem's.

Clem opened his mouth to speak, but the only sound that emerged was something between a growl and a whimper. As Nygerski watched in amazement, the old man dropped to his knees and pressed his hands to the sides of his head. Clem screamed, and the long yellow teeth at the back of his mouth distended, splitting his gums and sending streams of blood down his whiskered chin from the corners of his mouth. He writhed on the ground, his body contorting. His shirt ripped down the back. Moondog's jaw dropped. Clem's limbs bulged beneath his clothes.

His face contorted and stretched, a slobbering canine snout replacing his human features. Gray fur sprouted over his entire body.

"TIMMY!" Cassandra screamed. Then the scream became wordless as she, too, dropped to the ground. Nygerski watched in shock, clutching the silver pentagram in front of him. The beast that Clem had become let out a terrible roar. Timmy screamed, and ran for the car. Beyond the water, the red eye of the full Moon peered at them from just above the far shore.

The Clem-beast got to its feet. In three bounds it landed on Tim's back and dragged him down. "No!" Nygerski cried. But it was too late. A savage swipe of one paw took half of Timmy's face. The boy's screams died suddenly as the beast's terrible jaws closed around his neck.

Cassandra roared, and Nygerski looked at her. She was a woman no longer. The dark-furred wolf-thing reared up on its hind legs and fixed its canine eyes on him. Nygerski backed up, knocking over the gas can, stumbling into the outboard motor, falling over backward. The beast advanced on him, towering over him, its jaws dripping saliva. "Cassandra . . . ," he pleaded weakly. The beast roared. Desperately, Nygerski held up the silver necklace. Moonlight glinted off the shiny five-pointed star. The beast growled and turned away from him.

Beside Tim's body, the Clem-beast raised its blood-covered snout to the sky and howled.

The other werewolf leapt at him. They rolled in the gravel road, jaws snapping, feet kicking, the sounds worse than any dogfight Nygerski had ever heard. Petrified with fear, he backed away, clutching the necklace, as the two monsters staggered toward the cabin. They struggled by the knocked-over outboard motor, blood mixing with the gas on the ground. The Clem-beast swiped a paw at the other, but the dark-furred werewolf feinted away, then sank its teeth again into the soft area between shoulder and neck. The Clem-beast yowled in pain. As Nygerski stumbled toward the cabin, the wounded werewolf staggered and fell to the ground in front of the door.

Nygerski had backed right into the shack. He could smell the burning candles. The dark-furred beast licked its snout and stared at him. Nygerski held the pentagram in front of him, in full view of the creature. The gray werewolf pawed the air. One flailing arm hit the overturned gasoline can. The beast that had been Cassandra looked at him hungrily but made no advance on him.

The Clem-beast cried out and tried to regain its feet. Nygerski took a step back into the cabin and grabbed one of the floats with a burning candle in it. He hurled it at the gray werewolf.

The gasoline on the ground burst into flame. The gray beast howled as its fur caught fire. The flames spread to the outboard motor and the side of the cabin. Nygerski felt the searing heat.

He turned, and looked at the dark beast that was Cassandra. Their eyes locked for a moment, and then the werewolf whirled and ran away toward the water.

The fire roared up the near wall of the cabin. Moondog fled from the searing heat. A piercing cry from behind him made him stop. He turned. The beast that had been Clem had become a human torch. Through the flames, Nygerski thought he could glimpse the agonized face of the old clamdigger as he died. Then the flaming body toppled sideways to the ground and lay still.

The other werewolf—Cassandra—had disappeared into the darkness, somewhere down by the water. Tim's lifeless body lay on the road a short distance away. Moondog could tell at a glance it was too late for him. Half his throat was gone.

The heat was staggering. Clem's cabin illuminated the semidarkness all around him. In a few seconds the fire would spread to the nearby trees. He calculated his chances of getting to his car and driving away. They weren't good.

But the heat! He had to get out of there. Suddenly a tree beside the house exploded into flame. Nygerski watched as the near wall buckled, sending embers out onto the road. For several face-blistering seconds he stared into the inferno as flames shot skyward. Then he turned and ran.

A column of flame and smoke, brighter than the Moon, rose into the air behind him. A safe distance away, Nygerski slowed to a fast walk to catch his breath. His head throbbed; his lungs were burning. He had almost reached the first house when he heard the blast of a fire signal. A minute later, he heard the distant wail of approaching sirens.

CHAPTER 27.

SEASON'S END

Cassandra's mother flew out from Ohio for the funeral. Cassandra didn't look like her. Nygerski noted that she didn't really look like anyone in the family, except maybe Aunt Polly, whose hair had once been dark and who shared something in the eyes, the intimation of an ability to see through things. There was no reconciliation. The parents of the dead boy stood beside one another, not touching, as the small coffin was lowered into the rocky soil of the small seaside cemetery. Uncle Bill and his family were there, as were other cousins and relatives and the Woolfs and Grangers, the kids in a clump and the grown-ups trying their best to put on a show of solidarity. Almost everybody cried. But not Cassandra. She stood with her red-eyed parents, stone-faced and stoic in her grief, communicating with no one save for an occasional glance at Nygerski and Aunt Polly.

There had been a smaller, separate service for Clem Dyer days earlier. Cassandra and Nygerski had been among the half-dozen people in attendance. The police had questioned them both, and concluded that Clem had set fire to his shack and himself after murdering Tim. There were murmurings among the locals about Clem's alcoholism and how friendly he had been to young boys. Too friendly, as it turned out, they said, heads nodding. The old pervert had finally gone over the edge.

"Better they think that than the truth," Cassandra said to Nygerski during a private moment at the reception following Tim's funeral. "Fortunately for us, the body was burned so badly there was no way to tell how he *really* died."

"Is there someplace we can go?" Nygerski said. "We need to talk."

He was leaving right after the reception. The cops had no more questions for him, and he had the overwhelming feeling that he had worn out his welcome.

"The Green Cabin," Cassandra said. "The boats are in there, but we can sit on the porch." It was chilly, and most of the guests were in the house, around the spread of food on the big dining room table. Cassandra and Nygerski slipped out unnoticed and walked down to the water's edge. The tide was in, though not as high as it had been a few days ago, during the full Moon. A lobster boat bobbed on its mooring at the mouth of the cove. Low, gray clouds skidded across the tops of the islands. The wind whipped at their jackets and hair. They looked out at the water in silence for several minutes, and then, with a glance at one another, retreated to the porch of the cabin.

"I had terrible dreams," he said at length. "Before I came to see you. Only they're not dreams, are they?"

"No," she said.

"They're memories."

He looked at her, and she nodded.

"We did meet before."

She nodded again. "But not in this life."

"You gave me drugs," he said. "For a while I thought everything I was remembering was an LSD-induced hallucination."

"Acid doesn't work like that," she said. "People think it does. But people also think the world is linear and logical. And you and I both know it isn't."

Silence fell between them again. Nygerski watched several red leaves sail off a nearby tree and disappear across the field. "Why did you give it to me?" he asked her.

"So that you would see. So that you would know why you couldn't fall in love with me again."

"We were lovers once."

"Yes. But in another life. Your memories of it will fade. Pretty soon it will seem like a dream. More like a dream than it does now. You'll tell yourself it didn't really happen."

He pulled up a blade of grass in front of the porch and stuck the tender end between his teeth. "It was Clem," he said. "It was Clem who bit you."

She nodded. "I discovered that, when I got to San Francisco. Full Moon came around, and I was no longer affected. I wasn't a werewolf anymore, because Clem was dead. I allowed myself to think that everything would be okay. But Aunt Polly was right."

"There are always costs," he remembered.

She nodded again. "And now, somehow, we'll live our separate lives. Me as a werewolf. You as Cyrus 'Moondog' Nygerski, the best left-handed second baseman in all of Wisconsin."

"Not anymore." He felt miserable.

"It's not your fault," she said. But the words rang hollow in his ears. In a very real sense, he had caused her brother's death. How could they possibly live with that awful secret between them?

"There's something I still don't understand," he said.

She looked at him, waiting for him to continue.

"A person who survives the bite of a werewolf becomes a werewolf, right?"

She nodded.

"And it was Clem who bit you."

"In April," she said. "On the full Moon. I was attacked by what I thought was a dog on Williams Point. Only the silver necklace saved my life."

"And then you went back through the Hole and killed him?"

"That's right."

"But if you went back to a time before he bit you, how could you have become a werewolf and kill him? Logically—"

She put her hand to his lips. "Don't use that word," she said, smiling sadly, nothing like the full, toothy smile that had taken his heart. "Of course time travel is impossible. It defies all rules of logic. But impossible things happen. Like bumblebees being able to fly. Or the Red Sox winning the pennant."

"They have to beat Minnesota twice this weekend," Nygerski said.

"They will."

Nygerski stared out at the water, not knowing what to say. Baseball seemed far away. Like something from another life.

"What will you do?" he asked her.

"I don't know. Go back to California, I think. Someone like me can blend in there. You?"

"Don't know, either. Try to dodge the draft. Maybe go to college. Try to make sense of everything that's happened."

She smiled gently. "You won't learn that in school," she said.

"No," he agreed. "But it's a good holding pattern. Until something else comes up."

Another awkward silence descended. Nygerski sensed that it was time to go. Endings, he thought, are never satisfactory.

"Well," he said, and got to his feet. He held out his hands to Cassandra and helped her up. The simple touch of her thrilled his nerve endings.

"This is good-bye, I guess," he said as they walked slowly back to the house, side by side, a short distance apart.

"Have a good life, Moondog," she said when they reached his car.

"Thank you for giving it to me." He hesitated, and then put his arms around her, in full view of anyone who happened to be looking out the window. He didn't care. He would never feel quite so alive again.

The sky began to clear as he drove southward. The trees, bending to the wind, looked a good deal more bare than they had just a few days ago. His way out of Maine was punctuated by bridges: at Deer Isle, Bucksport, Bath, and the Piscataqua River, where Maine becomes New Hampshire. As he crossed the final span, he passed a Volkwagen bus filled with teenagers. The car had Massachusetts plates and a bumper sticker that read: GO SOX! Nygerski honked his horn and waved.